He turned her hand over and kissed the palm. The warmth of his mouth seared her cool skin. She knew she must take her hand away and could not—did not want to—could not break away. Without resisting, she allowed him to draw her into the circle of his arms.

Then he was bending his head to hers, and as their lips met, the ground beneath Melinda's feet seemed to dissolve into mist. There was no sound save the beating of her own heart and no taste or touch except that of his mouth. For a moment the world stood completely still and then deep in the fog of her mind, a voice of reason cried out in protest. *Miss Mel,* that well-known voice clamored, have you gone mad, then?

Also by Rebecca Ward
*Published by Fawcett Books:*

FAIR FORTUNE
LORD LONGSHANKS
LADY IN SILVER
CINDERELLA'S STEPMOTHER
ENCHANTED RENDEZVOUS
MADAM MYSTERY
GRAND DECEPTION

# A MONSTROUS SECRET

*Rebecca Ward*

FAWCETT CREST • NEW YORK

For Christy and Ash Shoop

A Fawcett Crest Book
Published by Ballantine Books
Copyright © 1996 by Maureen Wartski

http://www.randomhouse.com

Library of Congress Catalog Card Number: 95-96233

ISBN 0-449-28699-1

Manufactured in the United States of America

First Edition: May 1996

10  9  8  7  6  5  4  3  2  1

# Chapter One

"They were *devouring* sugar from the bowl, and when I taxed them with stealing, they *lied*."

Miss Vraye twitched like an outraged rabbit. Melinda eyed the two little girls that the music mistress had in tow and asked, "What was the lie?"

"It wasn't a whisker, Miss Weatherby," the braver of the Hanscom twins, Jenny, explained. "We just said that we were trying to see if it's true what Mr. Proctor always says about forbidden fruit being sweet."

Melinda felt the corners of her lips twitch, but she kept her face suitably grave. "And was it true?" Both little girls nodded vigorously. "That is most interesting. I shall look forward to reading an essay all about your findings. Two pages long, in your best hand," she added as the twins' faces fell. "I want it by this evening, if you please."

Miss Vraye gave an affronted little gasp as the children clattered away. "Miss Weatherby!" she breathed. "It is the outside of enough. Those wicked little girls should have been *punished*."

"I would consider having to stay indoors to write a dull essay punishment, especially on such a lovely day." Melinda drew in a breath of early spring air and smiled at Miss Vraye. "I have dipped into a sugar bowl myself. Haven't you?"

1

"Indeed I have not. You are altogether too lenient, Miss Weatherby. You leave me no choice but to inform Mr. Proctor."

She sailed away. Melinda watched Jenny Hanscom ape the music teacher's nose-in-the-air exit, and could not help chuckling. Jenny and Mary Hanscom were a handful, but she could not help sympathizing with them.

Miss Vraye had definite ideas of right and wrong. She never questioned established rules and regulations. Whatever the situation, Miss Vraye seemed always to know the right thing to do. "But what *is* the right thing for me to do about Zenobie?" Melinda wondered aloud.

A burst of laughter from a group of girls at play answered her. A bright blue butterfly, newly released from its cocoon, danced across the garden path to sip at newly opened spring flowers. Pleasant sights, pleasing sounds, familiar, comfortable, they had made up the boundaries of Melinda's world for the past three years. But now there was the problem of Zenobie's letter.

The letter had been addressed in a bold, flamboyant hand to Miss Melinda Weatherby, The Proctor Academy for Young Ladies, Sussex. "Melushka," Zenobie had written, "I have but newly moved to Dorset from London. I am lonely living all alone in this big old house. I, alas, have not been able to go calling on my new neighbors because of the wet and the problem of my health. Come to me at Kendle-on-Lake. Come as soon as you can."

It was more of a command than an invitation, but then that was Zenobie. Melinda pictured Zenobie grieving for her husband, the late Lord Darlington. She thought of the inclement weather and ill health keeping Zenobie imprisoned in a big,

2

gloomy house. She had reached out for help, reached out almost piteously. "But it is not so easy. I cannot just drop everything and go to Dorset," Melinda argued with herself.

And yet it was Zenobie's sugar bowl she had raided, so many years ago—a lovely, fat piece of china painted with forget-me-nots and roses. Worse, she had broken the lovely thing, smashed it to fragments. Her gray eyes somber with that memory, Melinda walked down the garden path to the door of the house, where a gray-haired, bony personage engulfed in starched apron and cap was awaiting her.

"Your tea's waiting for you, Miss Mel," she accused. "It's been waiting for half an hour."

"I'm sorry, Polly. I took a walk and forgot the time."

Small, bright blue eyes registered disapproval. A red-tipped nose grew redder. "On account of *her* letter," she stated.

Melinda did not bother to deny this. Without being told, Miss Poll knew everything. She had been Melinda's mother's maid and later progressed to being her nurse. She meddled, she infuriated, and she had also held a much younger Melinda when she cried.

In silence Miss Poll followed Melinda into the house and up the old stone staircase to the little parlor on the second floor. Usually, this parlor was where the academy's teachers had their tea together, but today no one was in evidence. "Had their tea and gone, most of 'em," Miss Poll grunted. "Ate everything as was on the tray. Good thing I kept back something for you."

She plumped up the cushions on the comfortably faded brocade sofa, whisked a drooping rose out of a

3

blue porcelain vase on the hearth, then busied herself with the tea things. "There's muffins and clotted cream and blackberry jam," she declared with satisfaction. "Miss Mel, what does the Rooshan want this time?"

"Zenobie wants me to come and stay with her at Kendle-on-Lake," Melinda began, but was interrupted by the older woman's snort.

"Just like that, you're supposed to leave Sussex. Ain't that just like the Rooshan?"

"Her name is Lady Darlington," Melinda reproved. "She writes from Dorset, where she is living in the house left to her when Lord Darlington died. She's all alone—and she's not at all well, Polly."

"If *I* had four husbands and buried all of 'em, I'd be wore out, too." Miss Poll rubbed the tip of her nose before adding, "You've worked that hard to get where you're now, Miss Mel. How do she think she can crook her little finger and you'd go running to her?"

"You forget she and Arthur took me in when Mother died. Zenobie—"

"—was always selfish, Miss Mel, and well you know it. I ain't blaming her, because life ain't good to them as always thinks on others first. True, she and your cousin gave you a home when you was in leading strings. But what happened after Mr. Arthur died? Didn't she leave you in the briars so she could go marrying that Frenchy weasel?"

There was a little silence during which the clock on the mantel chimed the hour. It was already four, time to call in the girls from their recreation so that they could rest and wash before dinner.

Melinda said slowly, "It wasn't her fault. After Arthur's death there was not much money." Miss

Poll muttered that she knew *who* had spent all of Mr. Arthur's estate, too. "Don't be unjust, Polly. It was not all Zenobie's fault that she had to remarry. She was used to living well and being dependent on a man."

Miss Poll jerked up her chin and leveled a direct gaze at Melinda. "Would *you* have gone away and left a young girl and an old besom like me on our own? If you had a child what depended on you, looked up to you, would you have left her to go marry a rich man?"

Reluctantly, Melinda remembered those difficult years. She had been thirteen when her cousin Arthur died, fourteen when Zenobie married Monsieur Vilforme. Old enough to feel the stab of rejection when Zenobie explained, through tears, that her husband did not want a child living with them. "You understand, do you not, Melushka?" Zenobie had pleaded. "If I do not marry Monsieur Vilforme, we will all starve." Then she had added, "I will not forget you. I will make sure you are provided for."

"She did send us money," Melinda mused.

Miss Poll clicked her tongue. "A pittance. Just enough to starve on. She *said* that was all her Frenchy husband would give her, but I'll wager she bought jewels and pretty dresses for herself."

"Enough, Polly."

"It's enough *now*," replied Miss Poll with heat. "Here you've got a nice little school and a nice living. A comfortable fire in winter and no worrying about where the next meal's coming from, neither. You done it all on your own, Miss Mel. Going for a governess when you was barely out of the nursery yourself. Working and working until the chance come along for you to teach at this here school."

5

There was a step in the hall, the sound of a man clearing his voice. At that self-important sound, Miss Poll raised her scant eyebrows, squinted down her nose, and pursed her lips in a parody of Mr. Augustus Proctor, headmaster and owner of the Proctor Academy for Young Ladies. Then she smoothed her face into a smile and dropped a knee as this personage entered the room.

"Good evening, sir," she murmured. "There's tea and scones buttered, just as you like them."

She winked at Melinda over Mr. Proctor's head and left the room. "An excellent woman," the headmaster declaimed. "These devoted old servants are like gold, ma'am. Like gold."

Melinda said nothing, the while thinking that Polly's wicked mimicry had sketched Mr. Augustus Proctor to a hair. She could feel her lips quirking shamefully as the headmaster perambulated into the parlor, carefully parted the tails of his bottle green coat, and deposited himself on the sofa.

"Our young charges are enjoying this fine spring day," he commented unctuously. " 'Where are the songs of spring?' quoth Keats. *I* say they are here, ma'am. It is a pity that the poet could not have taken tea at the Proctor Academy for Young Ladies."

He waited for Melinda to pour, requested two lumps of sugar, and selected a buttered scone. "I have been thinking, Miss Weatherby, that it has been three years since your arrival at the academy. How the time flies, ma'am. How the time flies." Melinda murmured assent. "In those three years," continued Mr. Proctor, "you have become an invaluable member of our staff."

He paused to wipe his fingers free of butter. Realizing that Miss Vraye had by then told him her version of the Hanscom twins and the sugar bowl, Melinda waited.

"But you are too tenderhearted, ma'am. Children need a stern hand. Spare the rod, as the saying goes, and spoil the child. The Hanscom girls are incorrigible."

"They have had many troubles in their lives lately," Melinda demurred. "They lost their mother this year, and now the father has remarried. Often children behave badly when they are confused and unhappy."

"We all have loss in our lives." Mr. Proctor leaned back and folded his short arms across his chest. "I agree with Miss Vraye that the girls must be suitably disciplined. I have set them to scrub the stairs on their hands and knees, and there will be no supper for them tonight."

He regarded her triumphantly. "But what will that teach them?" Melinda protested. "Besides, they are too little for such hard work. It would be difficult to clean those stone stairs."

"Rules must be obeyed." Augustus Proctor's voice rose a little. "We all are subject to rules, ma'am."

With an effort that was almost painful, Melinda bit back a protest. She held her breath, counted to ten, and watched the headmaster eating another scone and dropping crumbs on his brocaded waistcoat.

"I must ask a favor, Mr. Proctor," she said at last. "I wonder if I may have a fortnight's leave to visit my cousin in Dorset."

Mr. Proctor's baby-smooth brow contracted in a frown. His mouth grew pointed in thought. "A fortnight, ma'am," he repeated.

"I would ask Miss Tallison and Mrs. Gorse to take over my classes," Melinda explained quickly. "I

7

am sure they will agree when they learn that my cousin is unwell."

But Mr. Proctor was already shaking his head. "It is a difficult time of year. Spring makes our charges full of frisk, and all our efforts are required here at the academy. No, I am afraid it is not possible."

And that was that, Melinda told herself. Zenobie would have to manage for herself—as she no doubt would. Zenobie was a survivor, as were the Hanscom twins. She would not worry about them, either.

"I did not know you had a cousin in Dorset," Mr. Proctor was saying as he held out his empty teacup for her to refill.

"My cousin by marriage. She and my cousin Arthur raised me when my mother died. Now she needs my help."

Try as she would, Melinda could not keep her voice completely steady, and Augustus Proctor frowned. He was used to Melinda's competence, her devotion to her students, who all worshipped her. He had come to take for granted her brilliance in teaching languages, her skill in drawing. He had more than once congratulated himself for having discovered such a gem for his school.

And she was good to look at as well. With the judicious eye of a connoisseur, Mr. Proctor noted the petite Miss Weatherby's dark hair, coiled into a glossy chignon at the base of her graceful white neck. He admired her steady gray eyes fringed with thick, dark lashes and considered the slight tilt of her nose, the warm curve of her rosy mouth.

A gem indeed. Briefly he toyed with the thought of granting her request, but before he could speak, Miss Vraye came marching into the parlor.

The music mistress's watery green eyes were bright with satisfaction. "At last justice has triumphed," she crowed. "I saw Mary and Jenny washing down the stairs. Those wicked children will not soon tell lies again."

She and Mr. Proctor exchanged smiles. Melinda felt sickened. The bright sunshine, the muted laughter of the girls at play outside in the garden, suddenly seemed dull and lackluster.

Excusing herself, she rose and left the room. On the staircase landing she looked down and felt even more sickened to see the Hanscom twins on their hands and knees, scrubbing the stone stairs. This was hard work even for hands larger than theirs, and Mary was crying as she dragged a heavy iron bucket along.

Melinda closed her eyes. She forced herself to remember her happy days at the academy, the other teachers, her students, her work. She reminded herself of the days when she and Polly had been so poor.

Then she walked down the stairs, knelt between the little girls, and took Mary's rag from her hand. "You must hold the rag like this, and move your arm like this," she explained as the twins stared. "Come, we will make a game of it."

Energetically, she began to wash a step. Mary stopped crying. Jenny began to ape Melinda's movements. In a few moments both children were entranced as Melinda told a story of how she had learned to scrub floors.

"I did it to help Miss Poll," she explained. "It was a very cold winter, and Miss Poll had to go out to try and collect firewood for the stove. I got out the old wooden bucket and—"

"Miss Weatherby—pray, what are you doing?"

The headmaster had appeared on the hall landing and was gaping down at them.

Behind him, Melinda could see the astounded face of Miss Vraye. "They were not washing the floor correctly," she explained. "I am teaching them the right way to do it."

She returned to her efforts. "Miss Weatherby, you shall stop. I *demand* that you stop," commanded Mr. Proctor. "These children are being punished for their sins. They must learn to obey the commandment 'Thou shalt not steal!' "

Jenny Hanscom reared up, flung down her rags, and glared up at the headmaster. "Aw, muzzle it, you old bag pudding!" she shouted.

There was a loud gasp behind them. Turning her head, Melinda saw that the hall had filled with little girls. Some were pop-eyed with horror, some were giggling and poking each other with their elbows, and all of them were watching their headmaster turn a brilliant crimson.

"Get out, the lot of you," Mr. Proctor yelled. "Miss Vraye, get those little—take them away at once! Miss *Weatherby*, my study—immediately!"

Melinda looked at the Hanscom twins. "Impossible," she said clearly. "I must finish this floor. And then I must pack."

"Pack?" Mr. Proctor was beside himself. "You are demented, ma'am. Your mind has become unhinged. What are you talking about?"

Ignoring him, Melinda straightened her back and addressed Miss Poll, who had appeared on the scene. "Zenobie may have her faults, but I remember that when I broke her sugar bowl, she did not even scold. She hugged and kissed and comforted me instead. I'm sorry, Polly, but we must go to Dorset after all."

The Earl of Albermale's fashionable Mount Street residence was aswim with guests. Music and the sound of dancing feet vied with laughter and repartee; candelabra dazzled against brilliant jewels worn by exquisitely dressed ladies who plied their Angelica Kauffmann fans as they recounted the latest gossip. The gentlemen, as perfumed and as brilliantly plumaged as their ladies, helped themselves liberally to viands and spirits whilst arguing politics or the details of the hunt.

Against this assault of scent, sight, and sound, a newcomer might surely go unnoticed, but Lord Hartford's hope was a forlorn one. The Earl of Albermale, who had been loudly denouncing the want-wits who had bungled it and let Boney escape from Elba, broke off in midsentence to exclaim, "There he is, by Jove!"

Conversation slowed and heads turned as Albermale fairly trotted across the length of the drawing room to grasp his tall nephew by the hand.

"Good of you to come, Anthony," he wheezed. "Heard you'd just got back from Scotland."

"Barely returned. Dayce hasn't even unpacked." Lord Hartford looked around at the glittering assembly. "I thought you said it was urgent."

"Oh, it is, it is. I know y'must be exhausted after all that shooting and hunting, but it couldn't be helped. Y'see, they told me to—"

"I vow I cannot believe it. I am amazed into a spasm. Anthony, *dearest* boy, it is good to see you!"

A Junoesque lady in purple satin and a matching turban was descending upon them. Behind her minced a slight, bewigged and monocled gentleman in decorous satin knee breeches and a maroon velvet coat.

"Dished up, by Jove," groaned the earl. "Now you'll have to talk rubbish with your aunt."

"What's de Jermaine doing in your house?" Hartford wanted to know, but the countess gave her spouse no chance to reply. In her high, carrying voice, she demanded to be told exactly what her nephew had been up to in Scotland, how many hearts he had broken since he left London, if it was true that his older brother was carrying on an affair with a vulgar actress, and if his parents, their graces of Benwick, were in good health.

The earl stood by silently and admired his youngest nephew's poise. Not many men he knew could avoid Agatha's prying questions, but Anthony was her match. His dark eyes glowed with wit, his long, mobile mouth curved with humor, and anyone watching him might assume that here was nothing but a lighthearted, bubbleheaded young blood.

Which would have been very wrong. Of all of Benwick's brood, Hartford was the deepest, the hardest to bridge. Not the handsomest, since he had inherited the duchess's nut brown hair and dark eyes instead of the Benwick blue-and-gold, not the tallest, since he barely reached six feet. But Anthony had address, by Jove, he had, and presence, too. In his unexceptional black evening clothes, he looked *tray distingay,* as that mushroom de Jermaine might say.

And, talking of Frogs, he had a duty to perform. Albermale cleared his throat and interrupted his lady in midsentence. "All very well, m'dear," he declared, "all very fine, by Jove. But I have something to discuss with our nephew, d'you see?"

"Somezing of importance," lisped Monsieur de Jermaine. He bowed gracefully to Lord Hartford, and held out his arm to the countess. "*Noblesse oblige*, milor'. *Chère* Madame, I beg leave to claim zis dance."

Hartford bowed in silence as his aunt was led away. His lips still smiled, but his eyes were hard. "De Jermaine is undoubtedly a spy for Napoleon. Why is he still in England? And *why* is he in your house, Uncle?"

"Come with me and you'll see." Catching hold of the younger man's arm, the earl walked him out of the drawing room and down the hall to another room on the same floor. A bewigged footman opened the door and stood aside. "Go in, go in—you'll see what I'm talking about," the earl commanded.

Hartford paused at the door and looked around the room. That swift glance—it had become an instinctive reflex—took in a dark-paneled study furnished with shelves of books, ponderous mahogany furniture, and leather chairs. Candles in silver candlesticks reflected against portraits in heavy gilt frames.

Two men were in the room. The short, stumpy one with the mane of graying hair sat back in the shadow. The other, slight, fair, and elegant in dark evening clothes and a silver-figured waistcoat with diamond studs, stood with his back to the empty grate.

"Sir Orin Calworth," Hartford exclaimed.

"Give you good evening, dear boy."

As the fair-haired gentleman sauntered forward to shake hands, the shadowed figure snapped, "Has Albermale told you what you're to do, Hartford?"

"Admiral Kier." Hartford bowed slightly as he added, "What is this my uncle's supposed to have told me?"

"Steady, Hartford, all in good time, dear boy." Sir

Orin put a white, beringed finger on the younger man's shoulder. "The admiral and I approached Albermale and, after swearing him to strictest secrecy, asked him to arrange this meeting tonight. We thought it best that we meet in public—in full view of Monsieur de Jermaine."

"Tchah," snarled the admiral. "Bloody little spy. Should hang the bugger from the yardarm."

Silently, Hartford agreed. He felt a familiar tension rise in him as Sir Orin continued, "Hartford, you know without my telling you that you have my highest regard. The work you did for us in intelligence while you were still an officer in his majesty's armies was superb. Your efforts helped us put Boney on Elba. Unfortunately—"

"Unfortunately, his guards were cockle-brained nincompoops," snorted Albermale. "Slibberslobberers! Rabbit suckers! By Jove, if I had m'way—"

Sir Orin cleared his throat in gentle reproof. "*Unfortunately,* he has escaped and has reentered Paris. Now that the allied powers have declared war on Napoleon, the Circle will be needed again."

Hartford felt he had to interrupt. "I don't know where this is leading," he said, "but it's common knowledge I sold my colors when Boney was sent into exile. I've done with the Circle." He paused for emphasis before continuing. "I've just returned from a week's shooting in Scotland, sir, and tomorrow I leave for Benwick. My mother is celebrating her birthday and wants her brats around her."

"Naturally, dear boy, you must salute the duchess on her birthday. You need not go to Dorset immediately, after all."

Sir Orin stepped back, withdrew a gold snuffbox, and shook back a delicate pinch. He looked, Hartford thought dryly, and acted like a veritable tulip of the ton. Few people knew of the incredibly brilliant and coldly logical mind that plotted behind the lazy, half-closed eyes.

But *he* knew, and he could also play the game. Hartford met Sir Orin's hooded gaze with an ingenuous smile and replied that he had no business in Dorset, now or in the foreseeable future.

"That's what you think," growled the admiral. "Leave off diddling the man, Calworth, and tell him why he's been sent for. No—I'll do it."

He squared around, faced Hartford directly, and stated, "We've long suspicioned that there's a bloody traitorous organization that is selling secrets to our enemies. Not just to Boney, mind, but to *any* power that'll pay the highest price. No telling how many secrets these blackguards have sold."

"Are they Englishmen?" Hartford demanded sharply. Sir Orin shrugged.

"We don't know. We do know that the group operates here in England, but they have been remarkably clever in eluding us till now. Our Circle has come close, but always they slip through our fingers." He paused and added quietly, "Of course you remember what happened to poor young Latten. It was always believed that he was betrayed. This ring of spies may have sent Latten to his death."

Hartford said nothing, but his eyes had turned hard. Sir Orin continued. "Now, though, there has been a stroke of good fortune. My agents report that the widow of Hyacinthe Vilforme has taken up residence in a backwater Dorset town."

"Vilforme." Hartford's face grew even harder. "Boney's late and unlamented henchman. What would that bastard's widow be doing in England?"

"She remarried an Englishman after Vilforme

was lost at sea," Albermale interjected. He had been hovering on the fringe of the conversation, trying to get a word in edgewise. "Rooshan woman, married four husbands and buried 'em all. Married a Rooshan baron first time around, and he got chucked off his horse and cocked up his toes. Married a chap called Weatherby next, and wouldn't you know *he* pegged off, too. Then came that Vilforme fellow, and finally poor old Darlington."

The earl paused to draw breath. "Mind you," he added, "Darlington never had much in his brainbox. Had to be eighty if he was a day when he got leg-shackled to Vilforme's widow, and the excitement must've done him in. They used to have a residence in London, but now that he's cocked up his toes, his widow's moved to Kendle-on-Lake. That's just a stone's throw from Sir Rupert Blyminster."

He was interrupted by his nephew's exclamation of surprise. "You can't mean Flighty Blighty? Not the inventor fellow who's got a bee in his bonnet about inventing an underwater ship and nearly drowned himself in the channel a few years back?" When Sir Orin nodded, he began to laugh. "And I thought you were serious!"

Albermale popped open his mouth, but Sir Orin was swifter. "It *is* serious. My dear boy, reports of this underwater craft have aroused interest in several quarters. We of the Circle believe Lady Darlington has been sent to Dorset because of Blyminster's experiments."

"Barbarous invention," the admiral growled. "The Admiralty was right to refuse Fulton's *Nautilus* back in '04. Even that Frog de Pelle called undersea warfare immoral." He paused, glowering about

16

him. "If Boney gets his hands on an undersea ship, he'll blow us out of the water."

"Then you believe that Blyminster's invention will actually work?" Hartford demanded.

Sir Orin shrugged. "Perhaps, perhaps not. More important, here is a chance to trap the master spy of this pernicious ring. My agents have spread word that Blyminster's invention will revolutionize warfare. A double agent has sold reports on 'secret' experiments undertaken by Blyminster in Dorset."

"And you think Vilforme's widow has moved to Dorset because she's taken the bait?" Sir Orin nodded. "Let someone else unmask the lady as a master spy, Sir Orin. I'm no longer a part of Calworth's Circle."

Calworth ignored this. "It's all been arranged, dear boy, you're to stay with Blyminster. He's been told that you've been sent by the Admiralty to look into his invention—that's all he needs to know."

He paused and rested his hands on Hartford's shoulders. "Naturally, the very fact that a man of your reputation and standing is interested will give Blyminster credibility, and we feel sure that an attempt will be made to buy or even steal his invention." His voice grew soft, persuasive. "Of course you will serve your country once again, dear boy, will you not?"

With a depressing sense of déjà vu, Hartford recalled what serving his country had entailed. Not marches or charges or hand-to-hand combat in the hot blood of battle, but something much colder and infinitely more complex. Something that had left him with a bitter taste in the mouth and few illusions about human nature.

Aloud he mused, "I'd really hoped to have done with all of that."

"Tchah!" The admiral heaved himself to his feet and stood, glowering down. "England," he thundered, "demands that every man shall do his duty!"

That, too, had a depressingly familiar ring to it. The truly damnable thing, Hartford reflected, was that he could not in conscience turn his back on this miserable business—not while Bonaparte was loose and plotting to destroy England.

"I never doubted you for an instant, dear boy," Sir Orin was saying. He clasped the younger man's hand and wrung it. "Good man—true man. You'll do it, of course."

Hartford stifled a sigh. "Of course."

# Chapter Two

"There's one thing that can be said for Dorset," Miss Poll remarked grimly. "It's far from everything."

Melinda could not help but agree. Though the stagecoach was swift—they had covered an average of seven miles to the hour—they had been traveling since the previous afternoon. The night before they had put up in a noisy posting house near Eastleigh, and Miss Poll insisted that there were bedbugs in the bed.

She also complained that she had not had a wink of sleep all night due to riotous goings-on in the taproom below. Melinda, who had not spent a restful hour since announcing her intention to quit the Proctor Academy, forbore to point out that she had lain awake for hours listening to Miss Poll snore.

"It's not far now," she said soothingly. "The coast might be barren, but I am sure Kendle-on-Lake is going to be beautiful."

"*Kendle* Lake?" exclaimed a stout Yorkshire merchant who, with his wife, had boarded the mail coach at Eastleigh. "Not afraid of the Kendle dragon, arta, leddies?" Miss Poll sniffed. "I mean t'old boggle that lives at the bottom of t'lake. Oop it comes from the darkest depth with its black scales and leather wings and fiery breath."

"Stuff and rubbish!" Miss Poll rapped out. "As if there was such thing as dragons."

"Nay, it's no fib." Inspired by Miss Poll's scowl to higher heights of fancy, the merchant continued. "It's said that t'creature comes to warn t'country in times of peril. 'Twere sighted afore Hastings, and afore Agincourt, and when t'Spaniards sent their armada at us—"

Here he was interrupted by his round little wife, who besought him not to make such a pudding of himself. "Only thing t'be afeared of at Kendle Lake is floods and nasty fogs and mosquitoes," she said firmly. "And so I tell thee."

She looked about her for confirmation, but the other passengers inside the mail coach were either asleep or paying no attention. "Wonderful," Miss Poll muttered under her breath. "A dragon, the Rooshan, fogs *and* bugs. For this we left the best place we ever had."

Melinda ignored her companion's mumbled complaints until the mail coach drew up at the Royal Dragon in Kendle-on-Lake. Here she alighted, stretched her weary back, and looked about the neat, bustling town with pleasure until a handsome young fellow in livery approached, introduced himself as Lady Darlington's footman, and asked whether he was addressing Miss Weatherby. "My lady 'as sent a conveyance for you and your servant," he added.

His demeanor was supercilious and his manners just missed being impudent. Miss Poll's eyes narrowed alarmingly, but Melinda forestalled an explosion by replying, "I am Miss Weatherby, and this is Miss Poll, my *companion*. Please to see our baggage is properly bestowed."

Zenobie's elegant barouche had soft cushions.

Melinda leaned back into them gratefully and at last allowed herself to relax and admire the countryside. In sharp contrast to the often desolate Dorset coast, this was an area of softly rolling hills rich with trees and meadows, where horses were grazing. A lark sang from among the wildflowers, and the sun burst through clouds to turn the world warm and bright.

They soon came to a fork in the road and, swinging to the left, began to travel down a narrower road that skirted the rim of sparkling lake Kendle. Melinda noted that two large houses stood on almost opposite sides of this lake. The Cotswold stone of the house closest to them glowed golden in sun.

"Handsome is as handsome does," Miss Poll warned, but she thawed perceptibly as they drove into a broad courtyard. Here a groom came running to take the horses' heads and the young footman bestirred himself to set down the barouche steps.

"Welcome to Darlington Hall, madam."

Melinda looked up to see a tall, cadaverous personage descending the stone stairs of the house. He had a face like a disapproving walnut, and he all but creaked as he bowed, introduced himself as Russtin, my lady's butler, and added in a sepulchral tone that Lady Darlington was waiting impatiently.

"No more'n us have," Miss Poll began, but subsided at a warning glance from Melinda. Grimly silent, she trailed her former nurseling through the front door and an elegant ground-floor vestibule to a circular staircase.

"Her ladyship awaits you in her chamber," Russtin declared.

It was not like Zenobie to forgo a dramatic scene

of welcome. "She must be very ill," Melinda whispered to Miss Poll as they followed Russtin to the third floor, down a long, carpeted hallway and up to a closed door.

Here the butler knocked and a muffled voice exclaimed, "It is Melushka. Open the door, Sonya Vraskova—hurry!"

The door popped open, and a stout, middle-aged maid appeared to dip a knee and survey Melinda with watery blue eyes. "Miss Melinda," she said in a deeply accented voice. "How it is good to see you."

"I am glad to see you again, Sonya Vraskova," Melinda replied. "Where is Zenobie?"

The maid stepped aside to disclose a room hung with crimson velvet curtains and cluttered with Turkish carpets, ornate mahogany furniture, brass bric-a-brac, and an enormous four-poster. On this bed reclined a figure swathed from neck to toes in a shawl. A towel hid its countenance completely from view.

"Zenobie?" Melinda gasped.

"*Malenkaya*—my little one, I knew it was you!" The figure on the bed attempted to rise, then fell back. "Alas, I can't get up," she groaned. "Sonya Vraskova, don't stand there like a piece of furniture. Help me up at once, you tiresome woman."

Melinda had been prepared to find Zenobie ill, but not as sick as this. Hurrying into the room, she knelt beside her cousin to clench the small, beringed hand that emerged, groping, from under the shawl. "Zenobie, why didn't you write to me before?" she cried. "Are you very ill, dear? What is the matter with you?"

She was interrupted by the maid, who said, "The hourglass is empty, madame. The treatment, it is over."

22

At once the figure on the bed sat up, tossed aside towel and shawl, and flung open her arms. "At last, *malenkaya*," she cried.

Melinda stared at her cousin by marriage. Far from being at death's door, Zenobie looked to be the picture of health. Her face, under the upswept tangle of auburn curls, was rosy, her eyes were bright, and she was smiling. Nor did she show any signs of wasting away. The arms that hugged Melinda close were plump and strong.

"But—but I thought you were sick," Melinda stammered.

"Sick of boredom, my sweet one." Zenobie let Melinda go and smiled down into her worried eyes. "Ah, you think the treatment was for a disease? *Malenkaya*, it is for the worst disease of all—old age. To combat the wrinkles, I must put on my face the juice of pineapples mixed with spiderwebs and cover all over with a towel for an hour each morning. If not, I will soon come to look like Russtin."

Her laughter was so contagious that Melinda could not help smiling. Miss Poll folded arms across her bony middle and demanded, "So your *ladyship* ain't ailing?"

Sonya Vraskova bristled and glared at Miss Poll, but Zenobie ignored the sarcasm in the older woman's voice. She extended a hand, saying, "Miss Poll, I do not forget it is you who has taken so good a care of my *malenkaya*. Sonya Vraskova will bring us sherry and tea, and you shall tell me all about the difficult years."

Miss Poll pretended not to see the beringed hand. She curtsied and coldly stated that she had only done her duty. "And I'll be seeing about your luggage, Miss Mel," she added. "I don't trust that young bubblehead of a footman."

"Still starchy, still stiff in the rump," Zenobie commented airily as Miss Poll followed her maid-servant out of the room. "Does that woman never smile?"

Melinda herself did not feel like smiling. "Why did you make believe that you were ill?" she questioned.

Lady Darlington heaved a deep sigh. Expressive black eyes turned soulful, and her rosy, full mouth drooped. "It was not the whisker I wrote to you. I am so lonely, Melushka." She paused to press a whisper of lace against her eyes. "After Darlington died, my life has been an emptiness. All the time I lose the men I love in my life. Alas, I am accursed."

"I am sorry for that," Melinda said. "Really I am. But I don't see what I can do to—"

"Now that you are here, it will be as before. We will be so happy together, Melushka." Down went the scrap of lace and out came a brilliant smile. "Ah, the Poll woman may have the face of a Friday muffin, but she has at least done well by you. How beautiful a woman you have become, my sweet one. When we parted, you were such a child, all legs and angles and bones, and now!"

She clasped her hands in rapture. "Now here you are with such address, such hair, such eyes, and—and such *hideous* clothes. Bah! It will be my joy to golden the lily."

She jumped up from her bed to envelop Melinda in another scented embrace. "I am so very, very glad you have come," she whispered. "How I have suffered, *malenkaya*—I cannot tell you how much I have endured. But now that you are here, the sun shines, the damps and fogs do not creep up from the lake anymore. Life will be on the tops of the trees now that we are together once again."

* * *

"*She's* suffered, has she? What happened to her, then—tore the hem of her newest ball gown or maybe didn't have enough cream with her strawberries?"

"I beg you, Polly, hush." Melinda kneaded her throbbing temples with the tips of her fingers. Her interview with Zenobie had brought on a nagging headache that was not eased by the knowledge that Miss Poll had been right all the while.

Capricious Lady Darlington had never been ailing. She had just wanted some company. Because of this, Melinda had given up her secure position and, even worse, deserted the little girls who had looked to her for guidance and protection.

"You've got the headache again, ain't you?" Unexpectedly gentle fingers probed the ache at the base of Melinda's neck. "It's the tension what does it," Miss Poll grumbled. "All that worry as you've had, hurrying down here and all, not sleeping, hardly eating. And the Rooshan talks about how *she's* suffered."

Melinda resigned herself, and for the next five minutes Miss Poll catalogued what was wrong with Lady Darlington, her home, and her staff, which was, in Miss Poll's eyes, the laziest group of jumped-up good-for-nothings she had ever encountered. "And that Sonya Vraskova's as much of a sly-boots as ever she was. I don't trust her. I tell you, Miss Mel, save for Mr. Russtin and the cook, they're none of them better than they should be."

She paused for breath and asked without much hope, "Maybe you can talk that Proctor into taking you back?"

But they both knew that Melinda had burned her bridges at the academy. "Zenobie wants our visit to

25

last a long time. We can stay here until I find another post."

This could take some considerable time. Miss Poll was silent, and Melinda knew that the older woman, too, was remembering the anxiety, the frustrating delays, snubs, and petty humiliations that usually marked a search for suitable employment.

"I am persuaded that we will be lucky this time," she said with a cheerfulness she did not feel. "And my headache is much better now. Thank you, Polly. Zenobie is right—I would have been lost without you."

The pink glow intensified on Miss Poll's nose, but she only sniffed, "Stuff and rubbish. Stop trying to turn me up sweet, Miss Mel, and lie down while I go find you a good cup of tea and a compress for your head. It'll take me a few minutes to sort out them twiddlepoops below stairs," she added ominously, "so you may as well have a nap."

But Melinda was too nervous to rest. Instead, she looked about the room Zenobie had chosen for her. In sharp contrast to Zenobie's dramatic furnishings, this chamber was simply, even sparsely appointed. There was a narrow bed, a nondescript gray and blue carpet on the oaken floor, a grouping of rather elderly chairs around the hearth, and a desk set under a portrait of a portly gentleman with a drooping mustache.

Something in the disapproving countenance of this personage recalled Mr. Proctor. Melinda bit back a sigh. Best always to look forward rather than back, she told herself.

Rising from her chair, she walked to the window that overlooked the gardens. Her headache was almost gone so that now she could enjoy the sight of the sun dipping toward the west and sending golden streamers onto the curve of the lake below. In this hour of late afternoon the water seemed to shimmer with a silver haze.

"That is where the mythical dragon is supposed to dwell," she mused aloud, but in fact there seemed nothing ominous about the lake. It sparkled up at her in an invitation that was hard to refuse.

So why refuse? Without further delay Melinda slipped on her shoes, reached for her bonnet, and left her chamber. The impertinent young footman was busy flirting with a chambermaid at the bottom of the circular staircase, so Melinda let herself out of a side door. Then, standing on the top step, she admired Zenobie's estate.

Lord Darlington had left his widow with a fine property. From her vantage point Melinda could see that the garden spread all the way to the thick grove of trees that edged the lake. But when she walked down among the flower beds, she was surprised to see that they had not been weeded for some time and that the path that led down a gentle slope toward the lake was choked with brambles.

Zenobie should have a word with her gardeners, Melinda thought as she picked her way through those brambles. The walk to the lake, which should by rights have lasted a few minutes, took her a full quarter of an hour. But in the end the view was worth it, for framed by vines and trailing willow fronds, Kendle Lake was a gold blue picture. A blue heron, its neck folded into itself, eyed her warily as it stalked the shallows.

"Perfect," Melinda exclaimed. "Oh, this is perfect."

Gingerly, she made her way toward a sun-warmed tussock of grass by the water's edge, sat down, and let the last of the tension drain away from her. Time enough in the days ahead to think of what to do. In such glorious surroundings she could even feel glad that she had left Proctor Academy.

"I could not have stayed there anyway, not after what Mr. Proctor did to Mary and Jenny," she mused aloud. "I would have had to speak up. But, oh, the *poor* little girls. They will have cold comfort from Miss Vraye, I'm afraid."

As she spoke, she became conscious of a gentle splashing sound nearby. Looking up, Melinda saw that eddying ripples were forming on the lake's surface some fifty yards off. A fish? she wondered idly. But it would have to be a big fish, indeed, to cause such wide ripples.

Interested, she watched the ripples widen. "Perhaps a school of fish?" she conjectured.

The blue heron extended its neck and, with a single flap of powerful wings, flew off. But why would the bird fly *away* from fish? Melinda stared at the widening ripples and then caught her breath. Something was pushing up out of the water. Something long, dark, and snakelike—

*T'boggle that lives at t'dark bottom of lake Kendle.* "Impossible," Melinda exclaimed. "There are no such things as dragons—"

But the word vanished into a stifled scream as a huge black *something* boiled up out of the water. Melinda stared for a moment in frozen horror and then sprang to her feet. She tripped over a root, lost her balance, and began to fall backward.

"Easy, ma'am," a pleasant male voice exclaimed. Braced for a jolting fall, Melinda found herself propped up at the elbows. She dragged her eyes away from the monstrous dark object in the water and saw that a gentleman had somehow materialized at her side. "Don't be alarmed," he reassured her. "There's no danger."

Too shaken to respond, Melinda stared back at the large object in the lake. Now she could see that it was a partially submerged metal cylinder and most definitely man-made, *not* dragon-spawned. "I knew th-that all the time," she stammered.

"Naturally."

Melinda turned her attention back to her companion. He was tall and lean, and sported a double-breasted riding coat of fawn-colored superfine and buff riding breeches. Sunlight turned his thick brown hair to bronze.

How was it that she had not heard him approach? But, of course, her attention had been so riveted on the *thing* in the water that she would not have heard a thunderclap. "Are you sure you haven't hurt yourself?" he was asking solicitously.

A smile lurked just under the surface of those polite words. And why not? If the roles had been reversed, Melinda thought, she would have been laughing at the situation.

"For a moment I thought I was about to see the famous Kendle dragon." At her confession, the smile broke through, lighting his entire face. It was not a handsome face precisely, but pleasant to look upon. There was both intelligence and humor in his dark eyes and in the curve of his mobile mouth.

"I hope Sir Rupert's invention didn't give you too much of a fright." He apologized, "He intended to surface about a mile away, near Blyminster Cove. He must have drifted off course."

He paused, bowed, and added, "But I'm forget-

ting my manners. Anthony Hartford, ma'am—
yours to command."

Before Melinda could respond in kind, hollow
thuds and shouts began to emanate from the device
in the water. "Your friend seems to be in difficulty,"
she exclaimed.

"He probably can't get out of the dashed thing."
Mr. Hartford leaned back on his heels and watched
the bobbing craft with great interest. "Probably, the
hatch has gotten stuck again."

"How long has your friend been in there?" When
told, Melinda was aghast. "An *hour*? Then we must
lose no time in getting him out. He may suffocate."

But Mr. Hartford shook his head. "No danger of
that. Blyminster's invented a way to bring air into
his machine." He then added reflectively, "But it
must be fiendishly hot in there."

As if to underscore his words, louder thuds and
shouts came from within the metal object. "I'll get
help from the house," Melinda exclaimed.

"No need. I know what to do."

To Melinda's surprise, Mr. Hartford sat down on
the bank and commenced pulling off his riding
boots. Then, rolling his breeches up to the knee, he
waded into the lake toward the contraption.
Melinda winced as he stumbled and nearly fell. "Be
careful," she called.

She broke off in consternation as Mr. Hartford
suddenly sank waist-deep in water. "Not to worry,
ma'am," he called over his shoulder. Then, as the
water level rose to his chest, he added, "All in a
day's work. Now, where the deuce did the tow rope
get to?"

Melinda watched anxiously as he began to fum-
ble under the surface. "Ah, here it is."

He lifted up a stout cable to show her what he

meant and began to tow the cylindrical contraption toward the shore. It bobbed behind him until it had reached the shallows. An indistinct shouting came from the interior of the craft. "Steady on, Blyminster," Mr. Hartford called. "I'll soon have you out."

By now he had reached the shallows and had commenced to push at a section of the contraption. Nothing happened. Melinda could now partially understand the muffled shouts. "He's saying that you must pull and push," she said. "What does he mean?"

"Apparently it takes two people to open the hatch from the outside." Another volley of instructions came from the interior of the machine. "I'd better ride up to your house after all," he then said. "I left my horse along the path."

"But your friend is in distress. I can help you if you tell me what to do."

The dark gentleman looked surprised. "You'd have to wade into the water," he pointed out. "You'll get your feet wet."

"They have been wet before." Absorbed in removing her shoes, Melinda did not see the suddenly keen, measuring look that her companion bent on her.

"Be careful," he said as, in her stocking feet, she waded into the water. Sparkling blue though it might be, the April sun had barely warmed it. Underfoot, cold mud slithered and slid so that she could barely stand upright.

Melinda gave an involuntary gasp as she lost her footing entirely, but her companion caught her hand so that she fetched up against his side. In the scant second she remained pressed to him, she realized that she had to revise her first impression.

Anthony Hartford might be lean, but his tall body was solidly limned with muscle, and his grip was surprising in its strength.

"Did you twist your ankle?" he was asking. "I warned you not to come into the water. Lake Kendle *looks* peaceful, but looks are often deceptive."

There was a speculative glint in the dark eyes that looked down into hers from a distance of only a few inches. No doubt he was wondering what sort of lady went shoeless and padded about in the water, Melinda thought. "What must I do to help your friend?" she wondered aloud.

"Press that lever while I pull this handle. Push now. Er—put your back in it, ma'am."

Melinda pushed with all her might. There was a creaking sound, and all at once a hatch on top of the contraption popped open to divulge a red and dripping countenance. Lank curls, red mixed with gray, hung down into slightly protuberant green blue eyes.

"About demmed time," cried this individual testily. "What took you so demmed long to—ah, that is to say, ahem!—beg your pardon, ma'am. Didn't see you. Y'r most obedient, mean to say, egad—"

He broke off and goggled at Melinda. "Best get to shore, Blyminster," Hartford suggested. "No need to exert yourself further, ma'am. We have matters well in hand."

Seeing she was no longer needed, Melinda most gingerly retraced her steps to the bank. Here she wrung out her skirts and watched as Sir Rupert Blyminster dropped a rope ladder over the side of his device and cautiously descended.

"Mud's slippery," Mr. Hartford warned as the inventor splashed knee-deep in water. "What happened? I thought you were going to stay submerged near Blyminster Cove for another half hour."

"Decided to take it for a trial run around the lake, but the demmed—mean to say, the *dashed* valve in the air inducer got stuck again," was the aggrieved reply. "Had to come up in a hurry. Eh? Now I've got to rework the dem—the dashed thing again."

He paused and, with a furtive glance at Melinda, added in a loud whisper, "Did she see anythin' she shouldn't have, d'you think, Hartford?"

"If it wasn't for Lady Darlington, you'd be still stuck in that contraption of yours." Startled, Melinda looked up. "You owe her ladyship your thanks, Blyminster."

"But I am not—" Melinda was interrupted by the spluttering Sir Rupert.

"Lady Darlington, eh? Your most obedient, ma'am," he exclaimed. "Heard you was in the area—meant to call on you this long time. Beg you'll overlook m'deplorable manners. Fault of m'invention—it takes every minute I have, mean to say." He nodded to the device in the water. "I call it the *Subaqua*. Eh? Play on words, d'you see? It's meant to travel underwater."

Hartford coughed. Sir Rupert stiffened, gave a sort of wheezing gasp, exclaimed "Quite so," and then began to talk very quickly. "Quite right. Forgot m'self for a minute. Eh? Mean to say—m'invention isn't very good. Doesn't work. You saw how it didn't work just now. Useless, really. Probably never will work."

Completely baffled, Melinda watched as Sir Rupert Blyminster tipped a wink at his tall companion. Was the man merely an eccentric, she wondered, or dangerously deranged?

"Hartford is staying with me for a while," Sir Rupert dithered on. "*He* don't think the *Subaqua*'s any use neither."

"What Blyminster means is that he's putting up with my company for a few weeks, Lady Darlington," Mr. Hartford explained smoothly. "His invitation to Dorset rescued me from my boring life in Scotland."

Both men beamed at Melinda, who felt it was high time to put matters right. "Mr. Hartford," she said firmly, "Sir Rupert Blyminster, I am not Lady Darlington. My name is Melinda Weatherby, and I am Lady Darlington's cousin by marriage."

Sir Rupert looked astonished. Mr. Hartford said, "Ah," and for an instant, something seemed to shift in the depths of his eyes, changing his expression to—but before she could analyze *how* it had been changed, his pleasant smile returned.

"I beg your pardon, Miss Weatherby," he said. "I saw you on Lady Darlington's estate and assumed—but only a fool assumes the obvious." He took her hand and bent gracefully over it. "Forgive me. I hope you aren't the worse for wear after an encounter with the Kendle Lake dragon."

Her earlier reaction to the so-called "dragon" made her wince. Then she laughed at herself. "Not at all, sir, I thank you."

"But it's somethin', eh?" interjected Sir Rupert. He had been standing silent, staring at his invention and shaking his head. "Travelin' underwater like it was supposed to. Surfacin' when it needed to. It'll be all right and tight once I get it back to m'workroom."

He started toward his invention, re-collected himself, and bowed to Melinda. "Servant, ma'am," he said. "Beg you'll accept my thanks. Er, must be goin' now. Mean to say, have got to row the *Subaqua* home to Blyminster Cove."

"I'll meet you there," Anthony Hartford said, and Melinda realized that he was still holding her hand. As she disengaged it, he asked, "Are you visiting your cousin for some time, Miss Weatherby? In that case we'll doubtless meet again. As Blyminster said, we're neighbors. A paltry fifteen-minute ride away—"

He was interrupted by an exclamation from Sir Rupert, who by that time had climbed back into his invention. "I say, Hartford—forgot to untie the moorin' rope," the inventor called. "Would you get it for me, there's a good chap?"

As the tall gentleman obliged, Melinda began to climb the overgrown path back to Darlington House. Part of her mind was on what Miss Poll would say when she saw her former nurseling's ruined skirts.

"How she will scold. But," Melinda reflected, "it can't be helped. It's not every day that a lady meets with a scientific dragon. Nor yet with a latter-day St. George."

# Chapter Three

Whistling under his breath, Lord Hartford descended the stairs that led to Sir Rupert Blyminster's workroom. The stone stairwell held a chill in spite of the unseasonably warm early April day, for the workroom had been built only a few feet above lake level.

At the foot of the stairs stood a massive wooden door. It was closed, an enormous key protruded from the lock, and Sir Rupert's morose butler was standing guard. "Hard at it is he, Owens?" Hartford asked.

"Yes, milord, Sir Rupert has been in there since breakfast" was the dispirited answer. "His orders are that he is not to be disturbed."

"Then I'll make sure that I don't disturb him." As he spoke, Hartford turned the key and opened the door onto a long, narrow, low-ceilinged, flagstone-floored chamber. The light shed by half a dozen oil lamps illuminated a clutter of machine parts, piles of wood, and scrap metal. A metal safe stood in one corner, next to a table laden with papers. In the center of the room, set on a wooden platform with wheels, was the *Subaqua*.

There was no sign of its inventor. "Blyminster?" Hartford queried.

"Demmit." The inventor's muffled voice came

from within the cylindrical device. "Turn, you disgustin' piece of scrap metal, eh? Move, sirrah, if y'know what's good for you!"

There was a grunt, a curse, and a clinking sound. "A pox on you for a stubborn son of steel!" the inventor shouted.

Hartford strolled over to the *Subaqua* and called, "Having a hard day, Blyminster?" A moment later the inventor's choleric countenance emerged from the open hatch.

"Demmed valve's stuck tighter than a cent-per-center's fist. Can't shake it loose," he growled. As he clambered down the ladder he added combatively, "Don't stand there laughin'. Give it a turn if you think you can do better, mean to say."

Hartford took the proffered wrench, climbed the ladder, and entered Sir Rupert's underwater ship. Inside as out, the *Subaqua's* twenty-three feet of copper and iron chassis was lovingly polished. Two seats, buckled to the wall, were crammed together across from hand-turning propellers that were used to move the craft when submerged.

Underfoot lay bolts that could loose the metal ballast in case a rapid ascent became necessary, and overhead rose the long metal tube that Sir Rupert had invented to bring air into his machine. Crouching in the cramped space, Hartford reached up into the air inducer, found the stuck valve, and gave it a twist.

It turned almost instantly. "Can't get it, can you?" Sir Rupert was demanding outside the *Subaqua*. "Eh? Not that easy, is it?"

Hartford gave the valve a little tap with his wrench and tightened it slightly so that even the gentlest twist would set it free. "No," he called, "not easy at all. I can't budge it, either. It's stuck, as you said. So what will you do?"

"Have to keep tryin', I suppose." Sir Rupert sighed. As Hartford emerged, he added, "That's the first rule to inventin'—uncharted territory and all that rubbish just means y'have to put your backside into it."

He reentered the *Subaqua,* leaving Hartford to stroll across the flagstones to the workshop's one window. It was little larger than a porthole, but through it Hartford could see that the inventor had built his workshop to resemble a peninsula. It stuck out at right angles from the rest of the house and was surrounded on three sides by water.

Anyone seeking to pry into Sir Rupert's secrets would have to approach by boat. Instinctively, Hartford looked across the lake toward Darlington Place. "The stronghold of the enemy fair," Hartford mused. "By now she must be as curious as a cat."

Desiring to fan that curiosity, Hartford had carefully refrained from visiting any of the local gentry. His manservant, Dayce, who had spent his time making discreet inquiries in Kendle-on-Lake, reported that speculation and gossip was rife about Sir Rupert's visitor.

Hartford's thoughts were interrupted by a yelp of triumph behind him. "There, by Jove," Sir Rupert exclaimed. He climbed out of his machine, adding, "Knew I could do it, only had to persevere. Mean to say, perseverance and patience—that's the thing."

Patience—and a sense of timing. It was, Hartford decided, the right moment to call upon Vilforme's widow.

"You've done it, Blyminster," he said aloud. The inventor beamed. "A good day's work deserves a change of scene. We're going for a ride."

Sir Rupert looked taken aback. "But I don't want to ride, old chap. Mean to say, lots of work to be done on the—"

"We should ride," Lord Hartford interrupted, "over to Darlington Manor. You've said it yourself—you've been neglecting your neighborly duties. Besides, you owe Miss Weatherby more than casual thanks. She ruined her skirts to rescue you the other day."

Sir Rupert's face had grown gradually longer during his companion's speech. "I'm not used to talkin' to females," he confessed. "All that demmed polite conversation and gigglin' and gossip—makes me itch. Besides, Lady Darlington's some sort of foreigner, ain't she? Not our sort."

He went to the table and became absorbed in scribbling on a blueprint. Watching him, Hartford agreed that Lady Darlington was most definitely not Sir Rupert's sort. She could devour this well-meaning ditherer as easily as she could play piquet.

"Her cousin seems like a right 'un," the inventor was saying. "Small lady, but trim as a trencher."

Hartford could not help smiling as he recalled his meeting with Miss Melinda Weatherby. According to Dayce, who had made friends with the old butler at Darlington House, Miss Weatherby had only recently arrived at Kendle-on-Lake after leaving a position at a young-girls' academy in Sussex. On the surface of things, she did not seem the sort to be mixed up in her cousin's schemes, but then, few things actually were as they seemed.

*Trust no one, confide in no one, turn your back on no one.* With Sir Orin Calworth's prime directive firmly in mind, Hartford strolled forward to clap the inventor on the back.

"Come, Blyminster," he said bracingly, "time to show the flag, man. Keeping to yourself too much might arouse suspicion in the locals—and as you know, the Admiralty doesn't want anyone getting too curious about the *Subaqua*."

"If you say so. But," Sir Rupert added gloomily, "I'd much rather be doin' somethin' else."

"I thought you said that you were lonely," Melinda protested. "How can you be lonely with all these people coming to call?"

She indicated the silver tray that Russtin had just brought into the morning room. Zenobie reached out a languid white hand and ruffled the calling cards that reposed on that tray.

"What are these callers to me? But mere acquaintances. Bah! At the bottom of my soul, I ache with loneliness."

Her voice throbbed with feeling. Her dark eyes were studiedly soulful. Melinda did not believe her in the least.

Since she had arrived in Dorset, her cousin by marriage had entertained a great number of people. Each day Russtin brought in the silver tray, and each day Zenobie went through the charade of lamenting her loneliness. "Your house is always full of guests," Melinda pointed out.

"Full of nobodies, you mean. It is wearisome to see them all."

"Shall I say that you are not at home, milady?" Russtin wondered.

But milady shook her head. "No. Alas, one must keep up the appearance even if my health is suffering from it. My poor, dear Darlington would have wished it so. Show them to the Green Room, Russtin, and let refreshments be brought."

Zenobie, Melinda thought, did not look as if she was suffering. In fact, she appeared particularly handsome today in a muslin day dress of flocked damask embroidered with forget-me-nots. Moreover, as she read the cards, there was a pleased gleam in her eye.

"Ah-ha, we have amusing guests today. Here is little Ferridew, who is a poet, and my neighbor Mrs. Pennodie and her stepdaughter, Carabel, who is sadly a homely Jane."

Zenobie settled down to gossip. "Mrs. Pennodie is a rich widow. She will be quick to tell you that they are not enjoying the London season in her *expensive* London town house because she has hired the Briddle family of Yorkshire to make a little garden for her. The Briddles are all the cracks in the best circles, and Mrs. Pennodie thinks that hiring them will make her one of the ton even though her late husband made all his money as a grain merchant."

Zenobie's voice was heavy with an aristocrat's disdain for The Trade. "Mrs. Pennodie would like Carabel to marry well, but—ah, bah, here is Squire Parcher come again. You recall him, *malenkaya?*"

Indeed, Melinda remembered the squire. A short, stout, leering man past his prime, he had little to recommend him except broad lands that lay some distance away. "I do not think I will come down today," Melinda decided. "Pray give my excuses to your guests, Zenobie."

"But you must descend. I particularly desire you shall meet another neighbor, Dr. Theodore Gildfish, who lives in the town. He is a fine man and the son of Lord Macley, the Scottish gentleman."

To her surprise, Melinda realized that she was disappointed. When Zenobie had said "neighbor,"

41

she had immediately thought of Mr. Hartford and his friend the inventor.

It had been several days since that incident at the lake. When Melinda had regaled her cousin by marriage with the incident over supper, Zenobie had been excited and she had said that the elusive Sir Rupert would come to call, but so far neither he nor Mr. Hartford had manifested themselves.

"You must come down," Zenobie repeated, "and— by St. Catherine, I did *not* know that the Conte del'Anche was in England."

Melinda was surprised to see that Zenobie had turned pale. "No, I am quite well," the lady exclaimed to Melinda's anxious questions. "I am startled, that is all. I thought the *conte* was on the continent." Her color had returned, and she smiled roguishly at her cousin. "I met Paolo in Paris while I was still Madame Vilforme, and you must beware, for he has a reputation with the ladies. Come, we will go down and I shall make the introductions."

The ladies descended to the first floor from whence came the tinkling notes of a spinet being played. Zenobie winked at Melinda and then swept into the Green Room, exclaiming, "My friends, you are all welcome in my house."

The music stopped abruptly. A few steps behind her cousin, Melinda glanced quickly around the room and saw two men standing close together. One was youngish and in modest brown, the other older, fatter, and squeezed into a bottle green jacket and yellow corduroy breeches. A third gentleman rose swiftly from the spinet he had been playing.

"Madonna!" He exclaimed. "*Carissima, bellissima!* Lady Darlington, you are more beautiful than I 'ave ever seen you."

Near the door, a full-blown lady with improbably yellow hair and a mean, rabbity face simpered. "Does not the count make that foreign language sound elegant, Carabel?" She nudged the rangy, broad-faced girl next to her. "Get up and make your curtsy to her ladyship, you tiresome child."

"Ah, Mrs. Pennodie, how good to see you returned from London." Zenobie stepped forward, hands outstretched. "How sweetly you are looking, my little Carabel."

The young woman blushed as red as her expensive but unbecoming cherry-colored muslin gown. Her stepmother exclaimed in a high, affected voice, "Lady Darlington, my *dear*."

As the two ladies kissed the air beside each other's cheek, the spinet-playing gentleman advanced across the room. He was, Melinda noted, dressed with an understated elegance that flattered his dark good looks. Bowing over Zenobie's hand with almost feline grace, he began to murmur compliments in Italian.

"What nonsense you talk, *Conte*," Zenobie laughed. "Now I make you known to my little cousin, Miss Melinda Weatherby. You will not try to make love to my sweet Melinda, Paolo. I forbid it."

Melinda felt herself being appraised and measured by worldly eyes. But before the *conte* could speak, a plaintive voice exclaimed, "Who speaks of love?"

A fair-haired young man in gray was standing by the window. Melinda did not wonder that she had at first overlooked him, for he was so thin that he seemed almost as transparent as the glass he held in one hand. "I toast you, cruel goddess," he declaimed. "My Aphrodite with the coal black eyes and flaming hair. Love divine! Cruel, cruel love!"

43

"There you are, my little Ferridew." Complacently, Zenobie held out her hand and the young man also crossed the room—none too steadily, Melinda noted—and falling to one knee, pressed his lips passionately to Zenobie's knuckles.

"I have longed for this moment," he declared. "I have written a sonnet to the hand of my goddess, which I shall read—"

"Read it later. By my head, I can't stomach much of this mist and moonshine."

The fat man in green had stumped forward to greet Lady Darlington. Melinda stepped back to be well out his way, for Squire Parcher's loose-lipped, smug face and wet, warm handshake were all unappetizing. But even less pleasant was the way Mrs. Pennodie kept prodding and poking at her awkward stepdaughter.

"And the poet is foxed," she muttered.

"He's always in his cups. Something to do with the unendurable pain of living." The gentleman in brown had come up to stand beside Melinda. "Apparently poor Ferridew can't abide the philistines in the world."

He then paused to bow. "I beg your pardon. I'm Theodore Gildfish, ma'am, and your most obedient servant."

So this was Zenobie's doctor. Melinda was grateful that this gentleman, at least, was a study in moderation. Dr. Gildfish was handsome, but not excessively so. His handshake was firm without being importunate. His broad-shouldered, athletic form was dressed well but not extravagantly. And there was something both warm and diffident in his smile as he continued. "I understood that you had come to stay with Lady Darlington, Miss Weatherby. May I tell you that I'm glad of it?"

The slight constraint in his voice made Melinda exclaim, "Is my cousin *really* ill?"

The doctor's concerned brown eyes met hers squarely. "I know that Lady Darlington looks the picture of health, but she does have a condition of the heart. To give you words with no bark on them, Miss Weatherby, she could become very ill indeed."

And she had until then dismissed Zenobie's complaints as mere drama. Melinda's own heart contracted. "Please," she faltered, "will you tell me more?"

A burst of laughter drowned out the doctor's reply. Melinda glanced at the *conte,* who was toasting her cousin with sherry, and then back to Dr. Gildfish, who suggested that they repair to the back of the room. Once there, Melinda repeated her request.

"Lady Darlington's condition is not dangerous *now,*" the doctor replied, "but she must be careful. For one thing, she eats and drinks to excess."

Melinda glanced at Zenobie, who was reaching for another glass of sherry. "What can I do to help?"

"Get her to rest and not overexcite herself. She has lived such an *uneven* life that her constitution has been undermined." Dr. Gildfish broke off to add, "I don't mean to sound like a doomsayer, Miss Weatherby. Country air will do much for Lady Darlington—*if* she learns how to compose herself."

"I will do my best to persuade her," Melinda promised. "Thank you—I am so grateful that you are in Dorset."

"So am I. After some of the places I've lived in, Dorset seems a wonderfully peaceful haven."

Russtin had just entered the room with a silver tray laden with more sherry. He was followed by a maid who carried a platter of cakes, little sandwiches, and ices of which Zenobie was especially fond.

"You yourself have newly come to Kendle-on-Lake?" she asked the doctor.

"I've been here for a few months. Before that I was in Edinburgh and before *that* in Spain as a military doctor."

"How courageous of you," Melinda exclaimed, but he shook his head.

"Hardly that. I saw no fighting—I only treated our poor wounded men." He paused for a moment before adding, "After Napoleon was sent to Elba, I returned to my Edinburgh practice and found it too loud and busy. I confided this to a surgeon who had been with me in Spain, and he told me about a doctor who was selling his practice in Dorset. So I—"

Dr. Gildfish broke off. "Good Lord, Lady Darlington must *not* eat those rich pastries," he exclaimed. "Excuse me, Miss Weatherby, while I go and play the physician."

"Aye, do that, Doctor. I'll attend to the young lady."

Squire Parcher had stumped up to them. He carried a glass of sherry in each beefy hand. "A drop to warm you, Miss?" he leered. "Yer cheeks need to be rosier to tempt the bee, hey?"

Disgusted at the insinuation in his voice, Melinda turned to walk away. The squire followed. "You look down-pin, Missy," he suggested. "Homesick for Sussex and lonely, maybe?"

Before she could compose a satisfactory reply, Russtin announced, "Sir Rupert Blyminster and Lord Hartford."

And there, framed in the doorway, was the inventor. He had brushed down his carroty hair, but it still stood on edge around his long face. He looked uncomfortable in his navy blue coat, yellow waist-coat, and old-fashioned blue pantaloons.

"Eh, what?" he exclaimed. "Didn't mean to in-trude—didn't realize you was entertainin', Lady Darlington—best go away and come another day."

He hastily turned to depart and ran into the man who stood directly behind him. Mr.—no, *Lord* Hart-ford, Melinda corrected herself—looked the picture of a country gentleman in a simple but beautifully cut square-tailed coat and high-waisted, close-fitting pantaloons of light gray superfine. In sharp contrast to his perspiring companion, he seemed very much at his ease.

Melinda's thoughts trailed away as she realized that Lord Hartford was looking directly at her. He bowed and sent her a friendly smile before Zenobie closed in on him.

"I am enchanted—delighted," she caroled. "How kind to call on a poor, lonely old woman."

Lady Darlington was unlike any old woman *he* had ever seen. A handsome female, Hartford con-ceded dryly, who must have sent poor old Darling-ton's thin blood dancing.

And the old fellow's house was now cluttered with an assortment of rogues and toad-eaters. From his position by the door he had been taking inventory and had seen the old griffin with her un-gainly chick, the effete young tulip who was drink-ing sullenly in a corner, that aging country oaf squeezed into green and yellow—and del'Anche with his suave, catlike elegance.

The last time he had seen del'Anche was in Spain. Could it be coincidence that the man should turn up in Lady Darlington's parlor? Not bloody likely, Lord Hartford told himself.

All in all, it was as motley a collection of rascals

and care-for-nobodies as ever had assembled in a fashionable residence. With one exception. Hartford glanced back to the corner of the room where Miss Melinda Weatherby stood with her hands clasped lightly in front of her and was reminded of a rose blooming bravely in a patch of nettles.

He would have liked to walk across the room to greet her, but Lady Darlington was still expressing her delight at meeting him. She then bent a sparkling smile on Sir Rupert. "I had wondered when my neighbor across the lake would honor me with a visit. You are the gentleman who builds the boats, are you not?"

"And *you* are their graces of Benwick's son!" Mrs. Pennodie all but shrieked. "I knew I recognized the name. Pray, Lord Hartford, allow me to make you known to my little Carabel."

She shoved her stepdaughter forward so precipitously that the girl collided with the Conte del'Anche. With considerable aplomb the *conte* recovered, bowed aside Miss Pennodie's stammered apologies, and turned to the newcomers.

"I am Paolo del'Anche—at your service, *signori*. Milor' Hartford, we 'ave met before, but doubtless you will not remember such a triviality."

"On the contrary, Signor. I recall you very well." Smiling most pleasantly, Hartford added, "I didn't know you were in England. Did the continent lose its charm?"

"It lacks a certain panache these days." Del'Anche removed a snuffbox from his coat, shook a few grains out on his elegant hand, and sniffed. "And you, milor'? I 'ad 'eard you 'ad returned to your estate in Scotland."

There was a predatory glint in the *conte*'s eye, and a chill, prickling sensation—his foolproof presentiment of danger—began to play along the base of Hartford's spine. "Just now I'm visiting Sir Rupert Blyminster," he said.

"I, too, am visiting in the area. We will no doubt see more of each other, milor'."

There was a burst of coarse laughter from across the room. Hartford's lips tightened as he saw that the oaf in green and yellow had moved closer to Miss Weatherby and was waving a glass of sherry almost in her face. He had positioned himself so as to effectively block her escape and was standing so near that his meaty thigh was almost in contact with hers.

Enough was enough. Unhurriedly, Hartford bowed to del'Anche and strolled toward the lady and her importunate companion. Her eyes brightened at his approach, but all she said was "Good morning, Lord Hartford."

"Miss Weatherby, your most obedient servant."

As Hartford bowed, his elbow caught the stout man's arm. There was a cry of outrage and the furious squire stared at the sherry that was running down the front of his coat. "A pox on you," he snarled. "Don't you look where you're going, damn it?"

"Language," Hartford reminded him. "Lady's present."

The squire glared up at the young interloper to damn him again and encountered glacial dark eyes which made him hastily swallow his spleen. "An unfortunate accident," Hartford remarked as the squire stamped away.

Melinda raised her eyebrows. "There really was no need to spill sherry over him. A second before you appeared, I had resolved to stamp down on his instep with all my strength."

"That would have got his attention," he agreed gravely, and she tipped back her head and laughed.

She had, Hartford thought, a delightful laugh—warm, a little husky, and as he listened, the prickling sensation along his spine slowly eased. He drew a deep breath and found the air to be tinged with a delicate rose scent that emanated from her.

"How is the *Subaqua*?" she was asking. "Did Sir Rupert adjust the valve for the—I think he called it the air inducer?"

"He's working on it." Conscious of any ears that might be listening, Hartford spoke heartily. "According to Blyminster, the great danger in an underwater ship is lack of oxygen. He's devised a tube that allows air to flow from the surface into the submerged vehicle."

"But would not water flow in as well?" Melinda wondered, and Hartford explained that Sir Rupert had installed a valve that kept the *Subaqua* from being flooded.

"I see—so simple, and yet it would work." Melinda added thoughtfully, "I always thought it amazing to think of a ship beneath the sea. I am in awe of Mr. David Bushnell's *Turtle*—and naturally of Mr. Fulton's *Nautilus*."

Hartford was surprised. "I hadn't expected a lady to be knowledgeable in such things," he told her.

"I have 'scraps and bits' of information—" Melinda broke off in some confusion. She had almost added that such bits of information were useful to a governess.

A duke's son, no matter how pleasant and friendly, would consider governesses entirely beneath his notice—but then Melinda was exasperated at herself. Why would she care what Lord Hartford thought?

"Does Lady Darlington always have so many callers?" he was asking.

"Yes. She is not used to a quiet life and likes excitement," Melinda replied.

Hartford glanced over at Lady Darlington, who was deep in conversation with Blyminster. Perhaps it would not be long, after all, before the greedy mouse took the bait. Meanwhile, he might learn something of value from the cousin.

He smiled at Melinda and asked, "Has your life been as exciting, Miss Weatherby?"

The question was lightly asked. Melinda hesitated for less than a second before replying, "It has had its moments. For instance, the trick of stamping on an importunate person's foot was taught to me by my old nurse. She thought that it would protect me when I first began to work as a governess."

Now the duke's son would realize that she was Lady Darlington's *poor* cousin and thus below his notice. Melinda steeled herself for the snub that was sure to come and reminded herself of Miss Poll's greatest rule: Be honest, especially when it hurts.

But Lord Hartford only said, "I'd like to meet your nurse. Has your cousin taught you anything as interesting?"

Ridiculously grateful for the unchanged warmth in his voice, Melinda was about to reply, when a high-pitched, affected voice spoke almost in her ear.

"Tell me, dear Lord Hartford," Mrs. Pennodie was exclaiming, "how have you left their graces of Benwick?"

Without waiting for his lordship's reply, she gushed on. "I hear that her grace commissioned the Briddle family of Yorkshire to build her one of their lovely little gardens. By coincidence, I, too, have

51

contracted the Briddles to work for me. A coup, as I am persuaded you must agree, for they are in great demand. They do not work for just *anybody*."

Whilst chattering on, she all but shouldered Melinda aside. Perforce giving ground, Melinda bumped into Miss Pennodie, who ducked her head and whispered, "I beg your pardon, ma'am," in a frightened little voice.

Smiling reassuringly at the girl, Melinda made her way across the room to Zenobie, who was seated next to the inventor. "Oh, Sir Rupert, you are the tops of all the trees," she was exclaiming. "I never expected to meet the creator of such scientific wonders. You say that your invention is better still than the *Nautilus?*"

"The *Nautilus* don't have a feather on m'*Subaqua*, ma'am," replied Sir Rupert. He puffed out his thin chest as he added contemptuously, "The *Nautilus* couldn't stay underwater long—lack of oxygen, mean to say."

"And your craft can remain submerged?" the Conte del'Anche demanded. He had abandoned his pretence of talking to Dr. Gildfish and was now leaning forward in great interest.

Realizing that many eyes were on him, Sir Rupert turned scarlet and began to backtrack rapidly, "Well, no, not really. There's a problem—several problems, mean to say. The valve will stick, and the hatch and—best stick to sailboats, that's what I say."

Before del'Anche could ask another question, Zenobie exclaimed, "Sailboats—of course, sailboats. You are such a brilliant man, Sir Rupert, and you give me the rattling fine idea. You will be the admiral of my nautical party, will you not?"

The inventor blinked and muttered rather feebly

that he was proud to be of service. Zenobie beamed at him and spread out her arms in a dramatic gesture. "It will be a party of sailboats and boating in honor of the spring. I am inspired! I will invite everybody!"

Even Mrs. Pennodie, who had been prosing on and on to Lord Hartford, stopped to listen. Meanwhile, Melinda cautioned, "Perhaps you should think about this first, Zenobie. Dr. Gildfish says you must not become overtired—"

"Bah, what is there to think about? Besides, you will help me, Melushka." Zenobie's eyes glowed as she warmed to the theme. "It will be not the ordinary boating party, this. Sir Rupert and I will put our heads against each other to create most diverting things. Our guests will eat and drink and toast the fierce dragon that lives deep in the lake—and my little Ferridew will write an ode for us."

The poet raised his head, began to speak, then seemingly went weak in the knees. Like a folding accordion, he collapsed to the floor at the feet of Miss Pennodie.

*"Accidènte!"* exclaimed the *conte.* "The man is ill."

"No, he's just drunk," Miss Pennodie corrected him. "I remember that Papa used to—"

She gave a little squeak as her stepmother pinched her arm. "How disgustingly ill-bred of Mr. Ferridew," Mrs. Pennodie exclaimed in her affected voice. "If he *is* intoxicated, that is."

Dr. Gildfish was leaning over the poet. "I'd say he was dead drunk."

Philosophically, Zenobie shrugged. "Reach for the bellpull, Melushka," she directed, "and call the footmen. They will take the poor foxed little Ferridew to sleep awhile in the yellow saloon. Meanwhile, let us plan for the marvelous nautical party, *dear* Sir Rupert. I am persuaded that your ideas will be enchanting."

# Chapter Four

"Just look at those goings-on," Miss Poll sniffed.

Melinda set down her sewing and, stretching her back, looked out her window. The sun had long set, and the English gloaming lay like a shadowed wash over the garden and the darkening waters of the lake.

Zenobie's original idea for a nautical party had soon expanded into a full-scale extravaganza. A simple afternoon of boating and refreshments had been transformed into a lavish Event promising games and a feast to follow. The elaborate gilt-edged invitations penned by Melinda under Zenobie's instruction requested guests to appear in appropriately nautical fancy dress.

"Only there ain't nothing fancy about *this* dress." Miss Poll snipped a thread and held up the garment she had been sewing. "I don't know, Miss Mel. This thing isn't never going to make you look like anything except a dowd."

Melinda had chosen to go to the party dressed as a Puritan about to embark for the New World. "Puritans don't believe in bright clothes," she explained. Besides which, the costume was easily made out of one of her old day dresses.

"*She* is going as Queen Elizabeth. That Sonya Vraskova woman says that the Rooshan's wearing the Darlington pearls what costs a fortune." Miss Poll sniffed in disdain. "And then there's the cook making enough food to feed half of England."

Nor was the excitement confined to the house. Tents had been set up for the guests' comfort, and servants had hacked and pruned back the brush so that a wide path now led to the lake, where the games were to be held.

Zenobie was being almost childishly secretive about these games. She and Sir Rupert had put their heads together and devised something that they both seemed to think was inordinately clever. Neither Melinda, nor Lord Hartford, who often accompanied his inventor friend to Darlington House, were in on the secret.

At least this activity kept Zenobie happy. Melinda returned to her sewing whilst Miss Poll went on. "And who's coming to this party, I'd like to know. Fools like that poet. All *he* does is drink."

She was interrupted by a muffled Russian curse word that wafted down the stairs. *"Spulcheve!"* Zenobie was exclaiming. "You will make me to look as big as a cow. I am supposed to be the Virgin Queen, not a tugboat."

"Then there's the Eye-talian. I don't trust foreigners," Miss Poll continued darkly. "And as to the squire, he's a loose fish if I ever saw one."

Melinda smiled over her mending. Polly's assessments of character, though acerbic, were usually accurate. "Surely you can't object to Sir Rupert Blyminster?" she asked.

Miss Poll sniffed. "He's a Bartholomew baby, but there's no harm in him. His friend's another matter, though. Lord Hartford's a sharp 'un, and no mistake."

Melinda raised her brows. "Are you trying to warn me about something, Polly?"

"Don't go high in the instep with me, Miss Mel," retorted the older woman. "I saw the way he looked at you yesterday when him and that Sir Rupert came to call. *And* the way you brightened up when he paid attention to you."

"Lord Hartford was telling me about his experiences in Scotland," Melinda replied somewhat stiffly. "We share many interests. Zenobie and Sir Rupert were deep in plans for the boating party, so it was natural that Lord Hartford and I talk together."

"Miss Mel, I know that Lord Hartford's been coming to call here a lot. Maybe I say this as shouldn't, but—but dukes' sons don't marry governesses, and that's a fact."

Her nose redder than ever, Miss Poll resumed her sewing. Melinda set down her own work, leaned forward, and laid a hand on her former nurse's arm. "Don't worry," she said quietly. "I don't intend to marry Lord Hartford or anyone else. I shall never marry."

Miss Poll made a disbelieving sound. "No, really, I mean it. The moment a woman marries, she becomes completely dependent on her husband. Polly, I will never let what happened to poor Mama happen to me."

Miss Poll said, somewhat defensively, that Mrs. Weatherby had lived in different times. "Not so different," Melinda replied. "Even today women are considered ape leaders if they don't marry. Consider, Polly—Mama was twenty-eight when she met Papa. She knew from the start that he did not love her, that he was point-non-plus because of his unlucky ventures on the exchange and looking for a wife with a plump dowry. She *knew*—and married him anyway."

Suddenly restless, Melinda got up and stood by the window, seeing not the twilit garden but a self-effacing woman with a gentle face and sad eyes. "Even when Papa lost all her money on the exchange, poor, dear Mama considered herself more fortunate than women who were unmarried. She depended on Papa for everything, was governed by him in everything," Melinda went on passionately, "so that when he died and left us beside the bridge, Mama did not know how to cope. It wasn't illness that killed her—she lacked the will to go on alone."

There was an uncomfortable silence broken by Miss Poll, who said briskly, "Anyways, Miss Mel, you're young. When a gentleman comes to you with his hand on his heart and goes down on a knee, what will you say then?"

"I will say, thank you, but no, I like my freedom, such as it is," Melinda replied firmly. "Besides, if you are talking about Lord Hartford, he most certainly doesn't have his hand on his heart. I am persuaded that he wishes to remain fancy-free."

"Them's the worst kind. Them's the ones that have lightskirts and ladybirds and females that aren't any better than they should be." Miss Poll nodded darkly. "Governesses and schoolmistresses are fair game for such."

Which was, Melinda knew, an accurate description of most gentlemen of Lord Hartford's rank and station. It made sense to be forewarned—but tonight such common sense left her unaccountably depressed. She glanced at her sewing which lay in an uninspiring puddle on the armchair where she had been sitting and announced, "I'm going for a walk."

Miss Poll's insistence that she take her shawl and Zenobie's complaints to her dressmaker followed Melinda down the stairs. She paid little attention to what was said, for she was recalling that Miss Poll was right about one thing. Sir Rupert had visited Darlington House many times during the past two weeks, and the duke's son had accompanied him.

It was to discuss Zenobie's party, of course. "Lord Hartford was merely keeping his friend company," Melinda told herself stoutly. "Polly is making a mountain out of a molehill."

True, they had laughed and talked together yesterday. Lord Hartford had been witty and entertaining, as he could so easily be, Melinda remembered, but he had another quality that she liked even better. He *listened,* truly listened to what she had to say, as though her thoughts mattered to him.

Why should she not enjoy such a man's company just because he was a duke's son? Melinda wondered rebelliously at this as she stepped into the shadowy garden. "A cat may look at a king, after all," she mused. "And—and I refuse to think about this any further."

She concentrated on her walk, making her way down the broadened path to the lake and enjoying the liquid music of a nightingale's call. A stanza from *Romeo and Juliet* touched her mind, and she murmured aloud, " 'How silver-sweet sound lovers' tongues by night/Like softest music to attending ears.' "

Again the nightingale poured his song into the darkness. Melinda could now see lake Kendle before her, and as the rising moon trailed silver across the water, she realized that she was not alone.

Lord Hartford was standing in the shadow of some trees at the edge of the cleared path. He held a nautical spyglass to one eye, and for a moment she thought that he was looking lakeward, scanning the water for his friend's invention. Then, to her astonishment, she saw that the duke's son had his glass trained not on the lake but on Darlington House.

As the realization touched her mind, he quickly lowered his spyglass. Melinda saw a series of emotions chase themselves across his face, saw something very much like dismay give quick way to surprise and then to pleasure. "Well met by moonlight, Miss Weatherby," he exclaimed.

The genuine welcome in his voice brought a surge of happiness, quickly controlled as she returned his greeting. He came walking up the path toward her, and she noted that he moved swiftly and almost soundlessly. "Is the *Subaqua* submerged at this time of night?" she wondered.

"No, not tonight." Hartford knew that he should offer a palpable excuse for his presence near Darlington House, but her unexpected appearance had dulled his usually agile brain.

He had been thinking of her as he stood watch. No, *thinking* was too strong a word for the wisps of memory that kept superimposing themselves over the business at hand. He had to admit that instead of being completely focused on watching the Russian woman, he had been recalling the way Melinda Weatherby's eyes crinkled at the corners when she smiled.

Now here she was wearing the same simple round dress of pale blue muslin that she had worn the previous day. It had enhanced her pink and rose complexion by daylight, and by twilight it shimmered silver, like her eyes. "You look charming tonight," he told her.

Again the foolish happiness fluttered through her, and once again she repressed it. "Then you are not waiting for Sir Rupert to surface?" she asked.

He could not very well tell her that he and Dayce had been watching Darlington House for the past month. "I've been waiting for the Kendle Lake dragon to appear," he joked. Then he added, "Actually, I took a stroll after dinner and found myself here, hoping that you would come down to the lake."

He was smiling down at her. Melinda forced herself to recall the stern, pink-nosed countenance of her former nurse and said, "Indeed."

That cool little word, uttered in just such a tone, had defused difficult situations during her years as a governess. It had discouraged amorous older sons and once had stopped a lecherous old peer dead in his tracks.

But Lord Hartford merely asked, "Have you been listening to the nightingales? They put me in mind of some lines from *Romeo and Juliet,* and—but you're shivering. Are you cold?"

Melinda wished she had listened to Miss Poll and brought her shawl. "It is unusual," she parried, "to find a duke's son who reads Shakespeare. I have worked in many households where the gentlemen prided themselves in never opening a book."

If she thought that this reminder of the difference in their stations would give him pause, she was wrong. "That's true for many ladies, too," Lord Hartford pointed out. "My sisters read only the latest novels by Caroline Lamb, and your cousin

61

doesn't seem to be a bluestocking. You two are very unlike each other."

Grateful to shift the focus from herself, Melinda explained, "As I think you know, we are related by marriage only. Zenobie was married for some years to my cousin Arthur. He died, and she then married Monsieur Vilforme."

"Ah-ha. So you went to France with her?"

Melinda did not note the suddenly intent look in his eyes. She shook her head, adding quickly, "It wasn't Zenobie's fault that she had to leave me behind in England. Monsieur Vilforme wished it to be so."

"But of course she sent for you when she became Lady Darlington."

"Not—not exactly. She only recently wrote to me." Somewhat defensively, Melinda explained, "Zenobie has been in bad health, and so she wrote to me at the Proctor Academy, where I was teaching. But none of this has any bearing on why you read Shakespeare, my lord."

Abandon the little cousin and then, without thought to her welfare, yank her out of what probably was the first stable position she'd ever had. Selfish to the end, Hartford thought dryly, but what else could be expected of Vilforme's widow?

"Reading is a habit I picked up in Spain," he replied. "One of the officers I served with was my age. His father, an Oxford don, had given him a Shakespeare to take with him—and we had time on our hands."

There was a reminiscent note in his voice. "Dr. Gildfish told me that he was also in Spain," Melinda said. "Was your regiment there long?"

Too long, Hartford thought. Aloud he said, "Several months. I was attached to a special branch

62

headed by Sir Orin Calworth." He watched her face for recognition, saw none, and felt a stir of relief that she did not appear to know what this meant. "Between the action there were long periods when time hung heavy."

Melinda nodded. "Meanwhile you had time to read your friend's Shakespeare."

*Trust no one, turn your back on no one*—and yet he had befriended and trusted Latten, and poor Latten had trusted him. That memory twisted deep. Hartford drew a deep breath and pulled himself back to Dorset and Melinda, who was saying, "It can't have been easy for you—all that terrible fighting."

Her words had given him time to recover. Quite casually he said, "I wasn't involved in much of the fighting. I was in military intelligence."

Once more Hartford watched Melinda's face, but she only looked thoughtful. "You mean that you brought the news back from enemy lines? That was courageous indeed."

They were standing so close that he could draw in the subtle rose scent she wore. It reminded him of the beautiful Spanish countryside and the wildflowers that bloomed there. The memory made him say, "It wasn't all danger and bloodshed. There were wonderful nights like these, full of stars. I confess that I fell in love with the country, until—"

He paused. "Until?" she prompted.

"Until the time my friend—the one with the Shakespeare—was captured by the enemy near Astorga. He knew secrets that couldn't be allowed to fall into the wrong hands, so I was sent after him to try and get him away."

*Why* was he telling her these things? Hartford felt an uncharacteristic rush of confusion. He had never spoken of Latten to anyone outside the Circle. "It's too fine a night to think of war," he said.

She nodded agreement but added somberly, "Everyone is talking about it. The *conte* was saying tonight at dinner that the Duke of Wellington has left Vienna to go to Brussels. The *conte* feels that Napoleon will soon launch an aggressive war, and I fear I must agree."

Hartford knew he should ask what else the slippery del'Anche had said, but his heart was not in it. It was too heavy with what had happened long ago, of the terrible orders he had carried with him when he was sent behind enemy lines after Latten.

"No doubt the *conte* is right," he forced himself to say. "What else did he predict?"

"That many military men will be recalled to duty and be glad to go. Would you be glad to go back?"

He did not answer, and she was immediately contrite. "That was a foolish question. How could you be glad?" She paused, then asked gently, "Your friend who was captured. Did you—"

"He died in Spain."

He turned away from her as he spoke the bleak words, but she had glimpsed his face. It was hard with such pain that Melinda hurt for him. Impulsively, she reached out and put her hand on his arm.

Under her palm she felt his muscles tighten, but he did not turn to look at her. "Forgive me for bringing back such memories," she said in a hushed voice. "I am sorry, my lord, and truly sorry for your friend."

With this she would have taken her hand away had he not caught it and carried it to his lips. The mute gesture was so unexpected that Melinda looked up in astonishment. Their eyes met, and in

Lord Hartford's expression she saw something that made her catch her breath.

Still wordless, he turned her hand over and kissed the palm. The warmth of his mouth seared her cool skin. She knew she must take her hand away and could not—did not want to—*could* not break away. Without resisting, she allowed him to draw her into the circle of his arms.

Then he was bending his head to hers, and as their lips met, the ground beneath Melinda's feet seemed to dissolve into mist. There was no sound save the beating of her own heart and no taste or touch except that of his mouth. For a moment the world stood completely still, and then, deep in the fog of her mind, a voice of reason cried out in protest. *Miss Mel,* that well-known voice clamored, *have you gone mad, then?*

There was no other explanation. None! Just half an hour earlier she had been defiantly declaring that she would never marry, never be dependent on any man. And now here she stood, rooted to the spot, blind, breathless, and mindless in Lord Hartford's embrace.

With a little gasp Melinda pulled backward out of his lordship's arms. "I—I must go back to the house," she stammered.

There was panic in her voice, and Hartford silently cursed himself. What in the name of all the fiends of hell had he been thinking? Beyond any consideration of decent behavior was the fact that Melinda Weatherby was related to Lady Darlington. As such, she herself was not beyond suspicion in this broth of espionage and treason. *Remember that, dolt!* he told himself savagely.

He began to apologize. He blamed the moonlight, evil memories of the war, even her sweet sympathy, and all the while he was talking, Hartford battled an almost irresistible need to pull Melinda back into his arms. "I don't often talk about the old days because the memories are so strong," he concluded. "I thought myself back in Spain for a moment, and you were so kind that I forgot myself. I hope I haven't offended you past redemption."

He sounded so humble, so truly penitent and worried. With an effort Melinda calmed her racing pulse. What had happened, she lectured herself, was a mistake, an aberration caused by Lord Hartford's painful memories and the moonlight. A single kiss meant nothing to him and even less to her.

Aloud she said, "I understand—of course I do. I am not offended, Lord Hartford. But now I must really go back to the house."

Hartford watched her as she turned and walked up the path. She started resolutely, her back straight and her head held high. But halfway up the cleared path she slowed, paused, and almost but not quite glanced back at him.

That small, hesitant gesture caught at his heart, but before it could take hold, a cool-blooded voice nudged his mind once more. *If she's in league with her cousin, it's entirely possible that she engineered that little scene for your benefit, my dear boy. Remember the first rule of our Circle—trust no one, believe in no one.*

Hartford picked up the spyglass he had dropped. Even if she were not involved in her cousin's schemes, how would Melinda Weatherby feel when Lady Darlington was exposed as a traitor? *Focus,* he commanded himself.

No matter how reluctantly, for the time being he was once again a member of Calworth's elite Circle. He was here on a mission and the sooner he got it done and shook the dust of Dorset from his feet, the better.

"My guests will be arriving at any moment," Zenobie fretted, "and here I am a prisoner of this idiotish costume."

She flung her arms wide, nearly upsetting Sonya Vraskova, who had been arranging her mistress's lace ruff. "I should have listened to the voice of my own common senses," Zenobie went on darkly. "A local seamstress is useless. For this important event I should never have trusted myself to some ignorant country fool."

Noting that her cousin's color was more than usually high, Melinda said soothingly that she would go down at once and do the honors. At the door she paused to ask, "Zenobie, can you swim?"

"Of course I cannot swim. A lady has no need for such an activity. What makes you ask such a question, Melushka?"

"To venture out on a boat without being able to swim is hardly wise," Melinda pointed out.

Zenobie rolled her eyes. "You are too practical." She paused to look hard at her companion. "And you have the terrible taste, *malenkaya*. Not one ounce of the town bronze."

Melinda was wearing a serviceable high-necked muslin gown of dove gray, and a neat little white cap. "Why, oh, why, did you not accept from me a suitable garment to wear?" Zenobie lamented. "That costume makes you appear like someone about to be imprisoned for debt—"

She broke off suddenly to exclaim, "The guests arrive. Go outside at once, my little one, and keep them all occupied till I arrive."

Descending the stairs, Melinda walked out of the

house into a sunny day with patchy clouds sailing before a brisk wind. Tents afforded shelter from this breeze, and tables inside these tents were covered with delicacies to tempt the appetite of all the local notables that Zenobie had invited. Melinda shook hands with Ancient Mariners, water nymphs, sailors, and mermaids, and duly sent them off to enjoy these viands.

Among the few guests she recognized were Squire Parcher, a leering, rotund Neptune, and the Pennodies. Mrs. Pennodie, Melinda noted with some amusement, had elected to come dressed as Britannia, while Carabel wore a sea green gown with large pearls sewn to it, and a shawl of green gauze. Melinda could not guess what she was supposed to be.

The ladies had joined the squire in one of the tents when the Conte del'Anche, in the guise of Marco Polo, made his appearance. He kissed Melinda's fingers with his usual sinuous grace, murmuring, "I salute you, Signorina. And Lady Darlington? If I do not mistake, she is going to make the grand entrance when all 'ave arrived to do her honor."

Melinda smiled. "You know Zenobie well."

"She shone like a star at the court of Napoleon. But then, it is in the blood. Lady Darlington descends from a long line of Russian aristocrats who—"

"Mere mortals, be warned of the approach of divinity!"

There was a discordant, twanging sound, and Melinda frankly stared as the poet Ferridew approached. He wore a white and gold tunic cut short to the knees, and he carried a zither and a golden apple.

"I am Paris," he declaimed, "summoned by the goddesses to judge the fairest of them all. Ah, where is Aphrodite?"

He struck an attitude that showed off his legs dramatically. Several young ladies craned their necks to look and were immediately taken to task by their chaperones. Mrs. Pennodie pointedly averted her eyes and snarled inaudible commands to her staring stepdaughter.

"And 'oo is 'is 'Elen of Troy, do you suppose?" the *conte* wondered cynically as the poet tucked zither and apple under his arm and made off toward the food and drink. "But regard—'ere are coming more conventional guests."

Melinda's heart skittered nervously. Lord Hartford, dressed in a white shirt open at the neck, a broad red sash, and black breeches, was walking toward them. It was the first time she had seen his lordship since that evening by the lake, and though she had determinedly put that scene from her mind, the sight of him brought misgivings.

She was grateful when the *conte* defused some of her tension by exclaiming, "The costume becomes you, my lord 'Artford. You resemble the true buccaneer."

Just then Sir Rupert, dressed as Nelson, came trotting up. "Servant, Miss Weatherby—yours, too, *conte*," the inventor exclaimed. "Where's Lady Darlington?"

"*Dearest* friends!"

All heads turned, for Elizabeth of England was approaching. Her auburn hair was upswept and decorated with a jeweled tiara, and there was a deep ruff of lace at her throat. Ropes of pearls circled her neck and hung in her ears.

"It is she!" The poet fell on his knees and held

69

out his clasped hands in homage. "Gloriana! Aphrodite! Beauty has come to grace mere mortals."

"Nonsense, my little Ferridew, it is only I."

Preening herself, Zenobie began to greet her many guests. Sir Rupert hung back, shaking his head. "Stunnin'," he breathed. "Never saw anythin' like it, by Jove. Every inch a queen, eh, Hartford?"

Thinking that this was even better than Astley's Amphitheater, Hartford glanced at Melinda Weatherby. She looked very small and self-effacing in gray and white, with the little white cap hiding her glossy hair. What would she look like as Queen Elizabeth, he wondered, in that jeweled gown and those pearls around her neck?

For a moment the vision held him, and then another took its place. In his mind's eye he saw her looking exactly as she had the moment before he had kissed her by the lake.

*Folly.* With an effort, Hartford shook away the memory and realized that Blyminster was at his side, muttering into his ear. "What's that?" he asked absently.

"I was just tellin' you that you needn't worry about me," Sir Rupert said. "Got carried away the other day, but today will be different. Eh? Not a word about the *Subaqua* will pass my lips, old chap. Mean to say, you can count on me." He paused and drew a deep breath. "Well, have to go on with the games."

Sir Rupert squared his shoulders and marched forward to greet Lady Darlington, who offered her hand and purred, "I have *await* this day. It is your genius that helps make it a success, dear Sir Rupert."

Hartford felt a twinge of conscience as he watched his host dissolve into jelly. Poor old

Blyminster was no match for Vilforme's widow, and yet he was being coldly set up as bait.

"And 'ave you penetrated the secret?" Del'Anche was still hovering nearby. "I mean, of course, the mystery of Lady Darlington's nautical games. It is an enigma worthy of a man with your skills."

"Or of a man with your intelligence," Hartford parried, matching the *conte* smile for smile and bow for bow.

Melinda was perplexed by the undercurrent of hostility that simmered just beneath their polished manners and wondered at it as del'Anche took himself off and left them alone with the duke's son.

Would Lord Hartford now allude to the *contretemps* of the other night? Melinda felt another ripple of nervousness, but he only smiled and said, "You make a charming Puritan, Miss Weatherby."

"And you, my lord, are a very good pirate," she replied equably, thinking meanwhile that his costume suited him most tremendously. The duke's son had disappeared, and in his stead stood a handsome buccaneer with bold, dark eyes and wind-ruffled hair. He lacked only a sabre and a gold earring, and he could have commanded any pirate vessel—yes, and ravished many a landlocked maiden's heart with his kisses.

Involuntarily, Melinda recalled Lord Hartford's lips against hers and the strength and gentleness of his arms. "But should you not have an eye patch?" she continued hastily.

"I prefer to use both my eyes." Looking about him, Hartford noted that the tents were swarming with fancifully dressed personages who were eating, drinking, flirting, and gossiping. "Lady Darlington seems to have invited the entire county. How many people do you think are here?"

"Sixty-five," Melinda replied. "I know because I wrote the invitations. Everyone accepted, but I do not see Dr. Gildfish anywhere."

"There he is—dressed as a gondolier and talking to Mrs. Pennodie."

As Hartford spoke, there was the piercing sound of a bosun's whistle. "We are being called to attention," Melinda exclaimed. "I believe Zenobie's secret games are about to begin, and—oh, look!"

Down the lake came gliding several flat-bottomed boats poled by servants dressed as gondoliers. Immediately behind them glided a craft in the shape of a silver swan. It was propelled not by sail or by oars, but by some mechanism within the bird's body. Sir Rupert, looking self-conscious but determined, was seated in the prow.

Attached to the swan boat by golden strings floated a fleet of beautifully crafted miniature sailboats. "Friends, you now behold the game I have promised you," Zenobie announced. "Sir Rupert fashioned the swan and designed the boats, which were built by the best craftsmen in Dorset." She paused dramatically before announcing, "We will now have a race."

The crowd of guests hushed expectantly as their hostess explained that the little sailboats would race on the lake and that wagers would be made. The one who won the most money would have the honor of riding in the swan boat along with Sir Rupert.

"The so-elegant swan will lead all the other boats on a sail around the lake," she declared. "Come, is not that a merry idea?"

The applause was somewhat restrained at first, since the guests evidently thought that this amusement was much too tame. But the mood changed when Zenobie placed a substantial bet on a green and white sailboat. Now ladies and gentlemen eagerly approached the water's edge to examine the little boats and to conjecture their speed. Even Dr. Gildfish placed a wager with Russtin, who was recording each bet in a little book.

"So this is the famous secret," Lord Hartford mused as they watched Mrs. Pennodie trotting up and down the water's edge. "Are you going to make a wager, Miss Weatherby?" She declined and he added, "Then perhaps you'll help me make a choice."

But Melinda had noted that Miss Pennodie had remained behind when her stepmother went to examine the boats. She was sitting bolt-upright in her chair with an untasted plate of food in her lap and looked so unhappy that Melinda felt sorry for her.

Explaining that she should be seeing to Zenobie's guests, Melinda walked over to Miss Pennodie and sat down next to her. "You are not interested in boats?" she asked, smiling.

"Oh, it isn't that," the girl replied. She nervously smoothed her skirts with a square, broad-palmed hand as she added, "Mama says I must not get too close to the water or I will be sure to fall in and ruin my costume."

Mrs. Pennodie herself, Melinda noted, was bending over the water, intent on choosing her craft. "I am persuaded you would do nothing of the kind," she soothed. "Shall we walk down to the water together?"

The girl looked surprised, and then gave Melinda a smile that warmed her plain face. "I would like that above all things," she said eagerly, "but wouldn't you be bored? Mama says my conversation would put genteel society to sleep."

Stepmama, Melinda thought, was a griffin. "I don't believe that for a moment," she said firmly.

Miss Pennodie looked hopeful but unconvinced. "Mama believes that I should put my best foot forward and go out in society. She insists I go calling with her, but—but I think people are frightening. I much prefer to work in the garden with the Briddles."

"Zenobie mentioned the Briddles. Who are they?" Melinda wondered politely as the two began to walk toward the water.

"They are a Quaker family from Yorkshire," the girl explained. "Josiah Briddle's brother Nathanial is famous all over England for his wrought iron creations, and Josiah himself grows the most exquisite miniature trees and flowers. The two brothers and their families work together to make the most beautiful garden arrangements."

"I remember now. I believe the Briddles were engaged by Lord Hartford's mother."

"Oh, yes, and by the Prince Regent himself. Mama has waited a year for them to come to Pennodie House. They work slowly, for they hire no workers and do everything themselves—but they have let me help a little."

Melinda was astonished. As she spoke of the Briddles and their gardens, the awkward girl's shyness fell away. Her face glowed, and her small eyes shone with enthusiasm. "I should like to meet the Briddles, Miss Pennodie," Melinda said.

"Would you? Oh, please, come to the house and visit me," the girl begged. "And do call me Carabel, not Miss Pennodie."

Just then a shout went up from the waterside.

"The boats are off," Melinda exclaimed. She caught Carabel's hand in hers and urged her gently forward. "Which boat do you think will win? I like the look of that red one with the white sail."

"I choose the white and golden boat with the golden prow," a dreamy voice said at their elbow. "It reminds me of Aphrodite."

Glancing timidly at the poet, Carabel said, "The little blue sailboat is my choice."

Her voice was drowned out as shouts of encouragement followed the little boats. Mrs. Pennodie almost jumped up and down in her excitement. The *conte* forgot his aristocratic air and shifted from one foot to the other whilst Squire Parcher bawled at his chosen craft to get a move on.

"I believe Zenobie has chosen the winner," Melinda exclaimed.

Cries of disappointment as well as triumph filled the air as the other boats placed. Russtin began to dispense IOUs and vouchers. Meanwhile Zenobie, flushed with pleasure, declared that she was to lead the procession of boats over the lake.

"I am to ride with Sir Rupert!" she cried triumphantly. "I leave it to the rest of you to choose your partners for this event."

The poet shuddered. "I am afraid of boats," he was beginning to say, when a coarse voice behind them interrupted.

"Are you a man or a mouse?" To Melinda's discomfort, she saw that Squire Parcher had come up to them. He jerked his head at Carabel as he added, "Lady Darlington said we should choose our partners for the boat ride, young fellow. You and this young lady'd make a good pair, eh?"

"No. That is, I—I don't like boating, either,"

Carabel stammered before the poet could speak. "I would much rather stay on land."

The squire turned to Melinda. "What do you say to a turn about the lake with me, young miss?"

"Miss Weatherby has promised to boat with me."

Melinda looked up in heartfelt gratitude as Lord Hartford strolled over to join them. The squire scowled, opened his mouth to protest, then thought better of it and stumped away. "This makes the second time you have rescued me from that person," Melinda said thankfully.

Lord Hartford's white teeth gleamed in a distinctly piratical grin. "What buccaneer worth his salt would let an interloper carry a lovely maiden off from under his very nose?"

But Melinda knew this was fiction. The duke's son was still a duke's son even in costume. *And I'll bet he's kissed more girls than you've got hair on your head, Miss Mel,* whispered a cautionary voice in her mind.

Silently, she walked with Lord Hartford to the water's edge, where Sir Rupert was handing Zenobie into the swan boat. "Built her just for the occasion," Sir Rupert was saying. "It's a machine, d'you see? The boat moves forward when I paddle m'feet. Simple, really. Handles well, rides easy in the water. Mean to say, you don't need to fear it ain't safe, ma'am."

"I know I am always perfectly safe with you, dear Sir Rupert," Zenobie crooned.

The other guests were pairing up. The squire was partnered with a blond lady who kept giggling behind her fan, while the doctor had been captured by a buxom mermaid, and the *conte* was squiring a lady dressed as Circe. Only Mrs. Pennodie remained behind with her stepchild while Ferridew, golden apple in hand, assumed an attitude upon a rock near the water's edge.

"He's probably writing a poem about the race," Lord Hartford observed as he helped Melinda aboard one of the boats. He waved away the footman who was supposed to pole them along and instead took up a pair of oars from the bottom of the boat. "Be honest, Miss Weatherby. In your opinion, has the secret been a success?"

As a strong oar-stroke sent them into the water, Melinda glanced shoreward at Russtin, who was reading from his book to an excited gentleman dressed as a sturgeon. "People have been *enthusiastic*," she said. He chuckled, and she added, "Zenobie seems delighted, and so is Sir Rupert."

"I wouldn't have thought Lady Darlington would spend two minutes with a tongue-tied inventor."

"She has been lonely." Hartford raised his eyebrows. "No, really, she has. And she is truly interested in what Sir Rupert has to say," Melinda went on earnestly. "I know she enjoys his company."

Sunlight, Hartford saw, turned Melinda Weatherby's long, dark eyelashes to a dusty gold. It splashed more gold on her humble gown, and he was suddenly glad that she had not worn Lady Darlington's extravagant fancy dress, for Melinda was beautiful just as she was.

In silent tribute he plucked a small golden water lily that grew near the boat and offered it to her, and she thanked him with a smile so radiant that he actually had to catch his breath.

With some effort he reminded himself that his main reason for partnering Melinda and dismissing the oarsman had been to observe the Russian woman and maneuver closer to the swan boat.

"I can't think of anyone who looks less lonely

than Lady Darlington," he said aloud. "It seems to me that she's got more than one admirer dangling after her."

Melinda looked from the poet on the rock to Zenobie, who was laughing at something Sir Rupert had said. "She doesn't talk to me about her real feelings, but I do know she loved my cousin." Melinda smiled reminiscently as she added, "Arthur was such a dear man, good-natured and funny and kind. I know she mourned him when he died."

"And did she mourn Vilforme?" Hartford probed.

Melinda knit her brows. "I doubt it. I don't think she even liked him very much. But there was very little money after my cousin died, so she entered a marriage of convenience."

Money would matter to a woman like Lady Darlington. Hartford noted that she was hanging on every word Sir Rupert had to say. If the wretched woman would only take the bait and *act,* he thought impatiently, and then calmed himself. Patience was the cardinal rule of Calworth's Circle.

Out of the corner of his eye Hartford noted that del'Anche—who had also dismissed his oarsman—had rowed close to Sir Rupert's craft. He was not talking to his companion, which meant he was listening to everything that was being said in the other boat. Good, Hartford thought.

"I don't think you need to worry about your cousin," he told Melinda. "She's the sort of woman who will always fall on her feet."

"That is what Polly says."

"Your Polly sounds like my old nurse, come to it. Matter-of-fact, no-nonsense, and—why are you smiling?"

"I was remembering. Polly *is* very stiff and stern, but when I had nightmares, she would give me

78

milk and a lump of sugar. I confess that once in a *great* while I pretended that I had a nightmare just to have those treats."

"Madam Duplicity!" A fine, warm laugh Lord Hartford had, Melinda thought. The last lingering morsel of unease about the other night slipped away, and she leaned back in the boat and shut her eyes and let the sun dance across her face.

"It is such a beautiful day," she exclaimed.

"Oh, Aphrodite, most beautiful of the immortals!" Melinda's eyes flew open to behold Ferridew, who was now standing up on his rock. "For you, goddess of love," he declaimed. "For you, lady of the sea foam. I shall now read to you my poem of the love of Paris. But first, a tribute!"

Zenobie turned around just as the poet tossed the golden apple he carried to her. His aim was off, and the apple hit Sir Rupert directly in the center of the forehead. He gave a surprised grunt, fell backward, and cracked his head on the side of the swan boat.

"Sir Rupert!" Zenobie screamed as the inventor slumped down in his seat. Forgetting where she was, she jumped to her feet.

"Sit down!" Hartford shouted, but the warning came too late. Ladies began to shriek as the swan boat rocked, titled to one side, and deposited both Zenobie and Sir Rupert into the water.

"Oh, heavens!" Melinda cried faintly. She had half risen, when she felt her hand caught in a strong grip.

"Stay where you are or we'll be in the water, too," Hartford directed.

"But Zenobie can't swim. I must—"

Before Melinda could finish her sentence, there was a despairing cry of "Aphrodite!" followed by another splash. Ferridew had thrown himself from the rock into the lake. Almost immediately he resurfaced, choking and coughing and clawing the air.

"Another one who can't swim." Hartford looked swiftly around him. The footman who was propelling Dr. Gildfish's flat-bottomed boat was too far away. Del'Anche's companion had a stranglehold around his neck and was screaming at the top of her lungs.

No help from that quarter, either, Hartford thought. "Can you row?" he asked Melinda. When she nodded, he handed over his oars, directing, "Row over to the swan boat."

As he spoke, Lord Hartford began to peel off his coat. He kicked off his shoes and dived into the water. The boat rocked wildly as he plunged into the lake and sank out of sight, only to reappear a moment later, swimming strongly toward the floundering Zenobie.

There was no sign of Sir Rupert. Melinda gripped the oars and put her back into it, pulling as strongly as she could. But long before she could catch up with the swan boat, Lord Hartford had reached Zenobie and was lifting her chin out of the water. He then swam with her to the side of Melinda's boat.

"Help her in," Hartford told Melinda. "I'm going after Blyminster."

It was no easy task to get Zenobie into the boat, for she shivered and shook and clung to Melinda's hands. When the rescue was finally accomplished, Zenobie did not resemble a triumphant queen. Her fine clothes were sogging wet, her hair had come undone, and she shivered so hard that her teeth chattered.

"We will get you to the house soon," Melinda consoled as she wrapped her own shawl about Zenobie. "Are you sure you aren't hurt?"

"My costume is ruined," Zenobie moaned. "I am wet to the bones. Oh, Melushka, *where* is poor Sir Rupert? I cannot catch the glimpse of him."

Melinda, too, had been anxiously watching the lake. She caught her breath as Lord Hartford surfaced—alone—and once more submerged. "Oh, he is drowned," Zenobie moaned. "It is my fault."

"How could you know that the wretched boy would throw an apple at you?" Melinda consoled. "Lord Hartford will find Sir Rupert. He will not give up until he does."

She broke off as the duke's son emerged once more, this time towing Sir Rupert along. "He is limp, he does not speak, oh, he is dead," Zenobie wailed.

Del'Anche had managed to disentangle himself from his hysterical companion and was now helping Lord Hartford to get Sir Rupert into his boat. Melinda rowed toward them and was in time to hear Sir Rupert cough and sputter.

"Eh, what? Where's Lady Darlington?" he coughed.

"I am here—oh, I am here," Zenobie shrieked. "Oh, he is not dead, Melushka. Thanks be to St. Catherine, he is not dead."

Warning her cousin not to upset their boat as well, Melinda changed direction and made for shore. She was in time to see the poet being fished out of the water by two of the servants. One of his sandals had fallen off, and his blond curls were plastered to his head. He looked, Melinda thought, like a drowned mouse.

Melinda was about to row past him, when Zenobie caught her arm. "Wait," she said.

"Zenobie, the poor man did not mean to cause this disaster—" Zenobie interrupted Melinda's attempt at mediation.

"Little Ferridew," she called.

At the sound of her voice, the poet grew tense. He shook in every limb. Too dispirited even to offer apologies, he bowed his head for the ax blow he knew he deserved.

"I am sorry I did not catch your apple," Zenobie went on. "It was clumsy of me not to do so, my little one. It was all my fault that poor Sir Rupert was banged on his head."

She managed a watery smile, and Melinda's heart swelled with love. Zenobie could be exasperating, infuriating, *impossible*—and yet in the next breath she was capable of true kindness.

She continued to row to shore, where servants helped Zenobie out of the boat. Some distance away the *conte* and Lord Hartford were assisting Sir Rupert onto dry land. As she watched them, the duke's son turned his head and looked at her.

That one small glance was like the friendly touch of a hand. Lord Hartford was concerned for her well-being. He *cared* what happened to her.

With a warm feel in her heart, Melinda turned back to her shivering cousin. "Come," she said, "let us go to the house. A hot bath and bed, Zenobie, and you will soon be yourself again."

# Chapter Five

"A letter has arrived, ma'am," Russtin announced.

Melinda paused in the act of tying the ribbons of her bonnet. Since Zenobie's party had ended in near disaster for its hostess, dozens of gifts and letters had arrived daily.

So had the well-wishers. Ferridew had appeared to drink copious amounts of sherry, and recite his apologia in verse. The Conte del'Anche had come bearing hothouse flowers and fruit long after Dr. Gildfish had reassured Melinda that her cousin had come to no harm from her impromptu dip.

But this new letter was not addressed to Zenobie. "Good heavens," Melinda exclaimed. "It is from Mr. Proctor at the academy."

Before she could open the envelope, there were voices on the front steps, and Zenobie's voice crying, "Ah, Sir Rupert, you delight to be roasting me, yes?"

They came through the door arm in arm. Melinda, as she pocketed her unopened letter, noted how flushed and pretty her cousin looked and that Sir Rupert wore a bemused look.

Of all Zenobie's well-wishers, the inventor had been the most faithful. He had ridden over almost daily to see how Lady Darlington did, which was in sharp contrast to Lord Hartford, who had called only once. Melinda did not care for the sharp tug of disappointment she felt when she realized that once again the inventor had come alone.

She greeted Sir Rupert, who replied almost vaguely. He was plainly captivated by Zenobie. Even when he spoke to Melinda, his eyes barely strayed from the woman on his arm. "Ah, goin' out, Miss Weatherby?" he asked. "Quite the thing. The last two days have been full of rain and fog, but the sun's shinin' this mornin'. Fine day for an outin'."

"My cousin goes on an errand for me," Zenobie explained fondly. Then she added, "Do come into the Green Room, dear Sir Rupert, and let us have the cose. You must tell me more about your ship that rides beneath the water."

"What, more news about the underwater ship?" Sir Rupert looked disconcerted as del'Anche appeared at the door and bowed to the company. As usual, the *conte* looked elegant in dark superfine, and he carried a nosegay of roses and orchids in a silver holder.

"Beauty to beauty," he said, gracefully proffering the flowers to Zenobie. "You are the picture of 'ealth, *cara* madonna. I 'ope I don't intrude?"

Sir Rupert mumbled something under his breath, but Zenobie said, "Sir Rupert was about to tell me more about the most important achievement of the century. Alas, I can hardly comprehend all he says, but then, men are so much more intelligent than mere women."

"Nonsense, madonna," the *conte* said in a smug voice that said he agreed with every word she said. "It is only that you are too wise and beautiful to concern yourself with boring matters. Is it not so,

Signorina Weatherby? You prefer the fashions of silks and satin to machines."

Resisting the impulse to deflate the *conte*'s ego, Melinda merely said that she must leave to call on Mrs. Pennodie. "She has the cold," Zenobie explained, "and is not in plumped currants. I have asked my little Melushka to deliver a distillation of herbs to her."

"A recipe from your esteemed grandfather, Count Oblonski, no doubt," the *conte* murmured. "I believe you once told me, Lady Darlington, that 'is honor was most interested in 'erbs and distillations. I wonder what the count would 'ave thought of an undersea ship."

Melinda left the house to the cadences of the *conte*'s mellifluous voice. Zenobie's barouche was waiting, and as she took her seat in it, Melinda reflected how good it was to be alone. Miss Poll's sharp tongue had grated on her nerves that day, as had Zenobie's sugar-coated demands that her little Melushka fetch her this, or carry that away. It was almost as if she were in service again.

A rustle from her pocket recalled her unread letter. Hastily withdrawing it, Melinda slit the envelope and scanned the single sheet of paper. "Good heavens," she exclaimed. "He wants me to come back to the academy."

She reread the letter, but there was no mistake. In extraordinarily conciliatory terms, the headmaster of the Proctor Academy for Young Ladies wished to know how Miss Weatherby's cousin was feeling and whether Miss Weatherby might be free to return to teaching. There was no mention of the painful scene that had caused her resignation.

He was offering the olive branch. He wanted her to return to Sussex. And why should she not accept his offer? Melinda asked herself. Zenobie seemed perfectly well, and in any case, Dr. Gildfish was nearby. There was nothing to keep her in Dorset. If she wished, she could leave the next day. Melinda refolded the letter and returned it to her pocket, meanwhile wondering why she felt no joy at the prospect. I have grown too used to an easy life, she scolded herself.

The barouche had left the lake road and, turning at the fork, was approaching Mrs. Pennodie's house. Unfortunately, though Mr. Pennodie might have been as rich as Croesus, he had apparently had little imagination or taste. His enormous home squatted without charm of grace squarely in the center of an uninspired property.

Nor did the house improve when seen close up. Unusually ugly lions flanked each side of the massive marble stairs, and at the door a wooden-faced footman informed her that Madam was Indisposed and accepting no callers.

Melinda asked for Miss Pennodie and was told that the young lady was in the New Garden. Conducted along a garden path to the right of the house, Melinda was astonished. In sharp contrast to the rest of the property, this New Garden was truly charming.

There was an exquisitely detailed wrought-iron gazebo shaped like a castle—the work, no doubt, of Nathanial Briddle. Flower beds and a grove of miniature trees had been planted all around the gazebo so as to mimic a castle garden. A grave young man, blond and sunburned, was helping an older man with some fruit trees while two young women busily planted seedlings.

"Surely," Melinda exclaimed, "that cannot be Carabel!"

One of the women turned at the sound of Melinda's voice. "Miss Weatherby!" she cried. "Welcome!"

She jumped to her feet and, wiping her hands on her voluminous apron, came running over to greet her unexpected guest. "Have you come to see the gardens, ma'am?" she said, beaming.

Melinda could not get over the change in Carabel. She clasped the girl's outstretched hand and said, "First, I beg you will call me Melinda. Now, tell me—have the Briddles accomplished all this?"

Carabel nodded. "Isn't it splendid?" she enthused. "I wish you could have met Nathanial Briddle, but he has already gone on to his next commission." She added in a confidential tone, "That's the only reason Mama was able to prevail upon the family to work at Pennodie House, you know. Since they were already contracted to work near Dorset, the Briddles agreed to build the New Garden here."

This was not the shy, scared girl who had trembled in her stepmother's shadow. "I've always liked gardening," Carabel went on happily, "but I never thought there was so much to it. Come—I'll introduce you to the Briddles, but don't be surprised at their plain speech, Melinda. They're Quakers."

The three workers paused in their labors to shake hands. "I am glad to meet thee, Melinda Weatherby," the elder of the two men said gravely as he shook her hand. "These two are my son and daughter, Lucas and Hannah."

The tanned young man was as serious as his father, but the fresh-faced Hannah, who looked to be about Carabel's age, dimpled in friendly fashion. "I hope thee does not mind, Melinda Weatherby, but we must go back to work," Josiah continued in his slow, calm way. "There is much to do today, but thee can stay and watch if thee wishes."

As the family got back to work, Carabel explained, "Josiah Briddle spent his whole life perfecting his miniature trees. He's taught me so much—that is, whenever Mama isn't looking." A familiar shadow fell across her bright face as she added soberly, "If she knew I was out here now, she'd be in a real taking."

Without much enthusiasm, Melinda explained that she had brought Zenobie's herbal mixture and inquired after Mrs. Pennodie's health. "That's kind of you," Carabel said in a depressed tone. "Mama admires Lady Darlington so much. I'll give the medicine to her later, when I have the dirt off my hands."

"Then I shall take Josiah Briddle at his word and remain here with you for a few minutes," Melinda said. She looked about her with pleasure. "The New Garden will be truly beautiful when it is done."

Carabel cheered up almost immediately. "Do please sit here and I'll see about some refreshments. I'm so glad you came, Melinda. Mama has been difficult—"

Looking guilty, she broke off and hurried away. "Oh, blast that beastly woman to perdition," Melinda exclaimed wrathfully.

"You seem quite combative today," a voice said at her shoulder.

Startled, Melinda turned her head and looked up at Lord Hartford. "What are you doing here?" she wondered.

Lord Hartford raised his mobile eyebrows. "I could lie and say that I came to inquire about the ailing Mrs. Pennodie." He sat down next to Melinda on the stone garden bench, adding, "I take it you were referring to that lady when you spoke so earnestly just now."

Melinda nodded. "She has taken a splendid young woman and turned her into a timid creature afraid of her own shadow. Carabel is so competent and clever—only look at what she has helped to accomplish here! But her stepmama wants to turn her into an insipid deb."

Melinda's eyes flashed fire. Sitting so close to her, Hartford could distinguish her delicate rose scent above the other flowers that grew in the New Garden. He watched the flush stain her cheek and guessed that her skin would be warm silk. He *knew* that her mouth would be soft and sweet.

He had only to reach out in order to put an arm around her shoulders—Hartford shoved his hands into his pockets, out of temptation. "Foolishness," he sighed.

Melinda misunderstood. "Truly, it is foolish—but it is done all the time. The popular idea is that gentlemen like brainless bandbox misses." Melinda drew an indignant breath. "Before I left Darlington House, the *conte* intimated that women thought only about the latest fashions. Doubtless most people would agree with him."

"Not I," said Hartford. "I stand in great awe of women."

He obviously meant what he said, and Melinda looked at him in some surprise. "I am much too tongue-valiant," she apologized.

"You're a refreshing change from what I heard at Darlington House this afternoon. One gets tired of games." Momentarily Hartford reflected on the truth of this, then added, "I took to my heels as soon as your cousin told me you had gone to visit the Pennodies."

He had come here seeking *her*. A warm rush of pleasure ran through Melinda as his lordship continued. "Besides not agreeing with del'Anche about a woman's intelligence, I believe in her intuition. It's a sixth sense that few men have."

With no help from her female intuition, Melinda realized there was grave danger in being so close to Lord Hartford. Nothing could be less threatening than his lordship, who sat at his ease with his hands in his pockets and his long, booted legs thrust forward, yet he caused a turbulence within her.

Nothing in her life before had made her ready for what she felt whenever she was near him. It was the fault of that one kiss, Melinda realized, of that mistake best forgotten. But even as she tried to put the memory into perspective, she was aware that each of her five senses seemed to have come to vivid life. It was as if she suddenly stood on the brink of some wondrous discovery and found the world full of possibilities.

These were dangerous thoughts for a woman in her position. Melinda sought to shake herself free of them as Lord Hartford continued. "My mother, the duchess, is a tiny woman who barely reaches my father's shoulder. She allows him to bluster and give orders, but hers is the one voice that everyone obeys. When we were growing up, we all knew that if Mama was on your side, you would be all right."

"Her grace is a duchess," Melinda pointed out. "Other women are not as fortunate. My first position as a governess was in a home where the husband took every opportunity to belittle his wife. He called her a fool and worse in front of the children, and he trained the boys to treat all females with contempt. The oldest boy, especially, was insufferable."

"He was rude to you?"

When she nodded, Hartford felt a surge of raw anger. The reaction surprised him. Emotion was something he seldom allowed himself to feel when he was working. It clouded the mind.

"What happened?" he asked.

She matched his casual tone with a shrug. "Oh, the usual. He first tried to irritate me by insulting me. When I paid no attention, he accosted me in the garden one day and tried to kiss me, so I stamped down on his foot, as Polly had taught me. He limped for a week."

Melinda's eyes glistened with triumph, and Hartford gave a shout of laughter that made the Briddles look up from their work. "You are a redoubtable woman, Miss Weatherby," he said.

Just then Carabel came out of the side door, followed by a plump maid who carried a tray laden with cakes and small sandwiches. Carabel herself bore another tray with teapot, cups, and saucers. When she saw Lord Hartford, she looked startled and nearly dropped the tray. "Oh—I did not know you were here, my lord," she stammered.

Hartford rescued the tray from her, meanwhile greeting Carabel cheerfully. "Am I invited to tea, also?" he asked. "It's truly pleasant out here."

Relaxing under the friendliness of his lordship's smile, Carabel nodded. "Of course, my lord. Hilda, go and get another cup, and—and would you mind if the Briddles take their tea with us?"

The gardeners seemed to think it natural that they should sit down to tea with a duke's son. "For we believe all men are equal," Josiah explained, "aye, and women, too. We have no use for titles."

"Sensible," Lord Hartford commented, and passed the plate of small sandwiches. "I've heard of you and your brother, Josiah Briddle. My mother praises your work to the skies."

The older man only nodded gravely, but his daughter replied, "I'm glad your mama was pleased. She's a kind lady, with a good word t'say t'everyone. Thee has her merry eyes, Anthony Hartford."

Plain speech from a gardener's daughter to a peer she had barely met—Melinda was astonished and intrigued. Josiah, seeing her reaction, smiled his slow but gentle smile. "In our society, friend Melinda, t'women have the same rights as t'men," he said. "Aye, and they work wi' them in equality, too, like Carabel Pennodie, here."

He bent an affectionate look on Carabel, who agreed. "It's so. Even after they marry, women are considered equal to men. Can you believe it, Melinda? Lucas and Hannah have told me that wives don't have to promise to obey their husbands in the marriage vows. And—and if a girl doesn't wish to marry, she doesn't have to."

She spoke with such longing that Melinda's heart ached for her. But the ache gentled as she sat back and listened to Hannah and Lucas talking with Carabel and to Lord Hartford, who was asking Josiah's advice about dwarf apple and cherry trees he wanted to plant on his Scottish estates. A society where women were equal to men, where their opinions were valued, where they themselves were respected—it was an idea too extraordinary to take in all at once.

"It is a wonderful thought," she murmured.

As she spoke, the maid came out again to bring

more refreshments. She dipped a knee to Melinda's thanks but did not say a word.

"Hilda doesn't speak English—she is Belgian," Carabel explained. "Her brother lives near Antwerp and comes to see her from time to time."

"Is his name Vayrand, by chance?" Lord Hartford asked, breaking off his discussion with Josiah. "My manservant met a fellow by that name in town and they began to reminisce about their war experiences. It seems they met in Corunna back in '09."

Carabel looked puzzled. "Hilda's last name is Van Leyt. Her brother is a trader in wine, and I don't think he ever fought in the war."

The Briddles went back to their work, and Hannah called Carabel over to ask her a question. "I should be going, too," Melinda said, but she felt oddly reluctant to leave the New Garden. Besides, she did not relish having to face Zenobie with the news that she was going back to Sussex.

Involuntarily, she glanced at Lord Hartford and saw that he looked as though his mind were far afield. "Are you thinking of hiring the Briddles to beautify your Scottish estate?" she asked.

"I'd like nothing better. I offered Josiah double his usual fee just now, but he said that he never took more or less than his asking price. When he can find time, he told me, he'd come to Scotland."

Lord Hartford smiled down at her as he spoke. He had very clear eyes, Melinda thought, so clear that they reminded her of Kendle Lake. But the comparison was flawed. Though the lake could appear sunny and calm, there were depths to it, and dangers about which she knew nothing.

The thought of the lake recalled Zenobie. Reluctantly, Melinda got to her feet. "It has been such a pleasant afternoon," she said.

And an odd one. Hartford reflected that no other lady of his acquaintance would have sat so readily to tea with workers who had earth-stained hands. But then, Melinda Weatherby was a far cry from the insipid females whom he had met in polite circles.

Involuntarily he recalled that other Circle with its secrets and its dangers. Two worlds, Hartford thought, and do I truly belong to either of them?

He accompanied Melinda to the waiting barouche, saw her in, and then mounted his own horse with an unaccountable sense of gloom. If the noose tightened around Lady Darlington, he would be forced to hurt Melinda as well. And though Hartford knew that he was bound in honor to see this thing through, the fair day was suddenly bitter with the taste of betrayal.

"The thing is not to lose sight of why I came to Dorset in the first place," Melinda remonstrated with herself. "I came to help Zenobie, and now she does not need me any longer, so I must get on with my life."

Downstairs, Zenobie was saying good-bye to Sir Rupert and the *conte*. The two gentlemen had still been at Darlington House when Melinda returned, and they had both accepted an invitation to stay for dinner. Melinda noted that Sir Rupert's earlier dislike of the count seemed to have evaporated under del'Anche's charm, and that at dinner he had laughed heartily at the *conte*'s anecdotes of life on the continent.

Zenobie had been in her element, flirting with both men. Melinda envied the ease with which her cousin could play that charming game without in the least committing herself or acting the fool. "It's a gift," she sighed aloud.

A gift she, Melinda, totally lacked. She recalled her own afternoon spent in serious discussion with Lord Hartford and the Briddles. The Quaker idea of equality for the sexes was tantalizing, but so, too, was the coquettish way in which Zenobie could smile and flutter her eyelashes. What would Lord Hartford have thought if she, Melinda, were mistress of such feminine wiles?

"I am a perfect widgeon," Melinda exclaimed ruefully. "I must think of the academy and not of such foolishness."

"What's this about the academy, then?"

Miss Poll had come into the room with a small pile of mending. She regarded Melinda worriedly. "You're looking flushed, Miss Mel. Not caught that Pennodie woman's cold, have you?"

Melinda shook her head. "Polly, I have received a letter from Mr. Proctor. He wishes me to put bygones behind me and return to teaching."

Miss Poll's small eyes grew very round. "That old puff-bellows never said as much!"

"He did, however. Listen— 'It being the case that Miss Tallison is ill and Mrs. Gorse has been called home because of an illness in her family, we at the academy are Experiencing an Emergency. If you will return now, one would be grateful.'"

Miss Poll closed the door and leaned up against the door. "Are we going back?"

Melinda turned to look out the window. Zenobie had gone inside and the *conte* had departed. The gloaming was sweeping shadows across the land, and in her mind's eye she followed those shadows to the edge of Kendle Lake, where she had met Lord Hartford.

"I must," she murmured.

Miss Poll clapped her thin hands together and nodded so hard that her cap nearly bounced off her head. "Happy am I to hear you say so, Miss Mel. This Dorset is a pretty paltry place, and the Rooshan is just the same as she always was. She don't look sick or dying to me, and she isn't lonely as sure as my name's Jane Poll. You have your own life to lead and your living to make." She paused to take a breath. "When will you tell her?"

"Now. You always say that it's no use putting off a difficult task." Melinda attempted to smile at her old nurse, but her lips felt stiff. It took an effort to walk down the hallway to tap at Zenobie's door, where that lady was seated before her looking glass and unhooking the Darlington pearl ear-drops from her ears.

She turned with a welcoming smile, and Melinda spoke quickly before her courage faltered. "I have something to tell you," she said. "I'm going back to the Proctor Academy."

The pearls dropped out of Zenobie's hands. "Going back," she faltered. "Leaving me? *Malenkaya,* why?"

Melinda launched into a prepared speech about her cousin's health. "I was concerned, but now Dr. Gildfish has set my mind at rest," she concluded.

"Bah!" Zenobie rose to her feet and faced her cousin by marriage. "What do doctors know? I will miss you, Melushka. I will be desolate without you."

"Not desolate, surely," Melinda soothed. "You have many friends and admirers. Sir Rupert Blyminster and the *conte—*"

An odd look filled Zenobie's eyes. "Ah, yes. They are my admirers."

96

"You have many friends, too," Melinda pointed out. "Oh, Zenobie, please listen to me. Mr. Proctor is offering me my position back at the academy, and I would be foolish not to take his offer. I have to make my own way in the world. I would stay if I could, but I—I must go."

"Then go you shall." With one of her mercurial changes of mood, Zenobie enveloped Melinda in a smothering embrace. "I am a selfish woman, bringing you down here and trying to keep you when you so surely wish to be somewhere else. I am the old griffin, but I love you, Melushka."

Like snow under sunshine, Melinda's heart melted. "If you don't want me to go—" she stammered, "if you truly need me, I'll stay."

But Zenobie was shaking her head. "No. You have said the true words without peeling any eggs. Do not be concerned—I will get on famously. I have people all around me, and I am always admired. But one thing I must do before you leave. You will allow me to have a party for you, Melushka. No— my mind, it has been made up. One little night of joy and carefree enjoyment you shall have before you become the stern Miss Weatherby to a school full of horrid little girls."

Zenobie was not to be gainsaid. Next morning, immediately after breakfast, she sat down at a Louis XV desk, and, drawing out her cream vellum cards, picked up her pen.

"We," she announced dramatically, "will invite Everyone who is Anyone in Dorset."

She wrote two or three cards, professed herself exhausted, and relinquished her elegant gold and diamond-set pen to Melinda, who had perforce to write the rest of the invitations. Sixty-five cards were dispatched the next morning by the footmen, and Darlington House prepared itself for what Zenobie called "a small assembly."

Everyone prepared for this party in his or her own way. Sonya Vraskova put on such airs that Miss Poll asked her point-blank whether the party was in *her* honor. The cook retired to the kitchen, where he began to create a mountain of elegant viands. Russtin caused wines and spirits of every description and antiquity to be hauled up from the late Lord Darlington's cellar. Ices were sent for from London.

"For," Zenobie pointed out when Melinda protested the expense, "life is short. It is good to eat, drink, and be merrymaking, as my first husband, the Baron Osmanoff, used to say."

"And look where it got him," Miss Poll said later. "It fair gives me spasms to see how much is being spent on this party. You and me could eat off the stuff for six months, Miss Mel. Money flows from *her* like water out of that there lake at high flood."

As appalled as Miss Poll, Melinda refused Zenobie's offers of a new dress, but for once her refusal fell on deaf ears. "It is for you, this party," Zenobie scolded. "I will not be having my cousin, the guest of honor, in a dress that makes her look like a badly paid servant. It is an insult. So! To please me, you will accept this dress from me before you go away and leave me."

Zenobie summoned the local dressmaker and, amid temperament and inspiration, the dress was created. Even Miss Poll could not utter a single complaint about this garment, and on the night of the party she dressed her former nurseling with tender care. "Now," she approved, "you look as you were meant to look."

Melinda looked into the mirror, and an elegant

stranger stared back at her. The silver blue crepe dress scattered with seed pearls gently molded her petite figure and enhanced the darkness of her hair, which Miss Poll had dressed in upswept curls. Against the low but not immodest décolletage, her skin shone like ivory satin.

"Oh," she breathed, "oh, Polly, what a wonderful dress."

Miss Poll's nose was fairly crimson with pleasure as she smoothed the silver velvet sash that circled Melinda's waist and then dipped down to end in a bow near the hem. "It ain't just the dress," she said. "It's you."

Zenobie, resplendent in leaf green satin, agreed. "Did I not say that a little town brass would make you into a beauty? But a touch is needed here."

She set down a velvet box and lifted out a strand of pearls mixed with sapphires. "What is the matter now?" she asked, for Melinda was shaking her head.

"You have done enough. This dress is lovely—and I will float about in it like the princess in a fairy tale. But no jewels." She took her cousin's hand in both of hers and smiled up into her face. "I mustn't grow used to riches and good living."

"Why not?" Zenobie countered stubbornly. "You could with such ease marry a rich man. In fact, Lord Hartford owns three properties—two in England and the one in Scotland, which he likes best of all."

Melinda, who had been closing the velvet jewel box, looked up at this. "How do you know that, Zenobie?"

"Mrs. Pennodie told me when she called to thank me for the herbs and to accept the invite for your party." She paused to add with more than a hint of malice, "That woman cannot forget that her dead husband smelled of the shops. She makes herself important by learning the facts about every eligible young peer in England. But what can you expect of a counter-leaping mushroom?"

"Why invite her to your house, then?" Melinda wondered, and Zenobie puffed her cheeks like a contemptuous squirrel.

"Bah—she amuses me. And she gives the interesting parties from time to time. But, as I say to you, that woman knows of every marriageable lord, many not so young, either. Some of the suitors she would have for her poor Carabel are creaking old roués, my dear, but *you* will do better. I am persuaded that the handsome Hartford has a tendre for you."

"You are misinformed."

"How sternly you are talking. It leads me to believe I am right. Melushka, I will not be wrapping facts that are plain in white linen. Women have to marry well—or they are outside the bridge. That's the way of the world."

Melinda reflected on this as she took her place beside Zenobie to receive the guests, who were all attired in the stare of fashion. Mrs. Pennodie wore so many rings that her fingers could barely be discerned, and poor Carabel had been stuffed into a tight, stiff pink-brocaded gown.

Fine feathers seemed to mean a great deal to these people. The squire stared at Melinda with newfound respect, and Conte del'Anche for once seemed to mean it when he said, "*Che bellissima!* Signorina, Dorset will be desolate without your fair presence."

Even Ferridew deserted his Aphrodite long enough to promise an ode to the Lady with the Silver Eyes. "But where are our neighbors?" Zenobie fretted as the steady stream of guests trickled to a standstill. "Sir Rupert swore to me he would come early. And where is Dr. Gildfish, who promised to me he would fly to my side tonight?"

As she spoke, Melinda heard Mrs. Pennodie speaking across the room. "Oh, *yes,* my dear—would you credit it? Miss Weatherby's going away to Sussex to teach at a school for little girls. No better than a governess, really, though to look at her clothes one would think she is to the manor born."

Her voice was pitched so that Melinda was sure to overhear. "Borrowed feathers, my dear ma'am," that spiteful voice went on, "but what can you expect from the lower classes? Take the Briddles from Yorkshire—they are quite impossible. But then, you know, they are so much in demand and have created a garden for the Prince Regent himself. One must make allowances for artistic temperament."

Mrs. Pennodie was interrupted by Zenobie's shriek of pleasure. "But here you are—you have come at last!"

Sir Rupert, resplendent in a dark blue cutaway coat, brocaded waistcoat, yellow trousers, and stockings embroidered with clocks, was ascending the stairs. A step behind him came Lord Hartford, dressed in the subdued elegance of black and white. A diamond glittered in his faultlessly tied cravat as he stopped before Melinda.

" 'But soft, what light through yonder window breaks,' " he quoted. "But then, the words aren't adequate. You outshine Juliet tonight."

He bent over her hand. Melinda noted that the glittering guests were all watching, listening, holding their collective breath. She would have given much to know some clever rejoinder, something memorable to say to Lord Hartford, but her wits had seemingly evaporated.

Meanwhile, the musicians that Zenobie had hired were beginning to play, and ladies and gentlemen were pairing up for the first figure of the evening. Matrons with their husbands, young ladies under the keen eyes of mamas and chaperones and the speculative stares of eligible gentlemen—all were playing the time-honored game of matchmaking.

And Zenobie was also playing the game. Even at that distance Melinda could see her cousin's eyelashes fluttering up at Sir Rupert as everyone took their positions on the floor.

"Blyminster is in heaven," Lord Hartford remarked. "He insists that he hates parties, but when he got his invite from Lady Darlington, he brightened up as if he'd been summoned to paradise."

Then he added, "I meant what I said a moment ago—you're beautiful tonight. The other women here look as if they're dressed up for the stage."

"But the world *is* a stage, Lord Hartford, and I am part of the presentation. Tonight Zenobie has dressed me to play the part of guest of honor." He raised his eyebrows at this plain speech and gave her a quizzical little bow.

"I'm going to miss you when you leave Dorset, Melinda Weatherby—as Josiah Briddle would say."

And she would miss him! Stifling a sigh, Melinda glanced around the room at the pretty, eager young faces turned up to complacent male ones. "Zenobie is drinking too much champagne," she murmured. "Forgive me. I must remind her of Dr. Gildfish's orders."

She started to walk toward her cousin, but he forestalled her by saying, "Who is going to remind her not to drink too much when you're gone? She needs to exercise restraint on her own."

When he had learned that Melinda was returning to Sussex, Hartford's first reaction was that he was going to miss her. Then, in the same breath, he had felt relieved. Not only would Melinda be well out of the trouble that would soon befall Darlington House, but in her absence he would find it far easier to concentrate on the work at hand.

And this work was progressing daily. Thoughtfully, Hartford watched del'Anche detach Zenobie from the inventor's side and led her toward the floor. The orchestra had struck up a waltz, and as the sweet, slow strains filled the air, the *conte* and his partner began an animated conversation.

It would be interesting to hear what was being said. "Do you waltz?" Hartford asked Melinda.

She shook her head. "I never was taught. I used to watch parties sometimes and think how graceful the dancers were."

"Not all of them," Hartford pointed out as Carabel, partnered by the red-faced squire, lumbered past. Then he added, "When do you leave for the academy?"

"The day after tomorrow. Zenobie will come with us as far as Kendle-on-Lake, and there Polly and I take the mail coach." Melinda tried to sound eager as she added, "It will be good to see all the little girls again."

"Faster, play faster!" Zenobie suddenly called.

Surprised, Melinda turned around and saw that all the dancers except Zenobie and del'Anche had left the floor. "What dance is this?" Melinda exclaimed as the two began to prance about.

"A Russian folk dance, I think," Lord Hartford said. "I saw something like it while I was on the continent."

Zenobie was dancing with abandon. Her arms flailed, her legs kicked out. "She is certainly energetic," Hartford commented.

"Much too energetic," Melinda exclaimed in some alarm. "I should have stopped her from drinking so much champagne." Then, as her cousin's leaps grew even more inspired, she called, "Zenobie, stop dancing so hard!"

Her voice was drowned out in the wail of violins. Melinda started toward the floor, but once again Hartford held her back.

"Leave it to me."

He walked over toward the leader of the orchestra. Meanwhile the count, perspiring and panting audibly, kept up with Zenobie. Melinda noted that the younger gentlemen in the room had begun to make bets about who would tire first.

The orchestra stopped playing. Melinda glanced gratefully at Lord Hartford, then turned back to Zenobie, who had fallen dramatically on one knee.

The guests applauded wildly and Sir Rupert shouted, "Bravo! What? Bravo, ma'am. Never saw such dancin', mean to say—never *was* such a woman."

Zenobie turned her head as if to acknowledge the applause, and Melinda saw that she had turned very pale. For a moment it seemed as though she were trying to say something. Then she clutched at her heart and slumped down to the floor, where she lay very still.

# Chapter Six

"Zenobie!"

Darting to her cousin's side, Melinda fell to her knees. Meanwhile, in the instant of shocked silence before panic set in, Hartford took charge.

"Don't move her, Miss Weatherby. Blyminster, del'Anche, keep the others back—she needs air. You," he added to a gawking footman, "fetch the doctor immediately."

"I've just arrived, as it happens." Dr. Gildfish was shouldering his way through the crowd. He went down on one knee beside Zenobie, lifted her eyelids, then took her pulse. "Much too fast," he commented. "What has she been doing?" Then, as several voices began to speak at once, he added, "Never mind—she's coming to."

Zenobie opened her eyes and, looking about her dazedly, focused on Melinda's face. "Melushka?" she whispered. "What happened to me?"

Before Melinda could reply, Dr. Gildfish directed his patient not to weaken herself by speaking and ordered that she be taken to her chamber at once.

Sir Rupert insisted on helping the footmen carry the lady up the stairs to her chamber. Melinda, about to follow this entourage, suddenly recalled that she could not leave Zenobie's guests at sixes and sevens. She hesitated, but Lord Hartford took her by the hand and gently but firmly conducted her to the stairs.

"Go up and see to your cousin," he said. "I'll deal with the guests."

Melinda fled up the stairs and nearly collided with Sonya Vraskova in the doorway of Zenobie's room. "How is she?" she asked, and was answered in a stream of hysterical Russian. Pushing past her cousin's maid, Melinda saw Zenobie lying white and motionless on her bed.

The doctor was bending over her. "Don't worry," he was saying reassuringly, "you only fainted. I warned you that too much exertion could bring on this weakness."

Zenobie's reply was almost inaudible. "Will she be all right?" Melinda whispered worriedly.

"I hope so. But what brought her to this state?" Dr. Gildfish demanded. "What was she doing?"

"Dancin'," croaked a remorseful voice nearby, and Melinda realized that Sir Rupert was standing in the shadows near the door. "She was dancin' with that Italian fellow. And I *encouraged* her."

He tugged at his hair, causing it to sprout in all directions like a dandelion gone to seed. "*Encouraged* her, mean to say. Shouted 'bravo' or some such claptrap," he groaned remorsefully. "If somethin' happens to Lady Darlington, it's my fault."

"Nothing is going to happen," Dr. Gildfish said. He then added significantly, "The less excitement she has, the better, though. I must ask you to leave, Sir Rupert."

Head hanging, the picture of contrition and misery, the inventor slunk out of the room. "Poor Sir Rupert," Zenobie exclaimed. "Melushka, bring him back. He must see that he's not to blame."

She began to get up. "What are you doing?"

Melinda cried, alarmed. "You must lie still, as the doctor ordered."

"I cannot leave my guests in such a tub of pickles," Zenobie argued fretfully. Then, as Gildfish told her in no uncertain terms that she must remain in bed, she turned pleading eyes to Melinda. "Melushka," she entreated, "go down and see that the party moves forward. Tell Russtin to serve more drinks—"

Her voice trailed off, and she closed her eyes again. Melinda looked at the doctor, who nodded. Then, walking to the door with her, he spoke in a lower tone. "To cross her would only agitate her. Best to let the party proceed." Melinda hesitated, and he added, "Don't look so worried, Miss Weatherby. Lady Darlington is more frightened than ill. I'll stay with her and make sure she's all right."

"You are so kind," she exclaimed, but he shrugged off her thanks.

"Lord Hartford had everything in hand when I came on the scene. But then, a man of his training would know exactly what to do. Calworth's Circle is an elite group, after all." He added thoughtfully, "One can't help wondering why Lord Hartford was sent here to this quiet backwater. Sir Orin Calworth usually concerns himself only with major affairs of state."

Melinda realized that the doctor was speaking of Lord Hartford's activities during the last war with Napoleon. "Who is this Sir Orin Calworth?" she wondered.

"The leader of a group of extraordinary men. Not many know about Sir Orin's Circle," the doctor went on. "I myself heard of its existence only because I attended the deathbed of a wounded officer in a little town near Astorga. It seems that Lieutenant Latten and Lord Hartford were comrades in arms."

Lieutenant Latten must be the young man who had read Shakespeare—but before Melinda could refine on this, Zenobie once again begged her to go downstairs and see to the guests.

Obediently, Melinda went downstairs, where she conferred with the anxious Russtin, reassured him that Lady Darlington was in no danger, and gave orders for more drinks to be served.

"I'd advise against that." Lord Hartford had come out of the drawing room. "A number of the guests are half drunk already. Feed them instead, Miss Weatherby. After all, an army marches on its stomach."

Russtin looked uncertainly at Melinda, who gave the order. As the butler went away, she added, "That was sensible advice, my lord. Thank you."

"You need to thank Boney, since he coined the phrase." Hartford broke off as he saw her sway a little, and, reaching out, caught her around the waist to steady her. "Are you all right?"

His arm was strong and firm about her. For one weak moment she wanted to turn and bury her cheek in his shoulder, but Melinda knew she must not give in.

She had always stood on her own feet. She had always relied on herself—Melinda called forth a smile as she straightened her back away from the support of Lord Hartford's arm. "I am not the one who is ill," she pointed out.

"No, but you'll have a great deal on your shoulders for the next few days." Hartford frowned down into her pale face as he continued. "Blyminster has been giving me an account of Lady Darlington's condition that would make a deathbed scene at Astley's Amphitheater tame by comparison."

"Poor Sir Rupert. He blames himself, and he should not. *He* did not tell Zenobie to dance so wildly."

Hartford had meant to agree, but her brave smile and the way she squared her slender shoulders took the words out of his mind. Instead, he heard himself blurt out, "I suppose you won't leave for Sussex, now."

Melinda thought of that world full of little girls, of the ordered life and the sunshine-filled gardens, and wondered why she did not feel more regret.

"I suppose not," she said. "Not yet, anyway. Perhaps when Zenobie is better, and—and now I had better go and explain matters to the guests."

Silently, Hartford offered his arm and escorted Melinda into the drawing room, where the guests clustered about her, demanding news of Zenobie's state of health.

"It is my fault, I take the blame entirely," the *conte* exclaimed when she had told them all she knew. He drew out his jeweled snuffbox and took snuff with great delicacy as he added, " 'Ad we not been dancing that so energetic dance, this disaster would not 'ave 'appened."

"No, it wouldn't," Sir Rupert quoth belligerently. "Bacon-brained thing to do, jumpin' around like that. Not the thing, mean to say."

He looked daggers at the *conte,* who protested that the dance had been her ladyship's idea. "You probably talked her into it, then," persisted the inventor. "Saw you jawin' on and on at her. Botherin' her, I shouldn't wonder."

"Ah, you say so, when it was *you* she was talking to for so long," the *conte* countered. He spoke suavely, but his eyes glittered as he continued. "I wonder what it was that you were saying to her ladyship, Sir Rupert? Per'aps that you should like to see 'er dance the cossack dance which 'er grandfather, the Count Oblonski, liked so much?"

"Never did!" Sir Rupert shouted. "Don't known any demmed cossack dance. Mean to say, her ladyship was askin' me about my *Subaqua*—"

He broke off, turned crimson, and stammered, "I mean, about my inventions. Eh? She was askin' questions and I was answerin', that's all. I didn't make her dance like some fancy dancin' master."

Del'Anche's eyes narrowed. He said in a soft, silky voice, "If you 'ave any complaint about my be'avior—"

He took a step forward. The inventor took two. Like a bristling bantam, he eyed the taller, suave del'Anche and spat out, "Yes, I demmed well do."

"Oh, I beg you, stop," Melinda exclaimed in great distress.

"Up daggers, Blyminster," Hartford said. He strolled between the combatants, adding, "*Conte,* this is a house of sickness and not a time to be brangling. Let be, gentlemen."

The *conte* bowed and stepped back. Muttering under his breath, Sir Rupert followed suit. Hartford went on. "We're all of us concerned about her ladyship. Fortunately, there's no need for alarm. The doctor assures Miss Weatherby that Lady Darlington will make a complete recovery."

Melinda took her cue and announced that if the guests would repair to the dining room, dinner would be served. The guests looked at each other uncertainly until Lord Hartford professed himself extremely hungry, walked over to the oldest dowager present, bowed, and offered his arm to conduct her in to dinner. Seeing this, the others fell into place according to their rank and station.

It was, Melinda thought, a very odd dinner party. As if anxiety had whetted their appetites, the company fairly fell upon the food. Even Sir Rupert set aside his anxiety and remorse long enough to eat his way through two servings of roasted capon with herb sauce and three helpings of pickled crab.

Shortly after dinner, the party broke up, but del'Anche hung back to beg Melinda to convey his sentiments of respect and regret to Lady Darlington. "But 'ere is the doctor," he exclaimed as Dr. Gildfish came walking down the stairs. "She will recover, will she not, Doctor, the so-beautiful lady of the 'ouse?"

Assured that Lady Darlington was resting comfortably and would be better after a good night's sleep, del'Anche promised to return to call upon her and exited. Sir Rupert glowered over the departing *conte*.

"Demmed jackanapes," he growled. "Never trusted him. Knew he wasn't up to any good."

He turned to Melinda. "Miss Weatherby, would you offer her ladyship my warmest wishes for recovery? Hope she's back in good curl soon, mean to say."

He walked off, shaking his head. Hartford started to follow him, then paused to ask gently, "Is there something I can do to help?"

Once more Melinda fought a hen-hearted impulse to lay her head on his lordship's shoulder. "No, but thank you," she said warmly. "Thank you for being so helpful—and so kind. I must go up now and help Sonya Vraskova."

Hartford watched Melinda walking up the stairs

for a moment, then turned to Dr. Gildfish. "Is Lady Darlington very ill?" he asked.

"She'll be all right if she follows doctor's orders this time." Gildfish walked into the drawing room, unstoppered a crystal decanter of port, and poured himself a glass. "When I first took her on as a patient, I warned her against overexertion and excess. She has a condition of the heart. Apparently the result of a hard life."

"Lady Darlington has had an *active* life," Hartford agreed. The doctor raised his eyebrows. "Surely you've heard the neighborhood gossip? One of her former husbands was Hyacinthe Vilforme. He used to be one of Boney's less savory henchmen."

"That could explain it," Gildfish said thoughtfully.

Hartford asked, "Explain what?"

"Eh? Oh, some nonsense she spoke while she was coming around. A lot of it was in Russian, but she spoke English when she mentioned something about sacks of gold. 'I need more,' she said. 'Also always wants more, also is greedy.' Makes no sense, so I put it down for delirium, but perhaps it had to do with Vilforme. I've heard that he was a thoroughly bad hat."

"Indeed," Hartford said softly.

Dr. Gildfish was saying, "I've put her on bed rest and a restricted diet. She's too scared and sick to complain now, but when she feels better, it'll be a different story." He smiled ruefully. "I don't envy Miss Weatherby. Lady Darlington's not an easy patient."

Hartford agreed, thinking the while that Lady Darlington's illness could well be feigned and that he must send a dispatch to Sir Orin immediately.

112

If he was not mistaken, Vilforme's widow would make her move soon.

Dr. Gildfish had warned Melinda that Zenobie's convalescence might be a trying time, and the next few days bore out the full truth of this. Though pronounced out of danger after a day, Zenobie appeared pale, listless, and without appetite. Sonya Vraskova dramatically implored the God of Mother Russia to aid her mistress and generally "created," in Miss Poll's disgusted words, whilst declaring that Madam had *never* lost her appetite for food before, no, not even at the worst of times.

Mountains of flowers and fruit from Blyminster Cove arrived daily, and on the third day Sir Rupert himself appeared along with Lord Hartford. The inventor was all contrition and practically prostrated himself at Zenobie's feet. She rallied slightly, but as soon as the gentlemen had gone, she became restless and petulant and nagged Sonya Vraskova until the maid burst into tears.

Melinda took over Zenobie's care for the evening. It was a thankless task. Zenobie was fretful and demanding, and by the time she finally fell asleep, Melinda was exhausted. Wearily she walked down the hall to her own room, went to her desk, and picked up Mr. Proctor's letter of reconciliation.

"There's no help for it," she said. "It has to be done."

She was still at her desk when Miss Poll came into the room and accused, "You're writing to that there Proctor, aren't you, Miss Mel?"

Melinda straightened her aching spine and glanced at the clock. "Why are you not in bed?" she demanded. "It's one in the morning."

"Same reason you're up," retorted her sometime

nurse. She jutted her chin as she added, "You're refusing that Proctor's offer, Miss Mel, ain't that it?"

"It's the only thing I can do," Melinda sighed.

"That Rooshan woman's making you dance to her tune, Miss Mel. She knows your good heart and made herself get sick."

"You must not speak so of Zenobie," Melinda said sternly. "Dr. Gildfish says that if untreated, her illness could become grave. If I went away and she fell ill again, I couldn't forgive myself."

"Well, she took sick at a convenient time, that's all I say." Miss Poll shifted to a coaxing tone. "Look, Miss Mel, that one's selfish through and through. She don't take care of herself, yet she wants you to do it for her." Melinda said nothing. "You'd lose your chance for a really good post just so's you can carry her medicine and change her cushion under her head?"

Trying to ignore a sinking feeling that Miss Poll was right, Melinda spoke more sharply than she intended. "That is enough, Polly. I won't hear any more on the subject."

"Don't worry—I might as well spare my breath to cool my porridge."

As her former nurse huffed off, Melinda looked down at the letter in her hand. "It's the only thing to do," she repeated.

She could not possibly abandon Zenobie now. She finished her letter, signed and sealed it, and sat back feeling infinitely weary. "But," she thought out loud, "I should look in on Zenobie one last time."

The hall candles flickered dimly as Melinda left her room and stepped across to knock softly on Zenobie's door. No one answered, so she opened the door and looked inside, only to exclaim in consternation. Zenobie's bed was empty and there was no one in the room.

Where could her cousin have gone? Melinda stepped back into the hall and looked up and down, but there was no sign of Zenobie. Perhaps she had become disoriented and was wandering through the house? About to summon Sonya Vraskova, Melinda chanced to glance out the window and was surprised to see somone in the dark garden.

It could not be the night watchman, for the figure was definitely feminine. A servant girl meeting a lover? But a servant on a tryst would hardly dare to walk across the garden so boldly. "It must be Zenobie," Melinda exclaimed. "But she must not be out there—she will catch her death."

She ran downstairs, lifted a shawl from a hook by the door, and, wrapping herself into it, went to the side door. It was unlocked. Letting herself outside, Melinda softly called her cousin's name, but there was no answer, and in the light of the half-moon the garden stretched wide and empty. No one was there—no one at all.

Then she caught sight of something glimmering white on the ground. Reaching down, Melinda retrieved a small clump of white swansdown that had obviously torn free from a lady's costly pelisse. There was another bit of swansdown farther on and still another lay on the path to the lake. Could Zenobie simply be taking a walk down to the water's edge? But she had been so weak, so listless all day, and in any case the late April night was cool. Why would anyone want to be out at this time of night?

"Unless she's walking in her sleep," Melinda mused. The doctor's medicine might have induced sleepwalking—

Something ahead of her glimmered white, and Melinda glimpsed her cousin a few yards away walking slowly toward the lake.

"Zeno—" Melinda caught herself. She had remembered that to awaken sleepwalkers could be dangerous. Catching up her skirts, she skimmed down the path. But before she could reach her cousin, there was a rustling in the underbrush nearby, and a man's figure appeared.

Though she could not see his face, Melinda could smell the oddly pungent scent of the cigar he tossed aside before walking toward Zenobie. Thoroughly alarmed, Melinda started forward to try to protect her cousin, but before she had taken more than a few steps, Zenobie spoke.

"So," she said, "you are here. You have, then, received my note."

There was nothing sonambulistic or feeble about Zenobie's voice, and the hand she stretched out to the gentleman was steady in the half-moonlight. Melinda stopped where she was as the shadowed gentleman bowed gallantly over Zenobie's hand.

She had stumbled on a lovers' meeting. Both relieved and embarrassed, Melinda pulled her skirts close to her and began, as quietly as possible, to retrace her steps. As she did so, she could not help noticing that the gentleman was doing most of the talking while Zenobie listened. His voice was low, so that even if she had wanted to, she could not have overheard what he said.

"What a fool I am," she reflected. "To meet an admirer romantically by moonlight is like Zenobie. But if she is well enough for a rendezvous, why does she pretend to be so ill—"

Melinda stopped in mid-thought. As she walked, she had thought—*felt*—that someone was watching her from among the trees. She looked quickly about her but could see nothing. And yet she could *feel* those eyes.

She quickened her pace, but now there was a rustling beside her in the trees and underbrush that bordered the cleared pathway to the lake. Someone *was* nearby and following her.

"Who is there?" Melinda wanted to shout out this demand, but her voice emerged in a hen-hearted gasp.

"Can that be you, Miss Weatherby?"

Melinda felt her knees go weak with relief, for it was Dr. Gildfish who came walking down the path toward her. "Why are you walking alone at this time of night?" he wondered.

He sounded astonished, as well he might be. With an effort, Melinda forced herself not to glance over her shoulder toward the lake. She must not betray Zenobie's indiscretion.

"I needed a breath of air," she lied, "so I started to walk down to the lake. Then I thought I heard footsteps behind me and turned back."

"It's not wise to be outside alone, especially at this late hour," he told her somberly. "There are footpads and cutpurses about, even here in quiet Dorset."

"You are right. It was most unwise of me." Melinda wrapped her arms about herself to quell her trembling. "But you, Doctor? Why are you abroad at this time of night?"

"Unfortunately, country doctors are frequently about at all hours. I was summoned by Mrs. Pennodie earlier tonight and was kept in attendance for several hours."

His rueful look spoke volumes. "Her cold?" Melinda wondered without much sympathy.

"She acted as if on her deathbed. But she's apparently well enough to plan a party, for she's invited me to a morning gathering next week. She means to show off the garden that those Quakers built for her."

As he spoke, the doctor offered Melinda his arm, and they began to walk toward the house. "When I left Mrs. Pennodie," he went on, "I thought I might as well look in on Lady Darlington. I didn't realize how late it was until I got here and found even the grooms abed."

The doctor stifled a yawn. "I was about to ride back to town, when I thought I saw someone slipping furtively through the garden. I decided to investigate—and the rest you know."

No doubt the doctor had seen Zenobie. "I'm sorry you were bothered," Melinda apologized.

The doctor gave her a sympathetic look. "Nursing your cousin has exhausted your nerves. Shall I give you a mild sleeping draft?"

In the moonlight his face was full of kindly concern. "No, but thank you for escorting me through the shadows."

As the doctor walked away, Melinda uneasily recalled those shadows. She could not help believing that someone besides Dr. Gildfish had been watching her from the shadow of the trees. If she were right, that person—or persons—would be spying on Zenobie now.

Melinda was about to arouse the servants and have them search the woods, when her cousin came gliding up the path from the lake. She looked both ways to see if she was being observed and then made for the house.

Melinda called softly to her. "Who is it?" Zenobie

gasped, then put a hand to her heart. "Melushka, you startled me. Why are you not asleep?"

"Why are *you* not?" Melinda countered. "I saw that your bed was empty and came to find you."

"You sound like a foolish heroine in Lady Caroline Lamb's latest romance," Zenobie sniffed. "I desired to feel the fresh air, so I came for a walk."

"Just for a walk?" Melinda persisted. Her cousin nodded. "You didn't come out here to meet someone?"

"At this hour? Have you been sleepwalking, Melushka? It is a danger, the sleepwalking. I am told that you see and hear what is not there. You have been working too hard, my little one, and are *distrait.*"

Nothing could be more innocent than Zenobie's concerned gaze. Melinda thought dryly that questioning her cousin was like catching fish with a torn net. "But," she persisted, "I saw you meet a gentleman by the water's edge."

"Ah, bah! That I should have so little of the pride as to meet a gentleman at night dressed in my pelisse and bedroom slippers. You are not only *distrait,* you are mad."

Head high, she sailed past Melinda toward the house. But as she did so, Melinda noted that her cousin's face was white and set.

Something highly unpleasant had happened to Zenobie back there at the lake—involuntarily, Melinda glanced over her shoulder. It was no flight of fancy that she had felt those eyes watching her. She could feel them, still.

But asking her cousin any more questions that night would be wasted effort. Melinda went to bed and awoke the next morning to a wan, peevish Zenobie who spoke in a die-away voice and refused breakfast. She seemed so thoroughly an invalid that Melinda found herself wondering if she had indeed dreamed the happenings of last night.

She had little time to wonder. Zenobie kept Melinda running attendance all morning and then took a nap herself in the afternoon. This state of affairs continued for two days and caused Miss Poll to grumble that she hoped that Miss Mel would not regret her decision.

Melinda's spirits were at low ebb when Zenobie summoned her yet again. "She has been sick; she is not well," Melinda reminded herself as she went into the garden, where Zenobie, swathed in shawls and veils, was reclining on a wicker daybed and entertaining the Conte del'Anche.

The *conte* was just departing as Melinda came up to them. He bowed over Zenobie's hand as if she were a princess, vowed that after his so-tiresome trip of business he would fly to her side, and added that Lady Darlington would be always on his mind while he was away. But in spite of these protestations, Melinda sensed that he was angry about something.

"Have you quarreled with the *conte*?" she asked as he walked away, flicking at grass and leaves with the tip of his ivory and gold walking cane.

"Well-bred people don't quarrel," Zenobie snapped. "Where have you been? I saw you talking to that disagreeable Poll woman. If any of *my* servants spoke to me as she speaks to you, that servant would see the street."

"I don't consider Polly a servant," Melinda pointed out equably. "We have been comrades together for many years."

"So it is with Sonya Vraskova and me, but the lines of class are never down between us." Zenobie sniffed. "You are a gentleman's daughter and of the blue blood. You must not forget *who you are* and mingle with the servants, who come from no blood at all and must make the living with their hands."

"You forget that I, too, am in that situation," Melinda said somewhat coldly. Zenobie winced.

"I wish you would not say such things. It is not good ton to admit that you have to work for money."

"It is much worse ton to starve," Melinda said still more coldly.

"Ah, bah, as if you were in danger of that," Zenobie sniffed. "As if you don't have a handsome, rich lord dangling around you."

Melinda felt a rush of real irritation. Hot words leapt to her lips, but she stopped them in time. She was not going to argue with Zenobie, and anyway, protestations were never believed. "If you are speaking of Lord Hartford," she said, "I collect that he comes to see you with Sir Rupert Blyminster because Sir Rupert is too shy to come alone."

Her cousin raised herself on her elbow and stared directly at Melinda. "And do you stand there and tell me in words that have not got the bark on them that Lord Hartford—the rich, handsome duke's son for whom London mamas would scratch eyes out for—is not interested in you? Nor you in him?"

"No," Melinda snapped.

It was not a lie. Since that one evening by the lake, his lordship's actions had been entirely correct. But even as she thought this, she remembered the way he had looked at her on the night of the ill-fated farewell party.

Abruptly, Melinda asked, "Did you want me to do something for you?" Zenobie turned her head away.

"Is there something you need? If not, I have many tasks to attend to."

"Oh, if you are going to take that tone, go away." Melinda turned away, but had not taken two steps when Zenobie called her back.

"Melushka, forgive me," she exclaimed contritely. "I wear the Friday face. I am the sour pickles. Today nothing pleases me."

She held out her hands and after a moment Melinda took them. "Zenobie," she said unhappily, "we must us talk about the other night. I followed you to the lake and saw you met a man there."

Zenobie's eyes narrowed. "*You* followed me? You become, then, the spy?"

Melinda flushed at Zenobie's tone. "I thought you might be sleepwalking," she said stiffly. "I was concerned you would come to harm."

"Ah, I see how it was." Once more contrite, Zenobie smiled and squeezed Melinda's hand in a surprisingly strong grip. "It isn't what you think."

"I don't think anything," Melinda protested. "What you do or who you meet is not my concern, Zenobie. I don't wish to pry, but—but it seems that if you are well enough to keep a rendezvous with a gentleman, you should be well on the road to recovery."

To her surprise, Zenobie sat up on the daybed and tossed off her shawls and veils. "You are right, *malenkaya*," she exclaimed. "You are correct, my dear one. You will see—I am no longer sick. I am recovered. And the first thing we must do is stop living like hermits, which makes me cross as the crabs. Melushka, we must have a party."

"A party!" Melinda exclaimed in utmost horror.

"Well, not a *party*, then. Do not look so *farouche*, Melushka, we will make it a small dinner. Sir

Rupert and his friend Lord Hartford—otherwise my little one would pine."

Roguishly, she patted her cousin's cheek. "But," Melinda exclaimed, "this is insane. You are still not fully recovered and—and Dr. Gildfish would forbid it."

"Bah, we will invite him, too. And after our party for dinner, we shall look forward to another party—the invitation to which I this day received from Mrs. Pennodie, who wishes to show off her new iron castle and her expensive, silly little garden. That is just like a commoner, to show off, but her parties are entertaining. You will see."

Stretching out both arms, Zenobie hugged the reluctant Melinda and caroled, "Be going, dull cares! We will be merry and joyful now that I am well again."

# Chapter Seven

To Melinda's astonishment, Dr. Gildfish did not veto Zenobie's request for a dinner party. "A change may be what you need to raise your spirits," he said. "You can have your dinner party as long as you practice moderation."

Zenobie made a face. " 'Moderation' is such an odious word, but I will obey you, *dear* Dr. Gildfish. And may I attend Mrs. Pennodie's morning party? I must see this wonderful garden with my own eyes."

The prospect of her dinner, set for the night before Mrs. Pennodie's party, restored Zenobie's spirits and much of her health. "That is, if she ever lost it," the irrepressible Miss Poll sniffed to Melinda as she helped her dress on the night of the party. "I tell you, Miss Mel, the Rooshan's a sly one, and her servants aren't any better. Useless lot, if you ask my opinion, and Mr. Russtin's too old and soft to control them proper."

Since Melinda had dealt with Zenobie's staff during her illness, she was inclined to agree. She had tried to explain her servants' inadequacies to her cousin, who promised to take matters into her hands but did nothing. "I don't think she is happy, Polly," Melinda said slowly. "Yesterday I found her in tears. It isn't like Zenobie to be in the mopes."

A grim little smile hovered on Miss Poll's lips. "Perhaps she's in love again," she suggested. "Sure as my name's Jane Poll, she's got her mind set on being Lady Blyminster."

But Sir Rupert did not smoke cigars. Speculation about the man Zenobie had met at the lake followed Melinda downstairs into the as yet silent Green Room, where the guests were to gather before dinner. Here she discovered that the French windows had not been shut properly, and that a breeze, softened by earlier showers, was ruffling an arrangement of spring flowers. As she rearranged these blooms, Melinda remained deep in thought.

Whom *had* Zenobie met so secretively that night? Why did she pretend to be so full of spirits and then weep unobserved? Why?

"Why what?" a familiar male voice inquired behind her. "Was that a question to the world at large, or where you just thinking out loud?"

By now Melinda had become accustomed to Lord Hartford's silent tread. She gave him her hand, saying, "I did not know you had arrived. Is Sir Rupert with you?"

"He went down to the lake, mumbling something about water temperature." Hartford looked around the room. "This looks very pleasant. Your doing?"

The room lacked the opulent touches of which Lady Darlington was so fond. The heavier furniture had been banished, and comfortable, leather-upholstered chairs had been rearranged so as to welcome rather than impress. Instead of masses of flamboyant hothouse blooms, simple garden flowers filled the vases.

And in her simple gray crepe vertical gown Melinda was as lovely as the flowers. Hartford felt his heart lighten, as it always seemed to do when she was near. "Charming," he said.

The heartfelt approval in his voice made her ridiculously happy. "Zenobie is not yet feeling quite the thing," she explained, "so I have been trying to help."

He sketched her a courtly bow. "To the worker, the glory. Are the other guests late?" She explained that only the doctor would join them. "What, are del'Anche and Ferridew out of favor these days?"

"Mr. Ferridew keeps sending reams of poetry, but he has announced that he is involved in writing an ode and cannot commune with mere mortals. The *conte* has not come to call for a few days. I believe he said that he is traveling on business."

"Interestin'—just as I thought." Sir Rupert had stumped into the room. "Water temperature here's much warmer than it is at Blyminster Cove, and the wind's not as strong."

He then saw Melinda, begged her pardon, and professed himself her most obedient. "Good place to try out m'new glass eye," he went on. "Nice, quiet waters, mean to say—"

He broke off in midsentence as Zenobie entered the room. Her dress of deep emerald gauze spangled with golden embroidery floated over her silk slip-dress of lighter green. "Ah, dear Sir Rupert," she caroled. "Welcome."

The inventor's reply was incoherent, and Melinda observed that his eyes had a glazed-over look. He remained in this trancelike state throughout the evening, merely mumbling a greeting when Dr. Gildfish arrived. But not even his dazzlement took away from his appetite. Melinda watched with admiration as Sir Rupert sat down to table and proceeded to eat his way through a hearty soup followed by filet of veal, a serving of duck, prawns, and two enormous helpings of pickled crab, which Zenobie had asked the cook to prepare specially for his benefit. But though his jaws crunched away, and whilst he imbibed several glasses of the wine Russtin served up, the inventor's eyes never left Zenobie's face.

No one minded his silence, for throughout the meal Dr. Gildfish kept them amused with his experiences as a country doctor. It was only when the apricot puff was served that Zenobie guided the conversation to a topic that recalled Sir Rupert from his reverie.

"The sea—there's nothin' like it," the inventor rhapsodized. "Powerful, wild, as beautiful and as unpredictable as a woman. Been in water all m'life, love it, and lived in it. That's why I spent most of m'life inventin' somethin' that'll be at home in water. Eh? And m'*Subaqua*'s important, too. Mean to say, an underwater ship will change the world."

"So Fulton thought," Dr. Gildfish pointed out, "but the Lords of the Admiralty disagreed. Called the *Nautilus* a gimcrack, if I'm not mistaken."

"Bacon-brained, all of them," Sir Rupert retorted. "Mind, Fulton's design was flawed. Eh? If there ain't enough air in the dem—the dashed craft, the men inside'll suffocate."

Zenobie signaled for more wine to be poured. "But you have improved the design," she purred. "You have designed a new way to pipe in air from the surface through a long steel rod."

The inventor beamed at her. "You're talkin' about my air inductor. And there's another thing I've been workin' on."

Sir Rupert took a gulp of wine and lowered his voice to a whisper. "It's m'glass eye. Device that shows a fellow at the bottom of the sea what's happenin' on the surface. Mean to say—useful in times of war. Here—let me show you."

He called for pen and ink and, pushing his plate aside, began to sketch a diagram for the company. Zenobie, professing herself fascinated, leaned against his shoulder as he explained. "One end sticks up over the water—other end comes down here. There's a mirror placed here, d'you see? And here."

The doctor had risen and was looking at the diagram somewhat skeptically. "Are you saying that this, er, glass eye of yours really works?"

"In theory. Ain't tested it yet. I was waitin'—" Sir Rupert caught Hartford's glance, flushed, folded the sketch he had just made, and jammed it into the pocket of his coat. "Probably won't work," he mumbled. "All conjecture. Don't think it'll be good for anythin', mean to say."

Thoughtfully, Dr. Gildfish resumed his seat. "An underwater ship that has access to fresh air is equipped with a device that would allow a view of the surface—it would be deadly in war. What do you think, Lord Hartford?"

"That you're right." Hartford added, "Mind, I know less that nothing about science."

"Surely you're being modest," the doctor protested. "I would have thought that members of Calworth's Circle know everything that goes on in the world."

"And what, pray, is this Circle you are telling of?" Zenobie wondered.

With all eyes on him, Hartford explained that for a short time during the war with Bonaparte he had been involved in sub rosa activities for the crown. "It's nothing of any consequence," he added.

"Sub rosa—ah, you are meaning the espionage," Zenobie exclaimed. Her eyes had grown very round. "That is so romantic, Lord Hartford."

"Hardly that, ma'am." Hartford turned to Dr. Gildfish, adding, "I'm surprised you know about the Circle—or my involvement in it. How did you hear of it?"

"A military doctor hears many things." Dr. Gildfish's tone was apologetic. "Dying men tell us secrets they'd confide to no one else. I have never before mentioned the Circle, however, and I beg your pardon if I've offended you."

"Anyway," Sir Rupert cut in somewhat impatiently, "the *Subaqua* don't have to be used for war only. Think of bein' able to explore the bottom of the sea! Findin' treasure stored in ships that've gone down! It'll make England rich and powerful, mean to say."

He hiccuped and reached for more wine. "You are of such brilliance," Zenobie cooed. "Your country will honor you."

"More to the point, we must honor our hostess." Hartford lifted his glass so that the candlelight shined through the fine red liquid within. "The wine is really very good, Lady Darlington. If I'm not mistaken, these are Flemish grapes."

Zenobie looked pleased. "You are not mistaken, Lord Hartford. A Belgian wine merchant brings this wine when he can. We are lucky that Van Leyt's sister is in service to Mrs. Pennodie, because whenever he comes to Dorset to visit her, he supplies us with wine."

"That's fortunate for all of us." Lord Hartford rose to his feet. "I propose a toast to our lovely hostess."

Sir Rupert drank the toast with great enthusiasm and had to be restrained from casting his glass onto the floor. "Beautiful lady," he slurred, "diamond of the firsht water, egad. Daughter of the gods, divinely fair, or whatever rubbish the poets shay."

He hiccuped and held out his glass for more wine. As Russtin filled it, he added, "You're right, Doctor—the *Subaqua*'ll change the world. That's why I have to be careful, sh—see? All m'notes and diagrams about the invention are locked up in m'sh—safe in m'workshop." He tapped his narrow chest and hiccuped again. "I keep the key with me here—on a chain 'round my neck. Mean to sh—say—safe as a church!"

Dr. Gildfish now rose and announced that he had to leave the pleasant gathering since there was a patient he needed to see. "Don't let Lady Darlington stay up late tonight," he warned Melinda, who accompanied him to the door. "Since she's determined to attend Mrs. Pennodie's party tomorrow morning, it'd be best to have an early night."

"Sir Rupert will probably fall asleep soon in any case," Melinda pointed out.

Dr. Gildfish chuckled. Then his pleasant face turned grave. "Perhaps *I* had too much to drink. I should never have mentioned Calworth's Circle. I realized too late that Lord Hartford can't wish to discuss his mission here."

The doctor's words made Melinda feel vaguely uneasy. But, she reasoned, Lord Hartford's connection—past or present—with this mysterious Circle could have nothing whatever to do with her.

She returned to the dining room, where Zenobie and Sir Rupert were now sitting hand in hand. "You think of everything, Sir Rupert," Zenobie was purring. "With you I would feel safe for my first walk since that unfortunate night."

The inventor was so pleased that his eyes watered. "I'd be honored, ma'am. Proud to escort you anywhere, mean to say."

He got to his feet, swayed, and hastily sat down again. "It would be better to put off the walk," Melinda interposed. "Dr. Gildfish says—"

"Bah—the doctor is not here to see. Do not be the croaking raven, Melushka. To walk a few feet in the garden cannot exert even a snail. Doubtless you will come as well, Lord Hartford?" Zenobie added with an arch smile. "My little cousin is aching for a walk."

"She is impossible, but I suppose we must follow them," Melinda sighed as her cousin left the room to prepare for the Excursion. "If she overtaxes herself, she will be sick again."

"Proud to escort you anywhere—as Blyminster put it," Lord Hartford agreed gallantly.

They went into the hall and waited until Zenobie joined them, then left the house and walked through the twilit garden. Hartford offered his arm, and Melinda rested her fingers on his sleeve.

Such a light touch—but Hartford felt it in the depths of his being. He was more conscious of her walking beside him, her glossy dark head at his shoulder, than he had ever been of anything in his life. He glanced down at her to see if she had sensed his feelings and saw that she was following her cousin with her eyes.

"Don't worry so much," he told her gently. "She can't come to harm walking down to the lake with Blyminster."

But Melinda had been thinking of unseen eyes in the shadows. She shivered, and misunderstanding,

Hartford took off his coat and slid it over her shoulders. Enveloped in a warmth that carried his lordship's clean, distinctive scent, Melinda felt tremors that had nothing to do with fear.

"What troubles you?" he asked.

If he had so far read her thoughts, perhaps he could also sense her reaction to his closeness. Melinda felt a slow, treacherous glow invade her whole being. It was as if she were bathed in a warmth that brought both excitement and anticipation.

This must stop, she commanded herself. It must stop *now*. Aloud she commented, "It's a fine night now that the rain has stopped. There is even a moon."

"So I see."

"And it is quite warm." What am I saying? Melinda asked herself. Here she stood, exchanging banalities, when all she wanted was for him to draw her into his arms.

She darted a look up at his lordship and saw that he was watching her with an expression that pierced the defenses she had built around her heart. She knew in that second that she had not stayed in Dorset only because of Zenobie. She had stayed because she could not bear to be parted from the man at her side.

Hartford had been certain that he had regained his perspective, but he realized now that he had been wrong. One fleeting look from those moon-silvered eyes, and logic took French leave. His usually keen mind disintegrated, and he could no more think than he could fly.

"We should return to the house," Melinda said in a low voice.

"Do you want to?" Hartford questioned. She

started to nod, stopped, and gave a very small shake of the head. "Nor do I."

Melinda closed her eyes as Lord Hartford put his arms around her and drew her close. She recalled perfectly the taste and texture of his lips and the way their bodies seemed to meld into each other. She had thought—dreamed—of this moment so often before that now it seemed perfectly natural to be held and kissed.

Warmth and strength and gentleness—but even these impressions drifted away until only one reality remained. She was in love with Anthony Hartford. She had not wanted to be, had tried hard not to be, and yet it had happened. It was fate. Melinda leaned back in his lordship's arms and let destiny take what course it would.

There was a scream in the near distance and Zenobie's voice. "*Spulcheve!*" she shouted. "Cossacks! Criminals! Leave us alone!"

Almost simultaneously, Sir Rupert was heard to bellow, "Take that, miscreant knave—eh?"

Hartford dropped his arms from around Melinda and both of them ran down the path toward the noise. Near the water they found Sir Rupert struggling with several brawny men while another ruffian held Zenobie fast.

"Help," Zenobie shouted. Then she screamed again as one of the men fighting Sir Rupert hit him on the head. As the inventor sagged to his knees, his attacker grabbed at his cravat.

"Stay where you are," Hartford told Melinda. He then leapt upon Sir Rupert's attacker and felled him with a blow.

At once another ruffian jumped on him from the back, and simultaneously, a brawny arm coiled around Melinda's throat. "One move out of yer, and

I'll snap yer bleeding neck," a rasping voice threatened.

There was nothing to do but take a deep breath and pretend to faint. As the villain who was holding her instinctively loosened his grip, Melinda stamped down on his foot with all her strength. He let out a horrid yell and let her go.

She fell on her knees and rolled aside as the villain grabbed for her. She had a moment's impression of a flat, froglike face framed by bristly fair hair, and then he was bowled over by Lord Hartford, who demanded, "Are you hurt, Melinda?"

"No, I—'ware your back, Anthony!" Melinda cried, for two men were rushing toward them.

"Get behind that tree and don't move!" Hartford shouted at Melinda. He caught the first brute a blow on the chin that sent him sprawling back into one of his companions. As this villain attempted to extricate himself, Melinda hit him with a tree branch she had found on the ground.

Meanwhile, Hartford had knocked down the other man. "Didn't I tell you to stay hidden?" he demanded.

"You looked as if you might require my assistance," Melinda retorted. "Anyway, what good would hiding be when they knew where I was?"

Before Hartford could answer, Zenobie shrieked, "Help! They are taking Sir Rupert away!"

"This time, listen to me and stay *here*!"

The duke's son pursued the villains, who were limping away and dragging the unconscious Sir Rupert with them. Melinda ran to help her cousin, who had collapsed at the edge of the lake. "Do not worry about me," Zenobie gasped. "Stop those villains! They must not hurt Sir Rupert."

Melinda hauled Zenobie to her feet and together

the women hurried back up the path. Halfway to the garden they found the inventor sitting upon the ground, massaging his head. Zenobie clasped her hands to her bosom and begged him to tell her that he was unhurt.

"Nothin' the matter with me, never fear, ma'am," the inventor mumbled. "One of those blackguards whacked me on my brainbox, curse him. Was all aboard for a minute. All right now."

Hartford came running up from the lake at this juncture. "They've made off. They had a sailboat waiting for them." He added grimly, "I'd have given a great deal to have taken *one* prisoner."

"What did they want?" Melinda wondered.

"They wanted me to go with them," Sir Rupert answered, "but I wouldn't. Then they laid hands on Lady Darlington, and I lost m'head."

"Oh, you were a hero," cooed Zenobie. "No, you will not say it was nothing, for without your strong arms I would have fallen prey to those cossacks, and St. Catherine alone knows what they would have done to me."

While she was talking, Sir Rupert shoved his hand into his torn shirt and pulled out a key that hung by a chain around his neck. "They was after this," he breathed. "Didn't get it, though. I say, Hartford, the game's gettin' dangerous—"

Melinda saw Lord Hartford raise his head and shoot a quick, expressive glance at the inventor. Sir Rupert dropped his head back into his hands. "My head does ache," he moaned, "and I feel sick."

Belatedly, servants now came running out of the house. Zenobie ordered the footmen to fetch the town watch and then added, "We will return to the house at once. Come, dear Sir Rupert, lean on my arm. Lord Hartford will take your other arm,

135

and Melushka, please to run ahead and order Sonya Vraskova to make a poultice for the head. It is a secret remedy created by my grandfather, the Count Oblonski. Do not fear, *dear* Sir Rupert. I will soon have you in the plumped currants once again."

In the flurry of activity that followed, Melinda had no chance to reflect on all that had happened. Then, after the gentlemen took their leave, she had to deal with Zenobie, who was suddenly so exhausted that she looked like a pale rag doll.

"I told you that you should not do too much," Melinda sighed.

"How did I know that we would be attacked by cossacks?" Zenobie argued. Then she exclaimed, "Ah, what bad fortune. I have lost my golden bracelet. I must have dropped it down by the lake."

Melinda's promise that they would look for the bracelet in the morning made her cousin all the more agitated. "It was given to me by my grandmother, the Countess Oblonski," she mourned. "She swore to me that I would have the good luck while I wore it and horrible misfortune if I lost it. Sonya Vraskova's eyes are so bad, and I don't trust the other servants not to pocket it."

She began to get out of bed. "You must not exert yourself further," Melinda protested. "Let me go."

Bidding Sonya Vraskova to keep her mistress in bed, Melinda took a lamp and went out into the dark garden. It was good to be alone after all the tumult of the evening, but now that she could collect her thoughts, Melinda found small comfort in them.

So many things that were happening did not make sense. The attack on Sir Rupert was terrible, of course, but even more distressing to her was the look with which Lord Hartford had commanded the inventor's silence.

Sir Rupert had been mumbling something about a dangerous game before he was silenced. Melinda believed now that Lord Hartford had been sent there by Sir Orin Calworth to guard the *Subaqua*. But guard it against whom?

Belatedly, Melinda recalled the sensation of being watched on the night she had followed Zenobie down to the lake. What a fool I am to have come out here alone, she thought.

She had turned to go back to the house, when she heard a rustling in the underbrush nearby. The fears of that other night came flooding back, and her first instinct was to run, but she forced herself to stay where she was. She might not be swift enough to escape, and revealing herself would put her in even greater danger. With an effort Melinda calmed herself enough to part the branches of the bush in front of her.

Lord Hartford was standing in a small clearing beyond. He was walking about the area that had apparently been trampled earlier in the evening. As she watched, he leaned down and picked up something that glittered in the moonlight.

Then he said, "Why not come out from behind that tree, Miss Weatherby?"

"How d-did you know I was here?" Melinda stammered.

"When the wind shifted, it brought a hint of the rose scent you always wear. But you shouldn't be out here. It's not safe after all that's happened tonight."

Feeling even more foolish, she explained, "I was afraid that you were the ruffians come back, so I hid. But I saw you pick up something bright just now. Did you find Zenobie's bracelet?"

Without replying, he held out an object that glittered in the moonlight. "But that is a French coin," Melinda exclaimed, bewildered. "Those men who attacked us were English."

"Paid by Napoleon's friends, no doubt." He pocketed the coin. "Old habits die hard, as you see. I couldn't resist coming back to look at the scene of the attack."

"Then you really have retired from intelligence work?" Melinda asked.

"Why do you ask?" he parried.

Instead of answering, she gazed searchingly into his shadowed face. "Did Sir Orin Calworth send you to Dorset?"

She looked so troubled and so lovely that it almost broke his heart. Lies, practiced and easy, came to his lips, but instead of using any of them Hartford simply said, "Yes, he did."

Melinda felt a tightening in her chest. "The evening we met at the lake, were you—were you watching my cousin's house?"

Again the lies presented themselves, and again Hartford rejected them. Melinda Weatherby was too intelligent not to see through subterfuge.

"Why?" she cried, taking his silence for assent. "What has Zenobie have to do with your mysterious Circle?"

Hartford had always known that it would come to the point where he would have to hurt her. He let go his breath in what was almost but not quite a sigh. "I'm not at liberty to explain."

The tightness in Melinda's chest increased. She had no idea why Lord Hartford was interested in Zenobie, but one thing was now plain. From first to last he had been acting as an agent of Calworth's Circle. No doubt, Melinda thought bitterly, he had kissed her that night by the lake to stop her from questioning him further. And tonight—what of tonight?

"I must ask you to promise you'll keep our meeting to yourself," he was saying.

Hurt enough to be reckless, she cried, "Otherwise, what? Will you have to kill me to silence me?"

Even now his smile held a treacherous warmth that invaded her senses and made her remember the way he had held and kissed her. She steeled her heart against that insidious memory as he said, "Nothing so dramatic. I'd simply have to make sure you weren't believed. That would take a lot of time and trouble, so I would rather have your word to—forget."

"I will not give my promise to anything I don't understand," Melinda protested. "You were watching Darlington House that night. You cannot think that *Zenobie* wants to steal Sir Rupert's invention?"

She had guessed too much to accept anything but the truth. Hartford made his choice. "I see I will have to trust you," he said.

As he told her an edited version of the truth, Melinda listened in disbelief. "You can't suspect that Zenobie would be working for Napoleon," she blurted out. "She would never—"

Hartford interrupted. "Napoleon's beside the bridge. He's gambled everything he has, and he knows he *must* win a major engagement or be crushed entirely. That would make him more than ever interested in an underwater battleship." He paused. "Even you must admit that your cousin has appeared fascinated by the *Subaqua*."

"You are deranged, my lord!"

"Your loyalty to your cousin is very commendable but misplaced," Hartford said. "Consider that Lady Darlington has expensive tastes and that espionage is a lucrative field."

Melinda thought of Zenobie's midnight rendezvous by the lake. Doubtless Lord Hartford knew about that meeting, already knew the identity of that unknown man. Perhaps Lord Hartford had even been the watcher in the shadows whose hostile presence she had sensed.

Melinda felt an icy prickling across her spine, and with it came the harsh truth. All this time, Lord Hartford had been interested in Zenobie. He had never cared a rush about Zenobie's cousin.

I am a fool, Melinda thought bitterly. Polly was right all along. I should never have trusted a duke's son.

Aloud she said, "I do not hear one real bit of proof against my cousin. And—and I don't believe a word you've said."

The ice in her voice would have frozen an inferno, but Hartford could hear the hurt just beneath that anger. He wanted to take Melinda in his arms and soothe her hurt away, but he checked himself.

"I *don't* as yet have proof positive against Lady Darlington," he said somberly, "but the wine seller, Van Leyt, and his 'sister' are definitely French agents working for Napoleon. Now, take into account the fact that Lady Darlington abandoned her London home to come here to Dorset at the time the Admiralty put out word that it was interested in the *Subaqua*. Add to that the way she's gone out of her way to bewitch Blyminster—"

"She enjoys Sir Rupert's company. She finds him interesting!"

"She lured him out here tonight," Hartford continued inexorably. "She knew from the conversation at dinner that he carried the key to his safe around his neck. She must have arranged the ambush when she went out of the dining room to get her cloak."

This was not the man she knew. Melinda looked hard at Lord Hartford and saw a cold-blooded stranger.

"She—she did nothing of the kind," Melinda stammered. "Why should my cousin not enjoy Sir Rupert's company on a fine summer's night?"

*As we did.* The thought touched his mind, and though he tried to ignore that fleeting stab of conscience, she was staring at him with such large eyes and she looked so pale that he was afraid she might faint. "Melinda," he exclaimed, "I'm sorry. I wouldn't have hurt you for the world."

She turned her head away, and he caught the glint of tears on her cheek. Those tears cut him to the heart. Without thinking what he was about, he reached out to take her into his arms.

So bemused was Melinda that at first she had not even the wit to protest. Her chilled body registered only the warmth of his embrace. And though her conscious mind hated Lord Hartford as a treacherous government agent who could lie and cheat and connive to achieve his ends, her heart wanted nothing more than to remain in his arms.

For an instant she wavered, and then reality reasserted itself with a vengeance. Melinda jerked backward so forcefully that she stumbled and nearly fell.

"You don't care who you hurt, do you?" she accused him. "You are—you are despicable! I will

141

prove that you are mistaken about my cousin. You will see."

In the throb of pain that he felt at her words, Hartford realized just how much he had come to care for Melinda Weatherby. In spite of all his training, he had been fool enough to become involved.

Well, he would have to become uninvolved—and quickly. He schooled his features to an unreadable mask and spoke in a cold, indifferent tone. "I'd be grateful to you if you could," he told her, "it would make my mission much easier."

Then he turned on his heel and walked away, leaving her alone in the moonlight.

# Chapter Eight

Melinda stood for a long while, trying to quiet the turmoil within her. Then, when she could think again, she walked slowly back to the house.

Zenobie was waiting impatiently. "You took so long that I sent Sonya Vraskova to bed," she charged. "Did you find the countess's bracelet?"

All during the walk back to the house, Melinda had wondered how she was going to broach the question. Now she blurted out, "Zenobie, did you know any of the men who attacked us tonight?"

Lady Darlington stared as if her cousin had just grown a second head. "*Know* those dreadful cossacks? Of course not!"

"Then you didn't arrange that ambush?" Melinda persisted.

Zenobie sat up in bed. "You think that *I* made a trap for Sir Rupert?"

Her face began to quiver, and bursting into a flood of tears, she began to pound the bed with her fists. Sonya Vraskova ran into the room crying, "Madame, Madame, what has upset you?"

Zenobie broke into a stream of Russian, and the maid decreed, "You must allow Madame to rest now, Miss Melinda. It is not good, the excitement in her condition of weakness."

Heavy-hearted, Melinda left the room. "What am I going to do?" she wondered.

Lord Hartford was wrong. He had to be. But if there was even a grain of truth in what he said, if Zenobie *had* become involved in some way with Napoleon's agents, there was no help for her. Melinda felt chilled as she pictured her cousin apprehended, imprisoned, transported, or even hanged—

"No," she whispered. "It isn't true. I will prove that Lord Hartford is wrong."

The question was—how? Melinda went to bed in great ferment and lay awake most of the night. She finally fell asleep toward dawn and was awakened by someone shaking her shoulder.

"My little one," Zenobie's voice fluted, "you are the sleepyhead this morning. Awake and sing with the birds."

Melinda opened her eyes and peered groggily at her cousin, who continued. "Do make a haste to ready yourself. You remember that we are to attend Mrs. Pennodie's party this morning."

Melinda had forgotten all about the party and looked with disbelief at her smiling cousin. In spite of the fact that she usually lay abed until noon, Zenobie was not only wide awake but fully dressed in a smart green and white walking-out dress with puffed sleeves and a décolletage low enough to emphasize her deep bosom.

But behind her cousin's powder and rouge, Melinda could see definite signs of strain. "This is foolish," she protested. "How can we go to a *party* after what happened last night?"

Instead of replying, Zenobie turned on Miss Poll, who had just entered the room with Melinda's morning chocolate. "Why aren't you attending your mistress?" she demanded. "She should have been dressed by now. Servants," she added haughtily, "are not what they used to be."

She sailed out, leaving Melinda to pacify the irate Miss Poll and to resolve that she must speak with her cousin immediately. But as soon as she was dressed, she was swept into the waiting barouche, where Zenobie kept up a steady stream of prattle about every subject under the sun. It was not until they came within sight of Mrs. Pennodie's estate that Melinda was finally able to say, "We *must* talk about last night, Zenobie."

"What is there to say?" Zenobie shrugged her shoulders. "It is a terrible thing, that attack, but no one was hurt. I shall send a servant to ask if poor Sir Rupert is in plumped currants, and I shall send him some of the pickled crab which he loves."

By now the barouche had stopped in front of the house. With a sinking feeling in her stomach, Melinda watched Zenobie alight from their phaeton and sail up the stairs to meet Mrs. Pennodie, who had emerged to greet her guests.

"We have all been wondering where you were," that lady exclaimed in her most affected voice. "How ravishing you look in that gown, ma'am—so modish! And the hat—tell me where you acquired it, for I *must* have one like it."

Threading her arm through Zenobie's and almost but not quite snubbing Melinda, Mrs. Pennodie mounted the steps. As Melinda followed, she caught snatches of their hostess's compliments and her complaints about her stubborn stepdaughter.

"I promised Pennodie when he quit this vale of tears that I would take care of his child, but the chit is the outside of enough," she sighed. "She is stubborn and headstrong and thinks more of grubbing in the garden than of making an advantageous match."

Melinda looked sympathetically at Carabel, who met them at the door. She did not look headstrong at all, and her eyes were red, as if she had been crying. "I am very well," she whispered as Melinda asked after her health. "Only—"

She cast a frightened look at her stepmother, who was escorting Zenobie into a large room beyond. Apparently the Conte del'Anche had returned from his travels, for Melinda glimpsed him talking with Squire Parcher. Sir Rupert, who had advanced to greet Zenobie, showed no ill effects from last night's episode. Melinda was grateful to see that there was no sign of Lord Hartford.

At her side, Carabel gave a sudden sob. Melinda took one look at the tears that were welling in the younger girl's eyes, and grasping Carabel's hand, pulled her into a side room and closed the door. "Now," she said, "tell me the whole. What has happened?"

"Sq-squire Parcher has offered for me," Carabel whispered.

"You are joking me," Melinda gasped. "He is at least twice your age! Surely your stepmother sent him packing."

Carabel shook her head. "M-Mama says it is my fault that I haven't had any other offers. She s-says that she refuses to be saddled with me all my life just because I am too stupid to attract a husband, and so I must marry the squire."

She burst into a storm of tears. Melinda put her arms around the girl and held her tightly. "You can't be forced to marry that loose fish—it's not to be thought of. Surely, there will be another suitor."

"I don't want to marry anyone," Carabel wailed,

146

"but *she* says I must. Either that, or she washes her hands of me, and I will be put out into the hedgerows to starve."

Melinda doubted that. A woman like Mrs. Pennodie, so concerned with her standing in society, would not risk censure by treating her stepchild so basely. But she could—and doubtless would—make Carabel's life a hell.

And there was no hope that the girl could prevail against her stepmother. An unmarried female under the legal age and penniless had no rights and no power in the world.

Just then the door of the little room opened and Mrs. Pennodie looked in. "So there you are, Carabel," she exclaimed in her high, affected tones, "and Miss Weatherby, too. Our guests are going out to admire the New Garden, now, Carabel. Even you should know your duties."

Wiping her eyes, Carabel hurried out of the room, and Mrs. Pennodie looked after her with an exasperated expression. "I must apologize for my tiresome stepdaughter," she began.

"I don't find her tiresome in the least," Melinda replied shortly.

"Ah, well, but you are used to all sorts of people, aren't you? People in your circumstances can't be choosy about the company they keep."

Mrs. Pennodie let that rude little barb quiver for a moment. "Perhaps Carabel has told you that she has had an offer of marriage?" Melinda could not bring herself to reply. "Squire Parcher is a well-landed man," Mrs. Pennodie went on smugly. "He and Carabel will suit very well."

Nose in the air, she swept out of the room. After waiting several moments to compose herself, Melinda followed and, traversing the hall, exited a side door to join the guests, who were already admiring the Briddles' skill.

The Quaker family had lived up to its reputation. Melinda watched Mrs. Pennodie puff herself out with pride as her guests exclaimed over the beautifully crafted "castle" and admired the exquisite little flower gardens. She looked ready to burst with satisfaction as the Conte del'Anche exclaimed that he had never seen such fine fruit trees, not even in all the finest Italian gardens.

"Yes, they do fine work, don't they? But the Briddles tell me that they cannot accept a single commission more," Mrs. Pennodie boasted to one of her guests, who had begged to know how she, too, could hire the creators of so much beauty. "They are finishing some other work they have in Dorset and then they are moving on. A commission, I believe, by the Duke of Chisnaught. You see, my dear ma'am, they do not work for just *anybody*."

She paused to savor the moment and then besought her guests to refresh themselves in the tents that servants had erected nearby. Tables and chairs had been arranged inside these tents, and Melinda noted that Zenobie had already taken a seat. Sir Rupert had naturally gravitated to her side and the Conte del'Anche was talking to them both.

"Do you wish to sit down at piquet?"

Melinda turned to see Dr. Gildfish smiling at her shoulder. "I'm glad you are here," he said. "I have been looking forward to seeing you again, Miss Weatherby."

With an effort, she shook off her depression to return his greeting, and then glanced from Zenobie's table to another, where Mrs. Pennodie was dealing out cards. "I thought we had come to view the New

148

Garden," she said. "I didn't know it was to be a gaming party."

"Truly? But I forget that you're new to Dorset. The rest of us know that Mrs. Pennodie hosts the best gambling parties in the area."

Dr. Gildfish began to point to the various tables. "Our hostess is playing jeu d'enfer. Lady Darlington has chosen piquet. Are you familiar with any of this?" She shook her head. "Just as well that a love for games of chance isn't in your blood."

Was it in Zenobie's blood? Uneasily, Melinda watched as her cousin place a wager on the table, meanwhile laughing and joking with an almost feverish gaiety.

"Lady Darlington told me what happened last night after I left," the doctor was saying. "Luckily, she seems to have taken no harm. You're the one who looks pale, Miss Weatherby."

Zenobie was making yet another wager. "What are the usual stakes?" Melinda asked, then widened her eyes at the reply. "*So* much?"

"I've seen Lady Darlington lose more than three times that amount in the course of a morning."

"Folly!"

The doctor shrugged. "Gaming is a disease of sorts, as I said. Myself, I play only one or two games of piquet before my interest wanes."

The players with their intent and avaricious faces were spoiling the Briddles' beautiful garden. Sickened, Melinda excused herself and walked away down the garden path until she had left the gamesters behind. But though they were out of sight, she could not so easily escape her thoughts.

*Was* Zenobie an inveterate gambler? It was a troubling thought, for Melinda recalled one of her posts where the oldest son of the family had been a gamester. He had lost so much money that he had stolen and pawned his mother's jewels to try to pay his debts.

*Espionage is a profitable business . . .*

As Lord Hartford's cynical words echoed in Melinda's mind, she heard a passionate young voice cry, "I can't bear it any longer."

Carabel's voice was coming from the other side of a tall boxwood hedge. Standing on tiptoe, Melinda saw her talking to Josiah Briddle and his two children. "I wish I lived with you," Carabel was saying. "Then I wouldn't have to marry the squire. It makes my skin crawl to think of it."

Hannah took Carabel's hands in hers. "It makes *my* skin crawl, too, think on," she exclaimed. "Father, let's take Carabel wi' us. We can't leave her to be mistreated—we're her friends."

"That's so, Father," Lucas agreed. "We must help her get away from that squire."

Sadly, Josiah shook his head. "It grieves me, Carabel Pennodie, but we can do nowt for thee. Thee are thy stepmother's ward and must do as she says. That's the law."

Not wishing to eavesdrop, Melinda hastened to walk away. As she went, she heard Carabel mourn, "You have been so good to me. Kinder than anybody in my life since Papa died. And now you are going away and I—I will be left here with Mama and the squire."

And she could do nothing. Try as she would, Melinda could think of nothing she could do that would help Carabel. "I can barely help myself," Melinda sighed.

Then she broke off, suddenly aware that an oddly pungent smell was drifting toward her. She looked up and saw the Conte del'Anche smoking a cigar some distance away. "Ah, *peccato*," he exclaimed. "Do I intrude, Signorina Weatherby?"

He tossed his cigar into the bushes and strolled forward to bend over Melinda's hand. She gave it woodenly, and her replies to his exaggerated compliments were mechanical, for the scent of that cigar was unmistakable.

It had been the *conte* whom Zenobie had met by the lake. The *conte* who was now saying, "Alas that I behold so fair a lady only to say, *Arrivederla*. I am departing Dorset yet again on business. But I will not forget the kindness of Lady Darlington. To see 'er—and you, *bella signorina,* I will come from the ends of the earth."

During this flowery speech, Melinda painstakingly noted the *conte*'s body language. Her many dealings with employers had taught her to listen not only to what was said but how it was said, and the *conte,* while professing devotion and humility, exuded an almost predatory triumph.

Melinda was frightened. What exactly, she wondered, had the *conte* wanted from Zenobie that night by the lake?

Mrs. Pennodie's party lagged late into the afternoon, at which time the guests were offered a significant luncheon. Melinda noted that though Sir Rupert ate copiously, Zenobie herself barely touched her food and finally, to Melinda's great relief, professed herself ready to leave.

By now Melinda had a splitting headache that pounded so viciously, she put off the talk she meant to have with her cousin. Fortunately, the usually talkative Zenobie was silent on the way back to Darlington House, and Melinda could close her eyes in silence. This silence did not last long, for when Melinda returned home, Miss Poll pounced upon her.

"You look like a ghost," she accused. "The headache again, ain't it, and the Rooshan's to blame."

As sick as she felt, Melinda managed a rueful smile. "Why do you always blame her for my ills?"

"Because she's usually at the root of everything." Miss Poll paused to look keenly at her former charge. "But it's not just the Rooshan that's worrying you, Miss Mel, is it?"

Wretchedly, Melinda held her peace. Miss Poll narrowed her eyes and pursed her lips. "It's that there duke's son," she burst out. "Didn't I warn you about that one? 'Put not your trust in princes,' the good book says."

She went away to bring a cold compress for the headache, but Melinda knew that a compress would not help. She forced herself to get up and walk across the hall to rap on Zenobie's door. Here she was met by Sonya Vraskova, who declared in no friendly voice that Madame was resting. In no mood for explanations, Melinda stepped past the maid into the room.

"Is that you, Melushka?" Zenobie murmured from her bed. "I am very tired just now, my little one."

"Are you always so exhausted when you go to gamble?" Melinda asked. "But perhaps losing is less tiring than winning."

Zenobie's eyes popped open. She closed them again immediately. "What are you talking about?" she sighed.

"Dr. Gildfish suggests that the love of gaming is in your blood." When her cousin still did not answer, Melinda asked bluntly, "How much did you win today?"

Zenobie made a motion with her hand, dismissing her maid. Then she bluntly answered, "Only five hundred pounds."

Melinda's knees felt weak. She sank into a chair as her cousin continued. "I don't have gaming in my blood, no matter what that doctor says. I gamble in order to get the rollings of soft to pay for my expenses. You see, I don't have any money."

"No *money*? But—but the servants, the amounts you spend on your parties, the food, the wine—"

"You have to spend to catch money." Zenobie regarded Melinda with weary, worldly eyes. "You see, Melushka, Darlington's London house is entailed. His estate here is heavily mortgaged and can't be sold. His jewels, they are made of the paste." She heaved a deep sigh. "Darlington didn't tell me when we were married that he was already deep in the dunning territory. When he died, there was nothing left."

"B-but you have so many servants, Zenobie. How—"

"Russtin has been in Darlington's service here all his life. He begged me with tears in his eyes to let him stay on for his board, for the poor man has no place to go. The cook is in the same situation, and Sonya Vraskova is devoted to me. The others are hirelings from a London agency."

"Oh," Melinda whispered. "But if you had cut costs from the beginning, perhaps you could have—"

Zenobie sat bolt upright and pounded the bedclothes with her fists. "I cannot exist in this way. I won't do the scrimp-and-save and be the poor relation. I am not brave like you to go seek my bread. So, outside the bridge, I make a plan. I decide to marry a wealthy man."

"Sir Rupert Blyminster," murmured Melinda.

Zenobie regarded her cousin earnestly. "It is not only for the money, Melushka. I have come to care deeply for good, kind Sir Rupert. He is the only man I have felt affection for since your dear cousin was torn by cruel fate from these arms."

"What of Monsieur Vilforme?" Melinda prodded.

"Do not speak me of that monster!"

Two red patches burned in Zenobie's cheeks. "He was truly a squeezed crab of a man. A Captain Hackums who swore and beat me. He gave me just enough money to run his household and would never allow me to send you anything."

She paused for a moment. "Once, I defied him. I contrived to send Sonya Vraskova to pawn one of my jewels. You remember the little emerald heart that Arthur gave me when we were married, Melushka? I was desperate to send you the money from pawning it, but Vilforme stopped the letter I was sending to you and stole the money. He threatened to beat me if I did such a thing again."

As she listened, Melinda felt her eyes fill with tears, and a small, lingering tightness in her heart loosened and melted away. Zenobie was not heartless and uncaring, as Miss Poll made her out to be. But that had nothing to do with the matter at hand.

"So you really want to marry Sir Rupert?" Melinda asked. "I had thought that perhaps the Conte del'Anche—"

"No!" Zenobie shouted. "He is a leech, a vampire that sucks blood from me."

All these dramatics were causing Melinda's head to ache even more. "Zenobie," she pleaded, "*what* is your connection with the *conte*? I know you met him at the lake some nights ago."

All color drained from the older woman's face. "He is blackmailing me," she moaned.

Melinda could only stare. Zenobie went on. "While I was married to Vilforme, I—I was introduced to the *conte*. He was so charming, so amusing, so sympathetic that I trusted him. I must have said something to arouse his suspicions, for he began to investigate."

"Investigate *what*, for heaven's sake?"

Zenobie gave a sigh that sounded like a sob. "I am not really the daughter of a nobleman," she whispered. "My grandfather was not the great Count Oblonski, but Sergei Gregorivich, a groundskeeper for the count. The count was kind to me and had me educated with his children. Later, I—I pretended that the count was my grandfather so I could marry the Baron Osmanoff."

"And del'Anche learned the truth," Melinda mused.

Zenobie nodded. "I would have been ruined in society. Vilforme would have divorced me without a sou. I would have starved—or worse, so I paid the count for keeping his silence."

Melinda's heart had begun to lift. "Then you aren't—you are not connected with the ring of spies?" she cried.

"With—Melushka, what are you talking about?" Zenobie looked completely bewildered. "I have used my winnings today to pay the *conte,* but I fear he will return again, wanting more. No, Sir Rupert is my only hope. I believe he has the tender feeling for me, but, alas, he has not yet come up to scratching and proposed marriage."

She truly looked woebegone. Melinda asked gently, "Wouldn't it be better to make a clean breast of things? If Sir Rupert loves you, it should not make a difference who your grandfather was."

Zenobie closed her eyes wearily. "That shows you know nothing of the world," she declared. "If he learns the truth, Sir Rupert will disappear—pouf!—and I will read someday that he is marrying a horse-faced Honorable-Miss-Somebody. Ah, if I had only been nobly born."

Melinda thought dismally that gentle birth was no guarantee of happiness. Though her own blood was good, it availed her nothing, because a lack of money kept her as much trapped as Zenobie.

She rose as an indignant Sonya Vraskova bustled in to inform Melinda that Madame *must* rest, and she left her cousin's room with conflicting emotions. Lord Hartford had been wrong. True, Zenobie was deeply in trouble and needed money, but she was not involved in treason.

"But even if she is innocent, Lord Hartford won't believe her," Melinda sighed. "And since Sir Rupert is Lord Hartford's friend, he will never offer for her while matters stand as they do. She is truly 'outside the bridge' as she puts it."

Once again she recalled the young gambler who had stolen his mother's jewels. His fiancée had broken their engagement, and his friends had deserted him. Yet he had continued to gamble until he was forced to flee to the continent.

Melinda paused in mid-thought. "He fled to the *continent*," she murmured. "But of course. That's the answer to this mare's nest."

If Zenobie could get away from both del'Anche and Lord Hartford, she would be safe. The question was, *how* was she to do this? The more Melinda turned the question over in her mind, the more complex it became.

She was still trying to think her way past this Gordian knot, when she heard a knock on the outer door and Russtin's voice greeting the doctor. "Dr. Gildfish!" Melinda exclaimed. "My wits are slow today. Why didn't I think of him before?"

She waited impatiently until Dr. Gildfish had finished examining his patient. Then, meeting him in the hall, she requested a moment of his time and led him to the empty Green Room.

He gave her a concerned look. "You're looking ill," he said. "Did you, too, eat the pickled crab?"

Baffled, she shook her head. "Several people fell ill today after eating the pickled crab at Mrs. Pennodie's party," he explained. "I'm on my way to Blyminster Cove now—Sir Rupert is having a bad time of it—and I thought I'd better stop and see if you and Lady Darlington hadn't come to harm. Luckily, it seems she didn't eat any crab."

Melinda reassured him that she, too, had not touched the dish. "But there is something else that I need to ask you," she said. "Something in strictest confidence."

She proceeded to tell him about Zenobie's debts, carefully omitting all mention of Lord Hartford or the *conte*. As he listened, the doctor's face grew increasingly grave. "You aren't joking?" he asked, adding quickly, "No, forgive me—of course you aren't. If I understand you, you want me to write a letter in which I state that Lady Darlington must leave Dorset because of her deteriorating health."

Melinda nodded. "I know it is asking a great deal, but I have no one else to turn to. If Zenobie's creditors catch up to her, she will be ruined. She may even be sent to debtors' prison. I don't even know if I can get her away from Dorset, but I need to try."

Gildfish seemed to hesitate for a moment. Then he said, "It could be done. I am her attending physician, and if I signed an affidavit saying that Lady Darlington's condition is desperate and that she must go to London to see a specialist I recommend, no one would question it."

Once in London, it would not be too hard to drop out of sight. Zenobie could take a ship to Spain or Italy—but Melinda's thoughts broke off as she heard the doctor ask, "Am I right in thinking that debt isn't the only reason Lady Darlington wants to leave Dorset? Forgive me, but is Lord Hartford involved somehow?"

Melinda gave an involuntary start. "What makes you say that?"

"An educated guess. Shortly after he arrived here, Lord Hartford's manservant began to ask questions about Lady Darlington." The doctor gave Melinda an apologetic smile. "I know because my servant reported those questions to me. I thought it was only idle curiosity, but now—"

He broke off. "Now?" Melinda prompted.

"Now the pieces fit together, and I am afraid for you. Lord Hartford is intelligent and can be ruthless."

He paused and regarded her with unhappy eyes. "I think I mentioned Lieutenant Latten, the young officer who was in my care before he died near Astorga? He also was a member of the Circle, and Calworth sent him into enemy-held territory. He was captured. Since he had knowledge valuable to our enemies, Lord Hartford was sent after him."

So far, the story was familiar. With a sense of foreboding, Melinda listened as the doctor went on. "Lord Hartford's orders were, apparently, to bring

Lieutenant Latten back alive or kill him to prevent him from giving information under duress."

"No!" The cry was torn out of her. "He would not have agreed to such a thing."

"He was under orders, and it was a time of war," Gildfish reminded her. "I don't know what happened, but I *do* know that Lord Hartford came back to our lines alone. Lieutenant Latten was found much later and brought back, nearly dead, by some of our soldiers. He had been shot in the back."

"And did he tell you that Lord Hartford had done this?" Mutely, the doctor nodded. "I don't believe it," Melinda whispered. "Lieutenant Latten must have been delirious."

The doctor spread his hands in an eloquent gesture. "Terrible things happen in wartime," he said gently. "No doubt Lord Hartford believed he was acting for the good of our country."

He hesitated and then spoke again. "I tell you these things only because while Hartford's manservant was asking questions about your cousin, he was also making inquiries about you."

Melinda started. "About *me*?"

"At first I thought Lord Hartford was merely interested in a lovely young lady, but later I began to have doubts." The doctor's eyes became even more troubled as he added, "If he suspects your cousin of something, it's possible that he also suspects you."

Melinda felt the by now familiar tightening in her chest. The kisses in the moonlight, the long talks and confidences, the laughter—they had all been lies.

The doctor was watching her sympathetically. "What Lord Hartford did to Lieutenant Latten goes against everything I believe in. I'll write that letter and see if we can get Lady Darlington out of harm's way."

But Melinda was no longer thinking of Zenobie. Her stunned mind could grasp only one thought. She who had sworn to be guided by her head and not by her emotions had committed the ultimate idiocy. She had fallen in love with a man who was a cold-blooded killer.

# Chapter Nine

"Those little buggers have done for me," Sir Rupert groaned. "Goin' to cook up m'toes, no mistake about it."

For the past night and day Hartford had listened to the same complaint. "Gildfish says you'll be on your feet in a day at most," he said in what he hoped was a rallying tone.

"Man's a quack. He don't suffer from a pain in the belly," moaned Sir Rupert in an abyss of self-pity. "I'm dished up and m'work ain't finished, neither."

Hartford had had enough. He got up from his chair and announced his intention of taking a walk. "Oh, go ahead," the inventor replied peevishly. "Desert a man when he's down." He watched Hartford walk across to the door and then added, "Least you could do is stop by Darlington House—see if Lady D.'s all right."

"I'm not riding that way."

Sir Rupert opened his eyes at this. "No need to look so grim about it. All I wondered was whether Lady Darlington's feelin' the thing. Don't remember if she ate the crab or not. Never should have trusted crabs," he added petulantly. "Mean to say, nasty little brutes—all those legs and claws."

Hartford bade his host get some rest and walked

down the hall to his rook, where he reread the latest dispatches from London. Sir Orin wrote that Wellington was engaged in forming an invincible Anglo-Dutch army in Belgium and added that Napoleon was girding his loins in preparation for a massive assault against the allies. If he intended to steal the *Subaqua*'s secret plans, he would do so soon.

Yes, it would be soon. For an instant Hartford contemplated the moment when his net would close around the guilty, and then he thought of Melinda. Melinda with her gray eyes full of pain that *he* had inflicted.

There was an apologetic cough at the door, and he turned to see Sir Rupert's butler, Owens. "Lady Darlington and Miss Weatherby have called, my lord," Owens announced. "I have said that Sir Rupert is indisposed, but her ladyship insisted that I inform him of her arrival."

Hammer at a man when he was down—that would be the Russian woman's style of attack. "Where are they, Owens?" Hartford asked, and being told, went down to greet them.

At the doorway of Sir Rupert's drawing room, he paused for a moment. Seated on a sofa, Lady Darlington presented a portrait in elegance. Her Lavinia chip bonnet tied with sarcenet ribbons was in the stare of fashion, as was her azure walking-out dress. Pearls hung in her ears and looped across her bosom. A basket overflowing with flowers and fruit stood on the floor beside her.

She had most surely come a-courting—but Hartford's cynicism died when he saw Melinda, who stood by the window dressed in the pale blue muslin round dress he had seen her wear many times. She was watching a heavy fog drift over the lake, and much of her face was hidden by a bonnet of indeterminate age, but he could see the tension in her rigid posture and the way she clasped her hands tightly at her waist.

Hartford realized his own hands were clenched. Composing himself, he was about to step into the drawing room, when Melinda spoke.

"We shouldn't have come," she said in a low, urgent voice. "Sir Rupert is too sick to see us. We must make our apologies and leave—"

"Ah, bah." With a dramatic gesture, Zenobie dismissed such drivel. "How would it have been looking if neighbors did not come once to visit the poor man on his bed of pains? You English are too proper. You have no soul."

"Ladies, your most obedient."

Melinda clasped her hands even more tightly together as Lord Hartford walked into the room. She had schooled herself against the time when she would have to meet him face-to-face, and all the way to Blyminster Cove she had rehearsed this scene. Dr. Gildfish had warned her what kind of a man the duke's son really was, and forewarned was forearmed.

But now, here he was, bending over Zenobie's hand, and treacherous memories quivered deep in her heart. She struggled to rid herself of them as he turned to her, saying, "A pleasure to see you again, ma'am. You look to be in good point today."

Melinda could not believe that after their last encounter Lord Hartford could smile so pleasantly and talk as if nothing were amiss. And of course she must reply in kind and greet him as if nothing had changed between them. She *would,* except— except that now he was approaching to bow over her hand, and at the thought of his touch,

Melinda's unreliable heart began to beat so wildly that she was afraid he would hear it.

Hastily, she locked her hands behind her back. Mobile eyebrows rose at this, but Lord Hartford's smile did not falter. "Excellent point, in fact," he murmured.

Melinda's heart thudded even harder until it felt as though it must shatter against her ribs, but she managed to reply, "Good afternoon, my lord."

Her voice was brittle, and her gray eyes were stormy with confusion and hostility. Under their gaze Hartford felt his own composure beginning to fray and rather hastily turned back to Lady Darlington.

"I'm relieved to see you didn't eat the pickled crab," he told her. "Blyminster was concerned you might have become ill, too."

Zenobie clasped her hands to her deep bosom. "Ah, so good—so kind. He thinks of me even when he is ill."

"Think of you anytime, ma'am. Mean to say!"

Sir Rupert stood framed in the drawing room doorway. He had dressed and wore a smoking jacket above which his face was the color of old cheese. Rejecting Hartford's help, he staggered over toward Zenobie.

"Honored you should come and call on me, m'lady—eh?" he mumbled. "Miss Weatherby, too. Too kind. Better than any medicine in the world."

Catching the inventor's hands, Zenobie drew him down to sit beside her. "Oh, I have been so worried," she fluted. "I was afraid for you, dear Sir Rupert."

"Nothin' the matter with me."

The inventor thumped his chest and at once commenced coughing. "Zenobie," Melinda warned, "we must not keep Sir Rupert up a moment longer. We will return when he is feeling more the thing."

"Feelin' strong as an ox," the inventor persisted. He rang the bellpull near his chair. "Bring us some sherry," he directed as Owens materialized. "Refreshments, eh? That's what we need."

He gazed adoringly into Zenobie's eyes, and Melinda turned away to look out the window again. "The fog will probably lift soon," Lord Hartford said at her elbow. She made no comment. "Well, what shall we talk about, ma'am? The high price of sugar and flour? The deplorable state of the roads?"

In a low voice that the others could not hear, Melinda said, "I have nothing to say to you, my lord."

"Alas, a speechless lady." His voice sounded as carefree as ever, and his dark eyes expressed such indifference that Melinda hated him.

"I gather you didn't eat any of that benighted crab," he went on. "Unfortunately, Blyminster enjoys the dish. He came home from the Pennodie party looking green and summoned the doctor immediately." He paused to add reflectively, "Gildfish said that half the county was afflicted. It must have been a large party."

"I am surprised you were not there spying on the guests," she could not resist saying, but he remained unruffled.

"Gaming parties don't interest me. Unlike your cousin, I bet only on a sure thing."

With an enormous effort, Melinda checked the angry words that rose to her lips. "It's common knowledge that she won heavily at the garden party," Hartford went on. "No doubt she bought the *conte*'s silence with her winnings."

Melinda stared. "How—how did you know that?"

He shrugged. "The night she collapsed, Gildfish said that your cousin was delirious and murmuring something about needing gold for Also. *Anche* means 'also' in Italian, and it fit with what I already knew about the man. Five hundred pounds would scarcely satisfy him, so Lady Darlington must be desperate for money."

Melinda turned her head away and stared blindly at Kendle Lake. Nothing in Hartford's training could quell the ache of pity he felt for her, but if the truth hurt, it might also heal. Perhaps if she understood what her cousin by marriage was like, Melinda's fierce loyalty would give way to common sense.

"I'm sorry," he said gently.

Another lie. Angrily, Melinda swung back to face him. "Don't try to turn me against Zenobie," she warned. "Even if she were guilty of—of what you say, she is better than you, my lord. You are beyond shame."

"So I've been told."

She could not guess that his careless shrug hid real hurt. It pushed her over the edge, and she forgot caution. "Perhaps," she flung at him, "Lieutenant Latten thought so, too."

His eyes narrowed, but before he could speak, Sir Rupert exclaimed, "Just a short walk down to m'workroom. Mean to say, Hartford, Lady Darlington wants to see m'*Subaqua*."

Conscious of the watchful man beside her, Melinda suggested again that it was high time they were on their way. Ignoring her, Zenobie clapped her hands and cried that she would like above all things to see the undersea machine. "I have imagined so often how it would be down inside the working room of Sir Rupert. Now I shall see this with my own eyes."

"So you shall!" Sir Rupert rose and offered her his arm. "Comin', you two?"

Wordlessly, Melinda followed her cousin and the inventor out of the room. She could hear Hartford just behind her as they descended to the ground level and then down a flight of stone stairs. Finally they reached a stout wooden door at the end of a stone corridor.

"Ah, it is cold and damp here." Zenobie shivered.

"That's because we're at lake level," the inventor explained. He turned a key in the lock and the heavy door swung open. "Watch your step, ma'am—that window don't let much light in. Wait till I light m'lamps."

As soon as the lamps were lit, Zenobie began to walk around the cluttered workshop, admiring and praising the *Subaqua*. "It is such a feat of science," she gushed. "So much sense and such skill. May I climb inside and see this air inducer you have so brilliantly created?"

Beaming and blushing, his queasy stomach evidently forgotten, the inventor showed Zenobie how to climb the rope ladder. Helpless to prevent her cousin, Melinda watched Zenobie descend into the *Subaqua*. She did not dare look at Lord Hartford.

Everything Zenobie did or said today was damning her further in Lord Hartford's eyes. Melinda wished now that she had explained the situation to her cousin and told her of Dr. Gildfish's offer of help. She had debated long with herself before deciding to keep the matter secret for the time being. Excitable Zenobie, Melinda had feared, could easily let some hint fall in the hearing of those who would report their plans to Lord Hartford.

She must get her cousin away from Blyminster Cove—but when Zenobie emerged from the *Subaqua*, she once again ignored Melinda's suggestions and began to ply the inventor with questions about the air inducer.

"Bah, I have the brains of a cabbage," she sighed. "Your excellent words do not sink into my head."

"I'll show you what I mean." Sir Rupert went to his safe, unlocked it with the key he produced from around his neck, and drew out a sheaf of papers. "Here's the blueprints of the air inducer. Eh? Here's the valve that gave me so much trouble."

He paused and looked up at Hartford with a slightly guilty expression. "Mean to say," he said, "it's only Lady Darlington. No need to mind m'tongue in front of *her*."

"Of course not," Hartford agreed. "Lady Darlington is beyond reproach."

Melinda felt a stir of real panic as she watched her cousin study the blueprints. Though she could not believe that Zenobie was guilty of anything remotely connected to espionage, her absorption in the *Subaqua* could easily be misinterpreted. And she, Melinda, had been a fool to mention Lieutenant Latten, since to antagonize Lord Hartford could easily doom any chance of getting Zenobie away.

She was racking her brain to think of something that might break the tension between them, when there were shouts of "Fire!" on the stairs and Owens burst in to exclaim, "Sir Rupert, sir, the stable's afire!"

Zenobie put a hand to her heart and fell half fainting back into a chair. Sir Rupert exclaimed, "Fire in the stables—demmit, man, have they got the horses out?"

Lord Hartford was already racing up the stairs.

Sir Rupert followed. Melinda had picked up her skirts to do likewise, when Zenobie held her back.

"Melushka, I feel faint," she moaned. "Don't leave me."

"There was once a fire in a house where I was in service," Melinda said urgently. "It was terrible. I must go and help if I can, Zenobie. Let me take you upstairs—"

But Zenobie said that she felt too faint to move and would stay where she was. Melinda ran up the stairs. The side door was standing wide open, and she exited it into a scene of confusion. Smoke was billowing out from the stables in the back of the house, and servants were running here and there with pails, shovels, and picks. Frightened grooms were leading stamping, snorting horses toward the fog-shrouded paddock.

She saw Sir Rupert talking to a man who she surmised was the head groom and, hoping to help in some way, went toward them. As she did so, she heard a scuffling noise inside the still-smoking stables.

Thinking that perhaps one of the horses had been left behind in the confusion, Melinda lifted her skirts and hurried into the stable. It was dark there, and the acrid smoke made her cough violently and stung her eyes so that she could not see. As she tried to look about her, she felt someone grasp her arm. "What are you doing here?" Lord Hartford demanded.

"The horses—" but coughing made it impossible for her to say more.

He propelled her out of a side door nearby and then repeated sternly, "What in the devil's name were you about, going in there? The fire could blaze up again. It's madness to risk yourself like that."

Melinda drew a deep breath of pure air and managed to gasp out, "I heard something inside the stable and thought a horse had been left behind."

"They're all safe," Lord Hartford said. He had thrown off his jacket, and his white shirtfront was soiled with smoke and soot. "The fire started in a corner of the stables, but it's out now."

"I am so glad. I—I saw a stable fire once," Melinda explained in a subdued voice. "The poor horses were terrified. I can still hear them whinnying and drumming their hooves in panic."

"So you came to help." Her eyes were silver with tears from the smoke, and Hartford closed his mind to an almost irresistible need to kiss those tears away. "Well, no harm's been done. An undergroom grew careless and smoked a pipe near some straw. At least that's what Blyminster thinks."

"But *you* don't?"

"The grooms here are too well trained to endanger the horses like that." But he was not thinking of the fire. A spar of silver gray ash was caught in her hair, and he could not help reaching out to brush it away. "Melinda," Hartford heard himself say.

The sound of her name on his lips filled her with an ache of longing too deep to be ignored. Melinda felt that longing quiver in her heart as he went on. "You shouldn't have put yourself in danger. If something had happened to you—"

He broke off, and there was a moment's deep silence. Then Lord Hartford spoke in quite a different tone. "Tell me, Miss Weatherby," he said, "how did you know about Latten?"

The change in his voice brought her back to full watchfulness. It reminded her that she must go carefully with this man. Aloud she said, "Dr.

Gildfish mentioned that he had attended an officer by that name while he was in Spain. He said that you and Lieutenant Latten knew each other."

Hartford turned his head away from the smoking stables, not seeing the house or the fog-bound lake beyond, but, rather, watching himself and his friend, and how they had almost reached freedom unscathed that day almost six years before.

They had traversed treacherous terrain without incident and then their luck had run out and they had stumbled upon a hidden pocket of French soldiers. Hartford had been wounded in the shoulder, but Latten had taken a ball in the back. "You can't hope to make it back to our lines with me to slow you down," the boy had pleaded. "Leave me a pistol, Anthony, and go. Tell the pater I died well. And—and God bless you for trying to save me."

Melinda saw Lord Hartford's eyes fill with pain, and her heart ached for him. For a moment she grieved for the man before her and was desperately sorry for what she had said. Then she reminded herself that this man was threatening Zenobie.

"Leave us alone," she whispered.

That was what Latten had cried. "Leave me alone, Anthony—leave me be!" But Hartford had carried his friend on his back through the long night until they reached their lines. Toward the end he had gone on sheer nerve—crawling more than walking. He had been at the end of his strength when they finally reached English lines.

"I'm sorry for what happened," Hartford said aloud, not to Melinda but to the shade of the man he had tried so hard to save. "But what else could I do?"

His voice was bleak, heaving with a regret that Melinda interpreted as guilt. She felt chilled. Until now she had not really believed Dr. Gildfish. She had not *wanted* to believe that Lord Hartford had killed his friend to silence him.

"Hello—there you are, then."

Sir Rupert, his smoking jacket blackened with soot and his hair standing wildly on end, had come around the corner of the stable. "The horses are all right, thank heavens. I'd like to get m'hands on the demmed blighter that set this fire, though." He paused. "Better go tell Lady Darlington there's no cause for concern—and look, here's the sawbones' trap. Didn't hear him drivin' up in all the excitement."

Melinda began to walk toward the house. She did not want to look at Lord Hartford. She knew he was without principle or conscience and that she should hate all he stood for—but her heart ached so much that there was no room left for hate.

They found Dr. Gildfish examining Zenobie, who had made her way up to the drawing room. The excitement of the day had been too much for her, he said, and he sternly ordered her back to her bed.

Then he drew Melinda aside. "This fire is fortuitous," he said in a low tone. "It will give us an excuse for Lady Darlington's 'relapse.' I will write in my letter that she must leave Dorset *at once,* so be prepared."

Dr. Gildfish's letter *must* help her get Zenobie to safety. Once again Melinda debated the wisdom of telling her cousin everything, and once again she held back. Best to wait until she had the doctor's letter firmly in hand, she told herself. Time enough then to act.

Tensely she waited for the doctor to bring or send the letter, but nightfall came without a word. Perhaps, Melinda told herself, Dr. Gildfish was being cautious. Too many visits to Darlington House might arouse Lord Hartford's suspicions.

Next morning Zenobie slept late and arose after noon. In spite of her rest, she looked wan and dispirited. "*He* did not come up to scratching again," she sighed. "I thought for sure that yesterday after the fire—but he is too shy. I can only hope that del'Anche will not return and reveal to Sir Rupert the truth about my degrading birth."

Melinda waited all that day for Dr. Gildfish to visit his patient. When he did not, she resolved to take matters into her own hands and go to his house. In order to draw as little attention to herself as possible, she waited until Zenobie had retired to her room to lie down after dinner. Then she went out to the stables, had a horse saddled, and rode out alone toward Kendle-on-Lake.

It was only a little past seven, but a heavy fog had rolled in from the lake, and it was difficult to see. Melinda was glad of the fog, for no one saw her as she rode into the town of Kendle-on-Lake, but it also obscured the way. Though she knew the direction to the doctor's house, it was some time before she reached her destination. Here the manservant who answered her knock informed her that Dr. Gildfish had been called away on an emergency and might be gone for some time.

Melinda said that she would wait and was shown into the doctor's little waiting room next to his surgery. But though she waited for a full half hour, no sound of horses' hooves or carriage wheels disturbed the silence.

Had she done the right thing in coming? Should she wait longer or return to Darlington House? Too nervous to sit for long, Melinda paced about the little room. "I should have told Polly where I was going," she mused. "She will be worried if she finds me gone. Perhaps I should—"

She broke off as she heard voices from another part of the house. Thinking that the doctor had returned, Melinda hastened out of the waiting room. As she did so, she heard a deeply accented male voice say, "It does not matter that he is not here. Just tell your master that the rendezvous point has been changed. There'll be money and horses waiting for him tonight, but at a new location."

It was not the doctor—Melinda's heart sank. She was about to return to the waiting room, when Dr. Gildfish's servant said, "Keep your voice down— there's a woman waiting for the doctor. You're a proper lobcock, showing your face in Dorset, Van Leyt. 'Artford's got the town watch mobilized. They're looking for you."

Van Leyt was the Belgian wine merchant who Lord Hartford had said was an agent for Napoleon. Melinda stopped and listened tensely as the accented voice replied, "Damn Hartford. It's his fault that the meeting place had to be changed. See— here it is on the map."

There was the noise of paper crackling. Then the doctor's servant said, "All right, I 'ave it. Now get out of it, and be careful. 'Is nibs isn't dead—*yet*."

Melinda's involuntary gasp was muffled by the Belgian asking, "It happens tonight, *ja*?" His tone turned ugly as he added, "I wish I could see his lordship's face when he knows he's been trapped."

With mounting horror Melinda listened as the two men conversed. They spoke in low tones, but she had heard enough to realize the truth. *Dr. Gildfish* was the traitor that Lord Hartford was seeking.

It made horrible sense. A physician could come and go freely, ask questions without arousing suspicion. Men and women spoke freely to their doctor, told him secrets they would not share with anyone else, as the dying Lieutenant Latten had done.

Now the doctor was not only plotting to meet Napoleon's agents, but had also arranged a trap for Lord Hartford. She must warn him at once. Gathering her skirts around her so as not to make a sound, Melinda backed toward the front door and then hurried to her horse. She would ride immediately to Blyminster Cove. She would warn Lord Hartford in time—

"Miss Weatherby! Hoy, Miss Weatherby!"

Melinda's heart stopped in mid-beat. Looking back over her shoulder, she saw that a hackney had rattled out of the fog. Out of this conveyance leaned a familiar corpulent personage.

"Mr. Proctor!" she gasped.

The headmaster of the Proctor Academy for Young Ladies snapped something to the driver of the hackney. He then stepped down onto the road and regarded Melinda with exasperation tinged with triumph.

"Yes, Miss Weatherby," he intoned. "I have come myself. You have forced this long trip upon me, ma'am."

"B-but," Melinda stammered, "why, sir? I sent you a letter—"

"Pish!" With a flick of his hand, Mr. Proctor showed how little he regarded letters. "I could see between the lines, ma'am, and discern your desire to return to the academy."

Already unnerved by her discovery of the doctor's perfidy, Melinda could only stammer, "That is not so. My cousin—"

"I will speak to the lady myself," interrupted Mr. Proctor. "I will explain how necessary you are to the little girls. They miss you so much, ma'am. And the academy is shorthanded due to severe illnesses. I am afraid that you are sorely needed."

Without bothering to argue further, Melinda untied her horse and mounted it. Mr. Proctor watched her in dumbfounded amazement. "Miss Weatherby," he quoth, "hold a moment. You have not given me your answer."

"I am not going to Sussex with you. Pray get out of my way," Melinda declared sharply. "And take your hand from my bridle this instant, sir."

But instead of obliging, Mr. Proctor squared his shoulders and sucked in his prosperous belly. "Miss Weatherby," he said, "I see how matters stand."

"Thank heavens!"

"You are embarrassed about the ah, *contretemps* before you left the academy. You were outspoken then, ma'am. You were rude."

Mr. Proctor's small eyes hardened at the memory of the little girls who had giggled and laughed at their headmaster. They had called him a bagpudding—and in may ways that debacle had been Miss Weatherby's doing.

"But that is all forgiven," Mr. Proctor declared magnanimously. "I am not a man to nurse a grudge. Come, ma'am, do not stand in amazement. You are forgiven and your offenses are forgotten. But we must leave at once."

Melinda seized on the last words. "Yes," she exclaimed, "I beg you will leave at once, Mr. Proctor. I have no interest in returning to your school, I do not wish to do so, and I will not. I can't say plainer than that. Now, pray stand aside."

She was conscious, as she spoke, of a slowly

growing rumbling sound. It emerged from Mr. Proctor.

"Ungrateful woman!" he stammered. "To think I have come all this way to offer you forgiveness— nay, to extend the olive branch to you and give you another chance. And this is the thanks I get."

"Stand *aside*!" As Melinda fairly shouted the words, another male voice spoke out of the murk.

"Good Lord, what's amiss here?"

It was Dr. Gildfish.

# Chapter Ten

Before she could react or even think, he was at her side. "Miss Weatherby," he was saying in his pleasant, concerned voice, "my servant told me you were waiting for me. Is Lady Darlington ill again?"

As if sensing her inner turmoil, her horse snorted and tossed its head. Speaking soothingly to the beast, Gildfish caught hold of the bridle and smiled up at Melinda. "The fog makes the horses nervous," he said.

"Yes—yes, the fog," Melinda stammered. "Zenobie is restless, too. That's why I came to ask you for some medicine."

She hardly knew what she was saying. Foremost in her mind was a desperation to get away from Gildfish and warn Lord Hartford before it was too late. If it was not already too late. "I have been gone too long—Zenobie will be worried," she babbled on. "I will send a servant for the medicine."

"But if you would wait for a moment, I can give you the medicine to take with you," the doctor protested.

"There is no reason trying to reason with this person, sir," Mr. Proctor snapped. "I was mistaken in you, Miss Weatherby."

Gildfish surveyed the headmaster in astonishment. "Who is this person?" he wondered aloud.

The headmaster drew himself up and announced importantly, "I, sir, am Augustus Forthingay Proctor."

The doctor made a gesture that clearly asked, And who the devil is that? "He is the headmaster of the academy where I was employed before coming to Dorset," Melinda explained in a distracted voice.

"Quite so," interrupted Mr. Proctor. "Quite right. I came here to offer Miss Weatherby her position back."

Melinda perceived a glimmer of hope. "Perhaps," she told the headmaster, "if you accompany me to Darlington House, we can discuss the matter further."

"Are you saying, ma'am, that you may be interested in returning to Proctor Academy after all?"

Even Miss Poll would forgive this lie. "We could discuss it," Melinda repeated. "I may have been too hasty."

A look of malicious pleasure filled the headmaster's eyes. "Now I see that you are one of those females who says nay when she means aye." He wagged a sanctimonious finger at Melinda, adding, "I should have listened to Miss Vraye when she told me that you were not to be trusted. I comprehend now that you would not be fit to teach the young ladies at Proctor Academy."

"Let him go, ma'am," Dr. Gildfish said. "This *gentleman* clearly has business elsewhere."

"What is clear," shouted Mr. Proctor, stung by the contempt in the doctor's voice, "is that this young woman is out of her senses." He stamped back to his hackney, heaved himself in, and shouted a command to drive on. "Miss Weatherby, you will live to regret this day!"

She was already regretting it. Melinda's heart

shimmered like a slippery fish against her ribs as Dr. Gildfish chuckled. "A regular Captain Hackum," he said. "He should be on the stage."

He turned to her with a pleasant smile. "I know you couldn't mention it in front of your Mr. Proctor, but I have that letter you need to get your cousin away. I'm sure that is what brought you out, alone, on such a murky night."

He held out a hand to help her dismount, but Melinda stayed where she was. "Perhaps," she said in as firm a tone as she could manage, "you would be so kind as to get me that letter? My cousin will be worried and—and Lord Hartford is to call at Darlington House tonight. If I don't return soon, he will become suspicious."

There was a hint of smugness in Gildfish's smile. "Lord Hartford may be delayed."

Meaning that the ambush on Lord Hartford was imminent—or had already taken place. Desperate to get away, Melinda dropped her riding quirt. When the doctor loosed her bridle and reached down to get it, she snapped the reins over the horse's head and shouted a command. The animal plunged forward.

Behind her, she could hear Gildfish shouting for her to stop. Far from doing so, she dug her heels into the horse's flank and urged it forward. She knew that Gildfish would pursue her. If she could reach the lake road, if she could get a head start, she might have a chance—

Suddenly a man plunged out of the bushes and ran directly into her path. Her frightened horse reared up on its hind legs, throwing Melinda to the ground. As she lay momentarily stunned, she heard the stranger laugh and say, "Here we are again, then, missy."

The nasal, rasping voice was familiar—and in the moonlight his froglike face was likewise unforgettable. Here was one of the villains who had accosted her and Zenobie near the lake. Melinda scrambled to her feet, but as she did so there were muffled hoofbeats behind her.

"Help!" Melinda screamed. "Someone, help me!" But the sound thinned into a gasp as the frog-faced personage grasped her around the neck.

"One more sound and I breaks yer neck," he threatened.

Now the doctor's closed trap drove up, and Gildfish leaned out to command, "Get her in here—quickly, before someone comes."

Melinda's attempts to struggle were of no avail. She was dragged toward the trap and shoved roughly inside. "Be quiet, Miss Weatherby," the doctor threatened, "or, as Ralph Drekson put it, I will have to break your pretty neck. Luckily, the fog muffles sounds and by this time most honest folk are abed."

He then turned to the frog-faced villain. "Is it done?"

"I dunno, guv. I was delayed." Ralph Drekson lowered his voice to add, "You know that the roads out of Dorset are being watched? That Lord 'Artford 'as got the town watch poking their snouts everywhere. I 'eard some of 'em saying as that Belgie was seen around the town—I dunno if 'e managed to 'opp the twig or not."

"Van Leyt's too cagey to be caught so easily," Gildfish said, "but Hartford must be stopped. Join the others and report back to me if they've carried out my orders."

Ralph disappeared into the shadows. "And you are coming with me," Gildfish told Melinda.

Resistance was futile. In spite of his almost gentle voice, she had no illusion that the doctor would kill her without hesitation if she called out or tried to escape. "I gather you learned some things you should not have," Gildfish was saying. "Now, like Bluebeard's wife, you must pay the price."

He stopped the horses at his door, snapped a command to his waiting manservant, and, grasping Melinda by the arm, hustled her out of the trap and into his house. She forced down an impulse to scream. Not now, she commanded herself. She must bide her time and wait for a chance to escape and warn Lord Hartford.

"How much do you know?" he asked. She said nothing, and he pushed her roughly down into a chair. "I asked a question, Miss Weatherby."

"I have nothing to say to you," Melinda flung at him. She wanted to speak up boldly, but her voice sounded small and depressingly hen-hearted.

"She must 'ave 'eard me and Van Leyt talking," Gildfish's servant offered from the doorway. "Van Leyt was talking about meeting your contact, sir, and about plans for Lord 'Artford."

"And so you were going to run to his lordship to warn him, Miss Weatherby? Touching," Gildfish taunted, "but useless. It's my fond hope that his lordship is by now supping with the angels."

Her involuntary cry made him smile. "In love with him, are you? It may be some comfort to know he reciprocates your tender feelings, my dear. The note that lured him into ambush was a forgery. He thought that it came from you."

He went to a sideboard and poured himself some brandy. Melinda swallowed all the useless, angry words she wanted to hurl at him and forced herself to speak reasonably. "Zenobie will send servants to find me."

"By then we'll be well on our way."

"Traitor!" she could not help crying. He shrugged and downed his brandy. "Lord Hartford is not a man to be ambushed easily," she went on fiercely. "He will escape—and he'll find you. You won't be able to get away from him."

The doctor swallowed a second measure of brandy. "But I will. I've beaten him before, you know. In Spain."

His words brought a flash of insight that was staggering. "You have lied to me all along," she gasped. "Lord Hartford never shot Lieutenant Latten. It was you."

"Close—but not quite accurate." He drained a third brandy. "Let us say that I, ah, expedited young Latten's capture by the French."

"You s-sold him to Napoleon?"

"Not to wrap plain facts in clean linen, yes, I did. Unfortunately, Hartford got the boy out before he could talk." Gildfish's face turned ugly as he added, "He did his level best to bring Latten to safety, but the young man caught a French bullet in the back and died shortly after Hartford brought him back to English lines."

Even in such a place and at such a time, Melinda felt a searing joy. Lord Hartford had never compromised his honor even in the course of duty. He had not harmed his friend—he had tried to save him. But before she could savor her relief, there was a knock on the door and the frog-faced Ralph Drekson came running in.

"Well?" demanded the doctor. "Is Hartford dead?"

"I dunno. Guv, I come to tell yer something else. The watch 'as got 'old of Van Leyt, and they're questioning him. Lord 'Artford or no Lord 'Artford, if that Belgie talks, it's Tyburn tree for us."

"He won't talk."

Melinda did not miss the tension in Gildfish's voice. "Lord Hartford will know how to make him talk," she cried. "Van Leyt will confess, and you will be exposed."

"Be quiet!"

The doctor commenced gnawing on his lip. Melinda persisted. "Lord Hartford is not the kind of man to walk into an ambush, and you know it well. He'll hunt you down and punish you."

Ralph Drekson made a sound that was very much like a whimper. "Be still, you idiot," snapped the doctor. "There's no danger as long as we all keep our nerve." He turned to his manservant, who was hovering anxiously nearby. "All we need do is proceed with our plans and meet our contact at the new rendezvous point, as arranged."

Then all three men looked at Melinda. "You're tongue-valiant," the doctor said. He took a step closer to Melinda's chair, and she could not help shrinking back. "How shall I kill you? I wonder. By poison—or by strangling, or, perhaps, by pushing you into the lake. That might be best. It would seem as if your death was an accident."

He paused. "You see, doctors have many ways to kill."

"You are a disgrace to all doctors," Melinda cried. For a moment she forgot her fear in fury that this man was going to get away with treason. Treason for which poor Zenobie was going to be blamed. "Lord Hartford will follow you," she went on.

"We may as well hedge our bets." In a parody of his old, diffident courtesy, Gildfish bowed to Melinda. "I regret to say that you must come with

184

us, Miss Weatherby. In case he survives my ambush, we need a hostage that Hartford won't want to risk."

"I say, old fellow, I need to talk to you."

Hartford looked up with a frown. The inventor had chosen a most inconvenient time, for Dayce had just ridden in from Scotland and was making his report.

"What is it, Blyminster?" Hartford wondered somewhat impatiently. "Can it wait?"

Sir Rupert looked obstinate and shook his head. Instructing his manservant to find refreshment, Hartford dismissed him. "Well?" he asked.

The inventor walked up and down the room, alternately nodding and shaking his head. Finally he said, "Mean to say—have to do it. Man's got to screw his courage to the stickin' point, don't you know."

Still more impatiently, Hartford asked what Sir Rupert was talking about. "Talkin' about proposin'," the inventor promptly said. "Mean to go down on m'knees to Lady Darlington."

"You want to *marry* the woman?" Hartford exclaimed. "You're bamming me. She's buried three husbands already."

The inventor's jaw jutted pugnaciously. "Not her fault, is it, that they're cockin' up their toes? She's everythin' I want in a woman, suits me down to the ground. Light and fire and sweetness. I never thought," Sir Rupert continued, warming to his theme, "that I'd ever find someone like Zenobie— mean to say, Lady Darlington—except in m'dreams. And not even in them, don't you know, because I never had a dream like her before."

Hartford was speechless. Sir Rupert rambled on.

185

"Never thought a woman like that'd want an old duffer like me who knows nothin' but machines and nuts and bolts—unsatisfactory things, nuts and bolts, and machines will drift away from you, mean to say. But Lady Darlington's an angel, and she seems to return my regard. Eh? Have to speak up now or risk losin' her."

Listening to him, Hartford felt a spasm of guilt. If he had not pushed the two together, poor old Flighty Blighty would not be in this mare's nest.

There was no way around it. He *was* responsible—and he must therefore be the one to burst the inventor's rosy balloon. "Before you go any further," he said, "I've got something to tell you about Lady Darlington."

It was not an easy telling. Sir Rupert became agitated, strode about the room, and broke into Hartford's narrative to cry, "So what if she was leg-shackled to Vilforme? Not her fault, is it, that he was a scoundrel? Mean to say—it ain't fair, your cryin' her down like this."

Patiently, Hartford resumed his narrative, gradually moving from one damning episode to another. "Haven't you thought it strange that you were attacked by those men outside Darlington House?" he asked. "They knew just where to look for the key to your safe, too. Remember that you'd just showed it to Lady Darlington at dinner."

"Showed it to you and the sawbones and Miss Weatherby, too," Sir Rupert snorted. "Mean to say—could've been Miss Weatherby."

"She was with me at all times. Lady Darlington left the room to get her cloak, giving her the chance to arrange an ambush." Hartford paused. "And there was the pickled crab. Lady Darlington knew how well you like the dish. She could easily have added some substance to the crab that made everyone who ate it sick. *She* didn't eat crab, remember."

Sir Rupert waved his hands in agitation. "There's no demmed proof!" he spluttered. "What's more, there ain't goin' to be any. I tell you, Hartford—"

"She made you ill and used your sickness as an excuse to come calling," Hartford went on sternly. "That visit enabled her to see the *Subaqua* for herself. Don't forget how fascinated she was with your blueprints." The inventor shook his head stubbornly. "It's also my belief that she took several of those papers off with her under cover of that convenient fire."

"Didn't!" Sir Rupert shouted. "I'll prove it to you, what's more."

He fairly ran down the stairs to his workroom. Hartford followed in time to see the inventor unlock his safe and pull out his blueprints. "Mean to say, nothin's missin'," he began, and then stopped.

Hartford felt a profound pity as he watched Sir Rupert riffle through the blueprints and papers, counting and recounting. "Are they all there?" he asked at last.

"Must've put them someplace" was the muffled reply. "Must've mislaid them. Always jumblin' up these things, old sapskull is what I am."

He broke off and looked directly up at Hartford. "She played me for a fool."

Hartford could only say, "I'm sorry."

"I wish," said Sir Rupert miserably, "I'd never started workin' on the *Subaqua*. It's brought nothin' but trouble." He smoothed his remaining papers and blueprints with a shaking hand as he added, "Know what it is, Hartford? You think you're past your prime. Eh? Not going to walk into parson's mousetrap, not goin' to fill your nursery.

Maybe that wasn't of your choosin'—but there it is, and there's no use cryin' over spilled milk. And then you meet the one woman in the world."

His eyes glowed, and for a moment Sir Rupert seemed transformed from an ofttimes fuzzy-brained inventor to a young and ardent lover.

"It was necessary not to tell you," Hartford said unhappily, "but it must seem like a scurvy trick. I'm sorry, Blyminster."

Sir Rupert ignored this. "You know how it is, don't you?" he asked instead. "Seen you, by Jove, the way you looked when you was with that little Miss Weatherby." Hartford remained mute. "Mean to say, Lady D. seemed—I don't know. Under all that warmth and laughter and fire, she seemed lonely. Mean to say, lonely like—like me."

He rose and, moving like an old man, began to return the papers to the safe. Quietly, Hartford left the workshop and, returning to his room, summoned Dayce, who picked up the narrative where he had left off. Hartford listened silently for some time and then suddenly came alert.

"The devil you say," he mused. Astonishment and chagrin hardened his tone as he mused, "I've been a fool not to have followed that trail long ago."

There was a knock on the door. "Beg pardon, my lord," Owens announced, "but Sir Orin Calworth has arrived."

"Sir Orin!" Hartford exclaimed in astonishment.

"I've taken the liberty to conduct him to the drawing room, my lord. Admiral Kier is with him."

"What, the old badger, too? I suppose they've come for the kill," Hartford mused.

Pausing only to give Dayce some instructions, he descended to the drawing room. There he felt a flash of déjà vu, for here was Kier, hulked into a chair in the shadows while Sir Orin stood in front of the empty grate. And, as on that other night, both men looked at Hartford expectantly as he bowed to them both and said, "I didn't expect to see you here in Dorset, gentlemen."

The admiral rumbled deep in his throat. "Neither did we, dear boy," murmured Sir Orin. He looked, Hartford thought, more like a Bond Street tulip than ever save for the hard glitter in his eyes. "Frightful fog out there, upon my word," he drawled. "We almost surrendered to the elements, but we persevered. Your latest communiqué led us to believe that our spy is about to reveal herself."

"Or *him*self." Sir Rupert, looking combative, had come into the drawing room. Sir Orin raised his spyglass, looked the inventor up and down, then favored Hartford with a mildly reproachful look.

"I assume that you have had to take this gentleman into your confidence?" he wondered.

Hartford nodded. "Bad business," Admiral Kier grumbled. "No need to let every tomfool in England in on state secrets. We'll be shouting it from the hedgerows next."

Sir Rupert bristled still more, and Hartford made haste to intervene. "It was necessary to tell Blyminster. Our spy has the blueprints in hand now, and will probably meet his contacts tonight."

"Ah," Sir Orin exclaimed, his eyes as hard as flint.

"There are checkpoints on all the roads leading out of Dorset. In case our man takes to the water, I've posted members of the local watch along the lake. They have sailboats and orders to pursue any craft they see."

"And if the miscreant manages to elude your net,

189

every inch of the coast from Swanage to Torquay is guarded," Sir Orin said. "I believe that we—"

"But wait a minute," Sir Rupert interrupted. "You said 'he' before, Hartford, and just now you've said 'man.' You don't think it's Lady Darlington, then?"

"Slip of the damned tongue," growled the admiral, but Sir Orin raised his eyebrows questioningly.

Hartford explained. "Dayce has just returned from Edinburgh, where he's been making inquiries for me. The man we've known as Dr. Gildfish is an impostor."

"Eh—what? Not a sawbones?" Sir Rupert gaped.

"When I first came to Dorset, I made inquiries about him, but he'd covered his tracks well. He'd taken the name of Lord Macley's dead son—also a physician—ten years ago, established a practice in that name, and used it when he went to Spain as a military doctor. Nothing could be found against our man until we dug deeper and found that his real name is Fowarth."

"Fowarth!" mused Sir Orin. "Wait—I know that name. Cameron Fowarth was a Scots-English baronet who was as rich as golden ball until he gamed it all away."

"His son is also a gamester. Apparently he was at point-non-plus when he suddenly acquired unlimited funds." Hartford's voice hardened. "I'm convinced he had something to do with Latten's betrayal to the French."

"Tchah!" The admiral reared like an angry whale. "Are you saying that this bastard Fowarth sold Latten out? Run him to earth, damn it. Run him to earth before he takes to his heels—"

He was heaving himself to his feet, when Hartford checked him. "I've had Dayce dispatch two of the town watch to the good doctor's house. I was about to go there myself when you arrived."

"I'll come with you." Face aglow, Sir Rupert made for the door. "I'm goin' to Darlington Hall—not safe with spies and other raff and chaff hangin' about. Mean to see that Lady D.'s safe."

"If you go to her now, you'll spoil months of careful planning," Sir Orin protested. "No, Blyminster, you are too good a subject of the crown for that. Besides, the lady is still under a cloud. Nothing says that there are not *two* master spies."

Hartford watched the color drain away from the inventor's face. He put a hand on the man's shoulder and spoke quietly. "Hold fast. We're near the end of this tangle."

Sir Orin raised his eyebrows but said only, "Do you ride to town, then, Hartford. Meanwhile, Sir Rupert, perhaps you will tell us more about your *Subaqua*. The admiral and I have been following Hartford's dispatches about your invention with interest."

"What we want to know is whether the damned thing's not just a corkbrained gimcrack," the admiral added bluntly. "Hartford seems to think it's something the Admiralty might be interested in. Not convinced he's right."

Leaving the inventor to defend his *Subaqua,* Hartford went down the stairs and out the main door, where he found Dayce waiting with his campaign pistols, his sword, and two saddled horses. "I'm not a bit tired, m'lud," he said in answer to Hartford's questioning look, "and two hands are better nor one in a pinch."

He paused while his employer buckled on his sword belt and then added somewhat diffidently, "M'lud, this here note was just brought for you."

Hartford took the missive, opened it, and looked sharply up at his manservant. "Did one of Lady Darlington's servants bring this?"

"No, m'lud, it was that Mr. Ferridew, the poet." Dayce's tone left little doubt as to what he thought of poets. "He said as it was Miss Weatherby had given the letter to him. Something about her not being able to trust it to the servants."

Frowning, Hartford pocketed the paper and mounted his horse. As Dayce followed him into the dense fog, he was not thinking of Sir Orin's appearance but rather of the letter Melinda had written him. She had begged him to meet her at the fork in the road, but— "Why should she trust Ferridew?" he mused. "Was there no one else to send as courier?"

*Trust no one, turn your back on no one*—behind him, Dayce cleared his throat as his employer turned off the lake road. "Begging your pardon, m'lud, but that's not the way to the town."

"I've something to do first."

Hartford knew that it could easily be a trap. He had never seen Melinda's writing, and anyone who knew her could have put down words she might use. He was aware of this, and yet a part of him hoped that this was no trick and that Melinda truly wanted to see him.

"Begging your pardon again, m'lud," Dayce was saying, "but are you maybe meeting Miss Weatherby at the fork of the road?" Wordlessly, Hartford nodded. Dayce continued. "If I'm not making too bold, we'd best go easy. There was something about that poet I didn't trust, sir. He was stinking of liquor, and he didn't look me in the eye when he spoke—"

Dayce was interrupted by a shrill cry for help. "Melinda!" Hartford exclaimed.

He spurred forward. As he did so, the mist lifted momentarily, and he saw several shadowed forms attempting to drag a rider from the saddle.

Pistols were of no use in this fog—a stray shot might hit Melinda. Instead, Hartford leaned from his saddle and caught one of the villains around the neck, lifting him off the ground before flinging him backward. Then he cracked his whip down, again and yet again.

There was another scream as the villains succeeded in dragging Melinda from the saddle. Hartford could do no more than shout her name, for he was surrounded by a mob of attackers. He kicked one villain away, meanwhile drew his sword. Behind him he could hear Dayce swearing as he lashed about with his whip.

The battle did not last long. Infuriated that these brutes had dared to attack Melinda, Hartford laid about him with no mercy and soon several attackers lay on the ground. The others hastily beat a retreat into the shadows, and at a command from his employer Dayce rode off in pursuit.

Hartford then dismounted, assured himself that the men on the ground were dead or unconscious, and then strode over to the fallen rider's side.

She was struggling to sit up, and he put an arm about her shoulders to support her. "Are you all right, my love?" he began, then stopped, staring. "By the devil," he exclaimed, "Miss Pennodie!"

"They thought I was you," Carabel said.

"Most likely. Are you hurt?" he asked, and while she shook her head he tried to stifle his disappointment that Melinda had never wanted to meet him. It had been a trap after all, and poor Carabel, muffled by cloak and fog, had been caught in it. "But what are you doing riding alone at this time of night?" he went on.

Carabel gave a huge sniff. "I was trying to join them," she whispered.

"Trying to join *whom*?" Hartford asked impatiently. "No one is going to hurt you, Miss Pennodie," he added in a gentler voice, "but you must tell me. Where were you going?"

"To find the Briddles," she whispered. "They left after supper tonight. I—I was away with Mama, dining with Mrs. Spendagle, and they were all gone when I got back, but Hannah left me a note telling me she would never forget me—"

"I'm sorry," Hartford said.

She knuckled her eyes like a scolded child and added dolefully, "Then Mama shouted that I must marry the squire at once, and—and, oh, my lord, I couldn't bear it, so I ran away to try to overtake the Briddles and beg them to take me with them to Yorkshire."

Hartford drew a deep breath and let it go. "Don't cry," he said. Then, as hoofbeats signaled the reappearance of Dayce, he added, "They can't have gotten far in this fog. My man will see that you reach the Briddles safely."

Disbelief, hope, and then incredulous joy filled Carabel's tear-blotched face. "Then—then you won't send me back to Mama?" When Hartford shook his head, she seized his hand and kissed it, thanking him again and again.

"For they'll take good care of me," she cried, almost beside herself with relief, "and teach me their craft, and—and Hannah and Lucas will be my sister and brother. I have always wanted a sister, and—and I'll be so *happy* in their family."

Hartford gave Dayce instructions, helped the joyful Carabel up so that she could ride pillion, and watched them go. At least, he thought, someone will be happy.

Abruptly, he returned to the matter at hand. The forged note was undoubtedly Fowarth-Gildfish's doing. "Time to pay a visit to our doctor," Hartford said grimly.

But the men posted to watch the doctor's home said that no one was in. Had he already gone to earth? Hartford wondered. Staying only to dispatch some men to collect prisoners at the scene of the ambush, Hartford left the town and followed the dark road until a challenge rang out.

Hartford identified himself, and the watchman exclaimed, "Oh, it's you, me lord. Our sergeant's questioning that there gentleman over there. 'E tried to sneak by us, and when we told 'im to 'alt, 'e resisted."

Fowarth? But Hartford's hope that this might be the traitor was dashed as a high, affected voice nearby protested, "But I tell you, I am not a sh—smuggler. I, sir, follow my muse."

"Ferridew!" Hartford exclaimed.

He rode over to a trap that had been stopped by the side of the road. Next to it stood the poet, gloriously and profoundly drunk. He gesticulated wildly, his fair hair flew in every direction, and his clothes were in disarray.

Seeing Hartford, he struck an attitude and cried, "Thank the godsh—gods that you have come. Do convince these louts to let me go. They think I'm some sort of shm—smuggler. I assure you, sir, that such base material pastimes are as foreign to my nature as the shun—I mean, the sun to darkness."

" 'Is trap's full of bottles of rum, sir," reported the

interrogating sergeant of the town watch. "And 'e's that boozy 'e's talking gibberish, like."

"It's all right, Sergeant." Hartford leaned down from his horse and eyed the poet sternly. "Who really gave you that letter you handed to Dayce this evening?"

"The muse with the sh—silver eyes," Ferridew replied promptly. He wavered on his feet and sent a fatuous smile in Hartford's direction. "She looked at me and I fell at her feet. The goddesh with the dark silk hair demanded, and I could not refuse."

"So you won't tell the truth." The poet's smile broadened. Hartford turned to the sergeant. "Take him out into the woods," he directed, "and shoot him."

The words seemed to awaken Ferridew to instant sobriety. "You daren't!" he exclaimed shrilly. "No, you can't! Oh, take your hand from my shoulder, you *b-beastly* man. It was Dr. Gildfish gave me the letter. He said that Miss Weatherby had given the letter to him. I saw no harm—"

"And to make certain you kept your mouth closed, the good doctor supplied enough rum to keep you disguised for a month." Hartford turned to the waiting sergeant. "Let him go, but confiscate the rum."

"But—but you can't do that. An Englishman's possessions are sacred," Ferridew bleated. Almost in tears, he pursued the sergeant, who had begun to haul off the bottles.

"This is damnable, sir! Damnable! I am an English gentleman and it is my right to travel the king's highways freely. How dare you interfere with me in this way?"

A stout personage in a coat that shone green in the lamplight was being hustled up. Hartford turned questioningly to the watchman who accompanied this newcomer and was told that *this* one had been riding in a hackney that was driving hell for leather down the road. " 'E wouldn't give 'is name or state 'is business, neither," the watchman reported.

"I do not know this person," spluttered the man in the green coat. "Of course I refused to stop. I feared highwaymen!"

"What is your name, sir?" Hartford inquired civilly.

"I have been forced to stop, I have been searched, I have been subjected to indignities. I am Augustus Proctor, and I demand to know who you are, sir, and why an English gentleman has been subjected to such—"

"Augustus Proctor of the Proctor Academy?" Hartford interrupted. "Have you seen Miss Weatherby?"

The headmaster narrowed his eyes. "I fail to see that this is any concern of yours."

"Was anyone in the hackney with him?" Hartford asked the watchman, who shook his head. "Where is Miss Weatherby now?"

"I do not know or care. Unhand me, sir," shrieked Mr. Proctor as Hartford bent from the saddle, seized him by the lapels of his coat, and lifted him several inches off the ground. "How dare you— help! I am being accosted by a maniac!"

"Tell me about Miss Weatherby," Hartford said. He spoke very gently, but Mr. Proctor, who was about to protest that his business was entirely his own, saw the expression in his inquisitor's dark eyes and immediately told the unadorned truth.

"The devil and all his angels. She's with *him*—"

Hartford dropped the sputtering headmaster to earth just as hoofbeats announced another rider.

This man came from the east road. He saluted smartly and said, "Beg yer pardon, m'lord, but we've caught that Van Leyt trying to leave Dorset. He'd snuck into Dorset, seemingly. We're questioning him."

His ambush failed, Van Leyt taken—Fowarth would know that the game was over. "The roads are blocked, so he'll have arranged to meet a contact somewhere across the lake," Hartford mused. "Van Leyt will tell us where and when."

Calling the sergeant of the watch, he directed him to take several of his several men and fan out along the lakeshore. "Don't shoot no matter what the provocation," he added sternly. "He may have a hostage."

And, setting spurs to his gelding, Hartford plunged back into the fog.

# Chapter Eleven

Rough arms dragged Melinda out of the doctor's trap. Her hands were bound behind her, and a gag bit cruelly into her mouth. Still, she forced down panic. He can't be dead, she told herself fiercely. He'll come in time to capture these villains and— and in time to save me.

It was too murky to see much, but plainly they were near the lake. Melinda could hear the gentle lap of water nearby, and as she was propelled along the uneven ground, tree branches whipped against her face. Brambles caught and tore her skirt.

"Don't dawdle," the doctor gritted out. In spite of his bravado back at the house, he was clearly nervous. If he were so sure Lord Hartford was dead, he would not be in such a fever to escape, Melinda thought.

But her hopes fell again as they emerged from the woods onto the shore of Kendle Lake. A sailboat loomed, its mast a ghostly spar in the fog. She stumbled on something soft on the ground and Ralph snickered, "Now, look what you've gone and done."

Melinda was sickened to see that she had almost stepped on a man's hand. He lay sprawled on the ground, close to another man. For a moment she thought they were dead, but when Gildfish prodded one with his toe, the man grunted and gave a bubbly snore.

"Still sleeping off the laudanum I put in their ale," the doctor said with satisfaction. Then he ordered his henchmen to get Melinda into the boat.

Her struggles were less than useless. Bundled into the boat like sacking, Melinda was shoved to the bottom of the craft. Ralph cast off, then jumped in to take the tiller, and the sailboat slid away from shore.

Melinda twisted her hands behind her back, trying in vain to loosen the knots. Her tongue worked around her cruel gag until she nearly choked. A small moan was wrenched from her. Gildfish glanced her way, hesitated, then reached out to remove the gag. She took a deep gulp of air, choked, and coughed violently.

"You can scream if you like," Gildfish mocked her. "No one will hear you this far out on the lake, and no one will follow."

Melinda's throat felt as raw as the hands she was twisting behind her back. "Lord Hartford will find you," she croaked.

" 'E can't," Ralph interposed. "It's all bowman. While the watch was on the nod, I went along the lakeside and knocked 'oles in all the boats with which they was going to chase after us."

For the first time in her life, Melinda felt true despair. In the past there had always been something else to try, some other course to take. Now neither her wits nor her friends could save her.

"Your fault for being so busy," Gildfish pointed out. "If you'd been content to play the shy young cousin to that foolish Russian woman, I'd have buttoned up this scheme without involving you."

"Then Zenobie had really nothing to do with

this—" But what good did that do? Melinda wondered. Zenobie could not prove herself innocent of involvement in Gildfish's scheme. Even if she were not imprisoned, she would always be under suspicion.

She must stay alive for Zenobie's sake. With that thought came a rush of desperate courage, and her panic eased. I *will* survive this, Melinda swore. I *must*.

She now knew the doctor to be vain and boastful. If she played on his bloated ego, if she could gain time, perhaps a way to escape would open.

"You are a respected doctor," Melinda began. "What made you betray your country?"

"The money, of course." Gildfish looked back over his shoulder at the impenetrable wall of fog and asked, "Drekson, are you sure we're sailing for the new coordinates Van Leyt gave us?"

When assured that their course was true, he turned his attention back to Melinda. "I enjoy good living and gaming," he said, "and both require money."

"No wonder you were at Mrs. Pennodie's that day," Melinda exclaimed.

"That toad-eating harpy does give diverting parties." He leaned back in the sailboat and added smugly, "Of course, the stakes in this backwater are paltry things. There was one night when I lost three thousand pounds on jeu d'enfer at Crockford's and won it back at blind hookey."

"Indeed," she murmured.

"Oh, yes, *indeed*." His voice took on a reminiscent tone as he added, "I told you that gambling is a disease, didn't I? It runs in my family. My father was lucky and amassed a fortune. I, on the other hand, ran into a string of bad luck and lost all he left me.

I was fairly knocked into the horse stalls when some people came to see me with a business proposition."

*Treason,* she wanted to shout. Instead, she said quite calmly, "They suggested you become a spy."

"An agent, rather." He actually preened himself as he added, "They wanted me because, as a medical man, I would be valuable to them. Scruples are for the very rich who can afford them or the very poor who don't have anything worthwhile to buy or trade," Gildfish told her. "The organization has been more or less inactive after Napoleon was sent to Elba, but then we learned that Calworth had picked one of his best men to guard Blyminster's underwater craft. *That* was a clear sign that the *Subaqua* had worth."

He broke off and looked about him again. "Damn this fog," he muttered. "I can't see a bloody thing."

Ralph Drekson allowed that it was a queer fetch, but that they would soon clap their oggles on the rendezvous point. "See that we do," Gildfish snapped. "Remember the money that's waiting for all of us."

Perhaps if she acted foolish and weak and appealed to his vanity, the doctor might become careless. "Alas," Melinda sighed, "you did it all so cleverly that I never guessed. I thought you were so good and kind. I was even so foolish as to feel—" She broke off and dropped her eyes modestly.

"Never say you had developed a tendre for me," Gildfish exclaimed. "I thought it was Hartford who caught your eye." She could almost see him swelling his chest with the new thought.

"He is a duke's son. I knew he was only amusing himself with me." Melinda drew a deep sigh. "If only things had been different."

Then she held her breath, praying that he would believe her and would soften. For a moment she thought she had succeeded, for he sighed. "I grant you that it's a shame," he agreed. "To destroy something with so much spirit and loveliness—but it has to be done. I wouldn't be safe with you here to open your mouth to the authorities."

Melinda knew she was running out of time. "If only you could loosen my bonds," she murmured. "What harm could I possibly do against the three of you? And where could I possibly escape to?"

"Nowhere. Even so, you'll remain as you are" was the cool reply. Then he repeated, "A shame. It would have been pleasant to—enjoy your company."

Silently, she swallowed her disgust and renewed tugging at her bonds. She must free her wrists. If her hands were untied when she was thrown overboard, there was a chance she could escape—and she must escape somehow, Melinda thought. There was too much at stake for her to die now.

"Drugged!"

Hartford rose from examining three members of the watch who had been assigned to guard this quadrant of the lake. They lay at odd angles, snoring loudly, their weapons still clutched to their chests.

"This boat 'as 'oles knocked in the bottom, too, sorr," the sergeant of the town watch reported.

All along the lakeshore the story had been the same. "Fowarth has been busy," Hartford said grimly, and when the man did not comprehend, he explained, "The man we knew as Dr. Gildfish."

Hartford could picture the doctor riding around the lake, offering the watchmen ale laced with laudanum. Who would suspect a kind, friendly country sawbones of foul play? And who would refuse ale on a long, dark watch? Then, while the men lay snoring in their drugged sleep, Fowarth—or his accomplices—had knocked holes in their sailboats.

He had underestimated his enemy. Now, somewhere on the dark, fog-bound lake, that same enemy held Melinda hostage. And once her usefulness to him was over, he would kill her.

When he had found the drugged guards and ruined sailboats, Hartford's first instinct had been to plunge into the lake in the vain hope of rescuing her somehow. Failing that, he had wanted to ride like a madman to Blyminster Place and find a boat with a whole hull. Instead, he had sent a rider to Blyminster and himself remained behind to redeploy men all along the lakeshore.

This done, he now seethed with helpless rage, much of which was directed at himself. He should have trusted Melinda more. He should have suspected the doctor earlier. Yet his suspicions had not been roused until the night Gildfish-Fowarth had mentioned Calworth's Circle.

That night he had sent Dayce to Edinburgh, but— "Not quickly enough," Hartford gritted out. Meanwhile it had been the doctor, not Zenobie, who had tainted the crab at Mrs. Pennodie's garden party, thus giving himself unlimited access to Blyminster Cove. Gildfish-Fowarth, not Darlington's widow had set the fire. Now the spy and the blueprints he had stolen were out there somewhere on Kendle Lake, and he had Melinda. *Melinda*—

Out of the fog came hoofbeats, and Hartford strode forward to meet four riders, led by Sir Rupert, who was loudly complaining about the villains who had broken into his boathouse and damaged his sailboats.

Hartford's heart plunged. "*All* of them are damaged?"

"Exceptin' the rowboat that's always tied at the ramp by m'workshop. M'servants are rowin' it over here now, if they don't get lost in this demmed fog. Mean to say," Sir Rupert went on aggrievedly as Sir Orin and the admiral drew up, "demmed paltry thing to do, ruinin' all m'boats."

In a few terse words Hartford explained how matters stood. Sir Orin said in his soft voice, "Fowarth's clever—I'll give him that. But you've got the better of him, Hartford."

"How?" Bitterness rode Hartford's voice. "He's out there on the lake, and he has a—hostage."

"Tchaa!" The admiral grunted himself off his horse and stumped forward to push his belligerent face close. "Never mind the hostage. Got to catch Fowarth, damn it. Good of the many outweighs the good of the few, etcetera. *Do* something, Hartford."

In his gentlest voice Sir Orin pointed out that nothing needed be done. "Hartford has unmasked the villain. Fowarth will be stopped before he reaches the coast. Besides, even if he does escape with those blueprints, the *Subaqua* is unproven and could well be worthless."

Sir Rupert stopped in the act of dismounting from his horse and glared at Sir Orin. "My *Subaqua* ain't worthless. Thought I proved that back in m'workshop." Sir Orin shook his head in gentle denial, the admiral heaved his shoulders in a massive shrug. "If you think the *Subaqua*'s useless, you've got a leak in your upper works," Sir Rupert told them wrathfully.

Not waiting to hear Sir Orin's answer, Hartford walked back to the edge of the lake. A rowboat would not be a match for a smooth-sailing sailboat, but it was something. "I must find her," he muttered.

"Don't tear yourself to pieces, my dear boy." Sir Orin had dismounted and come over to stand beside him. "We all make mistakes when we permit ourselves to fall in love."

"Was it so obvious?"

Sir Orin shrugged. "Your communiqués sounded less and less like my finest operative. You were not only thinking and reasoning, Hartford, you were *feeling*. Dangerous for men in our Circle."

"I'm not a member of the Circle any longer," Hartford retorted. "I told you so at the onset, and—where in hell is that boat?"

Sir Orin internalized a sigh as he considered the shame of it. Anthony Hartford, who was the scion of a wealthy and noble house and who had charm, courage, and high intelligence, had chosen to fall in love with a genteel nobody. Even apart from the effects of this regrettable liaison on the Dorset mission, he disapproved for the young man's own sake.

Sir Orin was promising himself a long talk with his protégé when there was the sound of carriage wheels creaking above them on the lake road. A challenge was issued, but instead of answering, a distracted female voice screamed, "*Spulcheve!* Out of my way, you dolt! What have you done to my Melushka?"

"Lady Darlington!" Sir Rupert exclaimed.

Zenobie came running down the narrow path that led to the lake. Her hair was in disarray, and she wore a purple cloak under which peeped bedroom slippers. She was followed by a grim-faced Miss Poll.

The erstwhile nurse's nose burned deep red, and her eyes, as they sought out Hartford's, were bright and hard with fear. "The groom in the stable says that she rode out alone to see the doctor," she cried. "Rode out on horseback alone—*alone* at this time of night and in this fog—and that's the last anyone saw of her. Where is she, then, sir? What's happened to my Miss Mel?"

Before Hartford could answer, Zenobie uttered a cry of relief. "Sir Rupert—you are here! You, at least, I can turn to. Find for me my little cousin."

Weeping, she cast herself into Sir Rupert's arms, and everyone began to speak at once. Sir Rupert pleaded with Lady Darlington to stay calm. Zenobie wailed that her heart was broken and would never mend until Melinda stood before her. The admiral demanded to know who in hell were all these people. Miss Poll vowed that if her darling Miss Mel were not returned to her safely, she would tear whoever was responsible limb from limb. Sir Orin raised his glass to his eye and requested calm.

"Are you without blood that you can say to me to be calm?" moaned Zenobie. "Oh, Sir Rupert, *do* something. You who have invented the *Subaqua* and can make the swan boats can do *anything*."

Suddenly Hartford's paralyzed wits rushed back with such force that he felt dizzy. Fool, thrice fool, not to have thought of this before.

He strode up to the still-vociferating Zenobie, caught her hand, and kissed it. "Ma'am," he exclaimed feelingly, "you may command me in anything, for I'm the greatest jackass in the world. Blyminster, come with me. Your invention's about to be tested in battle."

"Eh? What's that? What's got into you, old chap?" bleated the inventor as Hartford proceeded to drag him toward the horses.

"Queer stirrups, all of this," the admiral rumbled as the two men, Sir Rupert still protesting, cantered off. "All these weeping females, and now Hartford's acting as if he's short a sheet. If you ask me, Calworth, the whole business is dished up and that bloody spy's going to get away."

"We should have reached the contact point by now," Gildfish fumed. "We're moving too slowly."

Ralph Drekson pointed out that here in the heart of the fog there was little wind. "Get out the oars, then, and start rowing," the doctor commanded. "We should have met our man and been on our way to the coast by now."

Suddenly Gildfish's servant exclaimed that he heard voices. "We must be near the point, sir," he added. "If we could just see through this muck—"

As if in answer to his plaint, a breeze sprung up and parted the fog curtain slightly so that Melinda could perceive faint lights glinting in the distance. "That's not our rendezvous point, that's Blyminster Cove," Gildfish exploded. "You bloody idiot, you've been sailing in a circle. Get us out of here!"

While she strained at her unyielding bonds, Melinda gauged the distance between herself and the lights. Perhaps even with her hands tied, she could manage to swim to shore. It would be better than waiting to be murdered, she thought grimly.

Surreptitiously, she kicked off her shoes, but her resolve had come a moment too late, for Gildfish had turned his attention back to her. "I know what you're thinking," he snapped, "but put it out of your mind. I need you here in this boat, madam."

What *she* needed was a distraction. But as Melinda gazed hopelessly shoreward, she noticed a long, thin object projecting out of the water.

Had she imagined it? Holding her breath, Melinda searched the dark, rippling water. There it was again, and much closer. Oh, yes! she thought exultantly, it *was* Sir Rupert's air inducer. Now, if she could prepare the ground a little—

"If I'm not mistaken, we're near the lair of the Kendle dragon," Melinda said aloud.

The quaver in her voice only made the statement seem more realistic. Gildfish ignored her words, as did his manservant, but the frog-faced Ralph laughed so hard, he almost fell out of the boat. "Of the *what*?" he guffawed. "You're whiddling me, missy. There ain't no such things as bogles."

"Oh, but there is," Melinda said. Pitching her voice to the low, sibilant whisper that had sent delightful terror into the hearts of many little girls at the academy, she added, "I've seen it."

"Garn," Ralph snorted, but she noted he looked about him whilst Gildfish's servant muttered contemptuously about not being such a Jack Adams as to be bedoozled by an old wives' tale.

"Oh, but I have truly *seen* the dragon," Melinda protested. "One evening when I strolled along the lake near Darlington House, there was a sound in the water. And when I turned, a great scaly head rose out of the depths—"

"Arr, that ain't possible," Ralph interrupted, but he sounded uncertain.

"The head was huge and round and misshapen," Melinda went on. She glanced at the water, saw that the metal tube had almost drawn even with the sailboat. "And then it lunged at me—"

As she spoke, the water seemed to cleave apart, and from the depths kraken arose. Ralph screamed as a big, dark, cylindrical mass cannonballed up next to their sailboat.

"The dragon! Gorblimey, it's the bleeding dragon!"

The doctor pulled out a pistol and aimed a shot at the "monster." "That's no dragon, you idiot," he stormed. "It's Blyminster's underwater craft. Get us out of this, I said!"

But Ralph sat completely paralyzed by fear. Gildfish's servant moved to take the tiller, but before he could do so, the hatch of Sir Rupert's invention flew open, revealing Lord Hartford.

"Anthony!" Melinda cried joyfully.

Before she could say more, Gildfish lunged forward, clasped Melinda around the neck, and pressed his pistol against her forehead. "If you come anywhere nearer, the lady dies."

Hartford checked, half in and half out of the *Subaqua*. "If you hurt her in any way," he swore, "I'll kill you by inches. Damn you, let her go."

"Not bloody likely, *my lord*. Not until I have safe conduct to France," Gildfish shouted. "Call off your dogs, Hartford, or say good-bye to your—"

Melinda stamped with all her force on his foot. The doctor yelped with pain and astonishment, and she twisted out of his grasp. Gildfish fired his pistol, but the shot went wide. Next moment, Hartford had launched himself like a projectile onto the sailboat and caught the doctor by the throat.

The boat tilted perilously, and Ralph yelled as he slid into the water. Melinda tried for balance, but her bound hands prevented her, and she, too, tumbled into the lake. Water clogged her ears as she sank. In vain Melinda kicked her legs to try to push herself to the surface. Her lungs were bursting. She was going to die—but as this thought filtered into her already-dazed mind, she felt an arm about her. A second later she was being propelled to the surface, where she gulped air into her aching lungs.

"Are you all right?" Lord Hartford was asking urgently. He pushed back the hair that had fallen into her eyes. "Tell me, Melinda—are you hurt?"

But all she could think of to say was "You're alive. Oh, Anthony, I was afraid he'd had you killed."

He caught her close to him and kissed her. There was nothing gentle or deliberate about this kiss, which was so passionate that the cold water of the lake seemed to turn to flame. Melinda felt as if she were caught in a fiery whirlwind, and in the heart of this wonderful vortex she heard him speak her name. "Melinda," Lord Hartford whispered, "my Melinda."

"I *knew* he could not kill you, Anthony. I knew you'd come—"

"If anything had happened to you," he told her passionately, "I'd never have forgiven myself." Then he kissed her again, so long and so thoroughly that Melinda's lungs once more felt as if they might burst.

"Hoy, out there! You alive, Hartford?"

Reluctantly, they broke apart and, turning her head, Melinda saw that Sir Rupert had left the *Subaqua* and was now standing on the sailboat. His pistol was aimed at Gildfish and his servant, who sat, hands raised, at the bottom of the boat. Ralph Drekson clung like damp sacking to the boat's side.

"Got these demmed villains where we want 'em," Sir Rupert shouted. "I say, Hartford, I can't see you. You ain't gone and drowned or somethin', have you?"

Still clasping Melinda close to him, Hartford swam for the sailboat. He lifted Melinda into the boat and climbed in himself, then cut Melinda's bonds and, taking the pistol from Sir Rupert, directed the inventor to sail for shore.

"We'll tow the *Subaqua* with us," he added. "There are some gentlemen onshore who are eager to meet Mr. Fowarth."

"Fowarth?" Melinda repeated, bewildered. "Who is Fowarth?"

"I'll explain later." The sailboat had begun to skim along the water, and now dark forms were running into the water and splashing toward them. In a few moments, eager members of the town watch had swarmed aboard and had taken charge of the prisoners.

Now Hartford turned to Melinda. "Now," he said, "finally, we can talk. I must tell you how I—"

"Melushka! Is that you, my dear one?"

Zenobie's voice penetrated the remnants of fog, and Melinda could see her cousin standing on the shore less than fifty feet away. Next to Zenobie were Miss Poll and two gentlemen. One of these was bluff, stout, and white-haired, and other slight, lean, and elegant.

"Well *done*," the latter one drawled. "Well done indeed, my dear boy. Blyminster, I confess myself deeply impressed. You and your underwater craft have caught the villains and saved the lady as well."

Melinda did not have to be told who the speaker was. She could tell by the way Lord Hartford straightened at her side. He said formally, "Miss Weatherby, may I present Sir Orin Calworth and Admiral Kier?"

The admiral muttered something incomprehensible and stumped off toward the *Subaqua*. Sir

Orin bowed with a grace that was both elegant and chilling. "Madam," he murmured, "your servant."

But, Melinda knew, this was far from the truth. She suddenly could see herself as Sir Orin perceived her—small, drenched to the skin, shabby, and *poor*. The frigid wind of reality rushed through her with such force that she shivered through the cloak that a clucking, tearful, scolding Miss Poll draped about her.

"Polly, please take me home," she whispered.

She did not dare look at Lord Hartford, who was giving orders to his men. What had happened between them in a moment of excitement did not count for anything. What did a few kisses signify? When those kisses were over and the man and woman stepped apart, one of them was still a duke's son and the other remained an impoverished gentlewoman forced to earn her bread.

Zenobie was meanwhile casting hopeful glances at Sir Rupert. Seeing that the inventor was deep in conversation with Sir Orin and the admiral, she shook her head and, sighing, led the way up the narrow path to the lake road.

As Melinda dispiritedly followed her cousin, she heard the clatter of horses' hooves and a man's hoarse voice calling a challenge. "*What* do you mean, who goes there?" a high-pitched, affected voice retorted. "I wish to pass. At once!"

"That sounds like Mrs. Pennodie," Zenobie said. "What can she be doing out here at this hour of night?"

They reached the lake road in time to see Mrs. Pennodie leaning out of her carriage. Facing her was a member of the town watch, who was patiently explaining that no one was allowed to pass without the express permission of Lord Hartford.

"Then go and get his lordship," Mrs. Pennodie fumed. "It is the outside of everything when an English gentlewoman may not travel unmolested along the common road."

She stopped, staring, as a dripping Melinda and her companions emerged from the bushes. "Lady Darlington!" Mrs. Pennodie gasped. "Miss Weatherby—can that by you? Is Carabel with you?"

"No—has something happened to Carabel?" But before Mrs. Pennodie could answer Melinda, Hartford, followed by the other gentlemen, also emerged onto the road.

"There's no need to be anxious, ma'am," he told the astonished Mrs. Pennodie. "Your daughter is quite safe."

"My Lord Hartford! But—but you are all wet," stammered Mrs. Pennodie in complete bewilderment. Then, realizing what he had just said, she demanded, "Do *you* know where my stepdaughter has gone to?"

Hartford enlightened her. Apparently his explanation did not fill Carabel's stepmother with relief, for she sputtered, "I knew it when she was found missing. I'll have those Quakers arrested. I will have them transported for coercing a child away from her home."

The events of the night had left Melinda with little patience for such histrionics. "Most likely Carabel ran away because she did not want to marry a loose fish like Squire Parcher," she snapped.

Mrs. Pennodie's indignant reply was drowned out by another challenge down the road. In answer came a calm voice replying, "Peace, friend. I am Josiah Briddle, and these are my children. We must pass on an urgent matter."

"It is he—the shameless villain! Arrest that man!" Mrs. Pennodie screeched.

No one moved as two conveyances came creaking out of the lessening fog. Lucas Briddle drove one, and Josiah the other. Dayce, who had been in the lead of the little caravan, spurred forward to dismount at his employer's side.

"I found them, as you said, m'lud," he reported, "but they decided to come back with the young lady."

"So I see." Lord Hartford strolled forward to greet the oncoming caravan and hailed, "Good evening, Josiah Briddle."

"Good evening to thee, Anthony Hartford." Melinda noted Sir Orin's start of surprise at this cavalier form of address. "My business is with Maria Pennodie. I have brought her stepdaughter back to her."

"How dare you speak of me in that familiar way?" Mrs. Pennodie demanded angrily. She leaned farther out of her carriage. "Well for you that you brought my daughter back. Where is Carabel?"

Just then Carabel emerged from the caravan. She stood there with her head bowed, the picture of dejection. Hannah, who had followed her, took Carabel's hand and held it tightly.

"She wanted to come with us back to Yorkshire and live with us," Josiah Biddle went on in his grave way, "but I told her she could not do so without thy permission, Maria Pennodie."

Everyone looked at Carabel, who drooped like a flower on a wilted stalk. Melinda was so sorry for her that she forgot her own troubles. But before she could do anything, Mrs. Pennodie hissed, "So, miss. You have returned like a dog to her vomit."

Her voice was so vicious that even the admiral looked taken aback. Melinda cried, "Shame!"

She ran to Carabel's side and put an arm around the girl's shaking shoulders. "How can you be so cruel and so wicked?" she charged. "You have always browbeaten Carabel and made her life miserable. No wonder she ran to the Briddles for comfort."

Mrs. Pennodie had had a trying night. Awakened by the news that her loathsome stepchild was not in her bed, she had sent her footmen in pursuit— and had been told that the roads were all blocked. Fuming, torn between her dislike for her stepdaughter and a reluctance to let such a fat fish as Squire Parcher go, she had perforce dressed and come in search herself.

Now, here was this jumped-up former governess calling her to task. Outrage pushed her beyond all control, and she screamed, "Be silent!" Then she turned on Carabel, adding, "Disgraceful, wild to a fault, brazen creature! This is how you repay me for all my kindness to you. I wash my hands of you."

"M-Mama," the terrified Carabel mumbled. "I'm s-sorry. I didn't mean to—"

"There is no use trying to turn me up sweet or worm yourself back into my good graces," Mrs. Pennodie raved on. "You have put yourself beyond the pale. I have done my best to fulfil my promise to your dead father, but there is no making a silk purse from a sow's ear. Go and beg in the hedgerows and sleep with the drabs for all I care."

This speech was followed by a shocked silence. Into this silence Josiah Briddle said calmly, "Stay, Maria Pennodie. Thee truly does not wish thy daughter returned to thee?" Mrs. Pennodie turned her head away. "Let all here witness that Carabel Pennodie has been cast out by her stepmother," he went on.

There were murmurs of agreement. "Thing's clear as a bell," the admiral gruffed. "Heard what she said; doesn't want the chit. Now, Hartford, come over here a moment with Blyminster. This is important."

As Lord Hartford turned his attention to the admiral, Josiah took Carabel's hand and said simply, "Come, child, it's time to go home."

From his perch, Lucas let out a heartfelt cheer. Hannah hugged Carabel and cried, "Don't fret thaself, Melinda Weatherby, we'st take care of her from now on. Carabel is one of our family now, sithee."

Melinda's heart was full as she saw her young friend's face flame into joy. Carabel was safe at last, loved and protected. From now on her life would be a happy one.

She clung to that thought as, still not looking at Lord Hartford, she followed Zenobie to the barouche. It made her own loneliness somehow easier to bear.

# Chapter Twelve

"You were so brave, Sir Rupert. No one in the world could have done what you did."

As Zenobie looked adoringly up into his eyes, Sir Rupert quivered like an aspen leaf, turned scarlet, and mumbled that he had done nothing, nothing at all.

"Not nothing! You *saved* my cousin, my sweet, dearest Melushka," Zenobie said earnestly. "But for you, that cossack Gildfish would have murdered my little girl. He would have fed her to the fishes. A very bad man, the doctor. And I never guessed."

"No one did—not even Hartford, at first." Sir Rupert cleared his throat several times. "Well, Gildfish—Fowarth, that is—is out of our hands now. Sir Orin's got him. And, ma'am, will you believe it, the admiral's really taken to m'invention?"

He expanded his thin chest. "It was all a hum to begin with—Hartford's comin' down here to pretend m'invention was somethin' the navy wanted. It was a plot to smoke the spy out, mean to say. But the other night, when we actually took the *Subaqua* out on maneuvers and stopped those scoundrels from escapin' and buttoned up the whole thing—well!"

He paused for dramatic effect. "Admiral Kier's convinced now that m'invention's somethin' the navy needs. He's invited me to come to London and show the *Subaqua* off to the Admiralty."

Appearing less than overjoyed at this news, Zenobie murmured, "When must you go?"

"In a sennight's time. Before I go, there's somethin'"—the inventor turned even redder, fumbled for words, and then burst out—"know I'm not much to look at, and speakin' frankly, I'm not young or—or—"

"You are," Zenobie interrupted feelingly, "a fine figure of a man. A *fine* figure."

"Ah, er, egad, mean to say, ma'am—would you do me the honor, that is to say—" Sir Rupert stopped dead, took a deep breath, and asked very quickly, "Will you do me the honor of bein' m'wife?"

Zenobie's speaking countenance lit up with joy. Then, suddenly, her eyes filled with tears, and her lower lip quivered. "Ah, it is no use, the pretence. I can't lie—not to you. Dear, *dear* Sir Rupert, I can't marry you."

The inventor blinked hard, nodded, and began folding into himself. "Oh, yes, ah. Knew it couldn't happen but thought—don't mention it, ma'am. Never mind."

"Oh, pray, do stop speaking so much and listen to me," Zenobie moaned. "It is not that I do not *wish* to marry you. It is that *you* will not wish to marry *me*." Sir Rupert looked at her blankly, and she said, "My grandfather was not a Russian nobleman. He and my father were both groundskeepers for Count Oblonski."

Sir Rupert appeared stunned. He opened his mouth, closed it, and goggled at his lady, who added desperately, "I made the lie. I told the whisker. In order to advance myself in the world, I said I was the granddaughter of Count Oblonski. I gave myself the rank and station that I did not deserve."

She had revealed her shame, the secret for which the *conte* had blackmailed her for so long. Zenobie waited for Sir Rupert to draw back from her in horror, but he only sat there, looking bewildered.

"I don't understand," he said at last. "You're a groundskeeper's daughter, you say. But—but what has that got to do with anythin'? Why can't you marry me?"

"The difference in our stations—"

"Oh, *that*," exclaimed the inventor, enlightened and vastly relieved. "I thought you was goin' to say you didn't love me." He dropped down on his knees and clasped her hands in his. "Lady Darlington— Zenobie—I love you madly," he told her. "Will you marry me?"

With a smothered Russian endearment, Zenobie fell forward into his arms. "My love," Sir Rupert sighed.

"My angel!"

"We'll post the banns at once. If—if that's all right," Sir Rupert added humbly. "Don't know much about females, eh? Mean to say, if you want a big weddin' with all the works, it's what we'll have."

Zenobie shook her head emphatically. "No, I do not. I would so love a little church, with cream and white roses, and music and champagne, and only a few friends. Like my Melushka and—oh, Sir Rupert, I cannot marry you yet!"

The inventor looked aghast. "What now?"

"Melushka." Dramatically placing her hands on her bosom, Zenobie explained, "My darling cousin has sacrificed so much for me. She risked her life for me. I cannot leave her alone in misery."

Sir Rupert, who had been attempting to follow

his beloved's line of reasoning, wondered aloud why Miss Weatherby was miserable. "Her heart is broken," Zenobie said.

"Oh—ah! Hartford," Sir Rupert exclaimed. "But I don't understand. Thought he was in love with her."

"You are so far-seeing, Sir Rupert. Yes, of course, as any cabbagehead with two eyes can plainly perceive, Lord Hartford is in love with Melushka."

"But—but if he's in love with her, what's the problem?" Sir Rupert wanted to know.

"Lord Hartford came to the house yesterday, wishing to speak with her, but Melushka would not see him. Instead, she sent that Poll woman with a chilly little letter, thanking him for saving her from Gildfish and wishing him the long and fortunate life."

Sir Rupert scratched his head. Though he had never pretended to have much in his brainbox, he had good eyesight. "I was sure I saw Hartford kissin' Miss Weatherby in the lake," he said. "Mean to say, wasn't pryin'—couldn't help seein' them, if you know what I mean. And I *thought* she was kissin' him back."

Zenobie rolled her eyes. "But yes, she kissed. Not to peel the eggs, she loves him, too. *But* she will not allow herself to see Lord Hartford." Seeing that her inventor looked even more confused, Zenobie paused to explain. "Melushka thinks a duke's son could not stoop to marry a lady who has not the money and who has been a governess."

"Tomfoolery. Eh? That's what it is. Demmed nonsense. What does that signify, mean to say? Why, I'd love you if—if your father'd been a—a chimneysweep."

Zenobie smiled mistily at her suitor. Then she sobered. "Melushka has not got such sense. My cousin would rather cry her eyes out at night and stay the independent woman. So she is going away to become a governess again, not daring to see Lord Hartford in case the sight of him should melt her heart and change her mind. And *he* thinks she does not wish to see him because she does not care for him, and his pride is hurt. So does he storm down her door and insist to see her? No, he becomes tiresomely English and is going away with Sir Orin Calworth to London."

Zenobie paused to draw a breath. Then she added, "It is tragic, no? Melushka and Lord Hartford are leaving Dorset separately, *away* from each other."

"Sad," the inventor agreed. He commenced chewing on his knuckles until Zenobie leaned forward and grasped his hand.

"We must bring them together. We must make a plan. You will help me, my angel, so that they can be happy and we can be married soon."

"Eh—but really, I don't know about that," the inventor exclaimed, looking alarmed. "Mean to say, can't force people into doin' things they don't want to do. Besides, *I* don't know what to do."

Zenobie smiled. "But I do."

"She knows as you've got to make an early start tomorrow morning," Miss Poll grumbled. "So why does she have to drag you all the way to Blyminster Cove tonight?"

Melinda looked up from the nightdress she was folding. "She isn't dragging me anywhere, Polly. Zenobie knew that I had much to do, so instead of my going with her early this afternoon to

Blyminster Cove, she suggested that I join her and Sir Rupert for dinner."

"If I was you, Miss Mel, I'd stop where I was."

As she spoke, Miss Poll looked worriedly at her sometime nurseling. Ever since Dr. Gildfish's—no, Fowarth's—arrest, Miss Mel had been too calm. It was as if she were withdrawing into herself and taking all her emotions with her. Now, with the last of the day's light shining on her face, she looked beautiful but pale, like a maiden carved out of snow.

In spite of her cousin's fervent invitations, requests, and even demands, Melinda was leaving Dorset. The money that Zenobie had insisted she accept would keep them comfortable until she could find a new post and begin once more to earn her bread. And then what? Miss Poll wondered. Was Miss Mel to have nothing in her life except dreary work?

"I can't disappoint Zenobie," Melinda was saying. "And you needn't worry. Lord Hartford left for London this morning."

It hurt to say the name, but she must say it, Melinda knew, for facts had to be faced. Even so, her heart ached as Miss Poll muttered, "I dunno, Miss Mel. Maybe if you'd seen him that day when he come to call, 'stead of sending me down with that note—"

"What would have been the point?" Melinda tried to speak briskly, but she could not help the quiver in her voice. "You said it yourself. Dukes' sons don't marry governesses."

Miss Poll was heard to mutter that such talk was stuff and rubbish, but her sharp eyes were moist. "At least you should've found out why he came to see you," she grumbled. "Lord Hartford moved heaven and earth to rescue you from that Gildfish. My guess is that he's in love with you and meant to offer for you."

"Unlikely, Polly. Besides, I will never marry."

Miss Poll remembered how her young mistress had spoken those words just two months earlier. Then, she had been sure of herself, her clear eyes staring an uncertain future full in the face. Now those eyes were sad, and though Miss Mel's back was straight and her head held high, her self-assurance had dimmed.

She was in love. It was bound to come someday, and now it had. Miss Poll ached for her nurseling, but there was nothing she could do or say. Like the smallpox, unfulfilled love left bitter scars.

"Help me dress for this farewell dinner with Zenobie and Sir Rupert," Melinda said. Attempting a lighthearted tone, she added, "I can't show a Friday face when they're so happy with each other."

Zenobie had been in such joyful spirits when she and Sir Rupert announced their engagement last night. Melinda thought of this as she stepped into the carriage Sir Rupert had sent to convey his guest to Blyminster Cove. Zenobie, like Carabel, had at last sailed into a calm and happy port.

She tried to let the joy of this thought warm her as the carriage rattled along the lake road. The sun had already set, and the gloaming was soft on the water, and as Melinda watched those gentle shadows, she could not help remembering the first day she had come to Dorset. Then she had watched the sun setting into Kendle Lake, and Anthony Hartford had come—

For a moment she drew back from that memory and then forced herself to recall every moment of their first meeting. If she faltered now, there would always be ghosts of what might have been in her mind.

"I must look to the future," Melinda told herself firmly, "but I must never fear the past."

She repeated this maxim inwardly as the carriage bowled up to the steps of Blyminster Cove and a footman hurried to let down the steps of the carriage. Tonight was for Zenobie. Melinda summoned up a bright smile as she descended from her carriage to meet Sir Rupert, who was walking down the steps of the house to greet her.

"Miss Weatherby, your most obedient."

It was not Rupert. It was— "Lord Hartford," Melinda stammered. "B-but—but you have left to go to London. Zenobie said—"

She broke off in confusion, her defenses crumbling, and with them all her careful rationalizing. Useless to say that she would forget him, when the mere sight of him caused her heart to race so wildly.

"Lady Darlington's mistaken. I leave tomorrow." Hartford had steeled himself for this moment ever since Blyminster had arranged this infernal dinner party. His first instinct had been to refuse to be present, but the inventor had insisted, and besides, it was best to see Melinda once more and end it cleanly.

All of which was sensible, and yet it took all Hartford's will to smile and take her small, cold hand and bend over it. "I hear you're leaving Dorset as well," he told her.

How calmly he spoke, Melinda thought. No doubt he had already forgotten his brief infatuation with her. "I'm eager to return to work," she managed to say.

"And I to return to Scotland." Though he did not

look at her as they walked up the steps together, he had never been more aware of her presence. The rustle of Melinda's skirts, the light fragrance she wore, were reminders that at any moment he could throw restraint and pride to the winds and sweep her into his arms.

But she did not care for him. Reminding himself how it had hurt to read her cool, carefully correct letter of thanks and dismissal, Hartford said, "Shall we go in? Lady Darlington and Blyminster are waiting in the drawing room."

But no one was in the drawing room and Owens announced that Sir Rupert was downstairs with my lady in the workshop. "They will come up in due course," Hartford said. "Perhaps a glass of sherry, Miss Weatherby?"

It grieved her to hear him call her by that formal name, hurt to have him so close to her and not feel the touch of his hands or his arms around her. *Idiot*, Melinda named herself, oh, *twice* idiot. What would you have him do?

"Will you return to Scotland, my lord?" she asked politely.

"Yes, after a brief stay in London," he replied. "It'll be good to get home."

But would it be home, after all? Hartford looked down at the diminutive woman beside him and despaired. Sir Orin had been wrong. What he felt for Melinda was not an infatuation arising out of the excitement and danger of a mission. She had wound herself into his life so completely that wherever his thoughts drifted, they could not but help touch her.

Unable to stand so close to her without taking her into his arms, Hartford walked over to the window. "You might be interested to know that I've severed all connections with the Circle," he told her. "I've lost the touch. I should have investigated the doctor from the start. My lack of perception put you in grave danger, Mel—Miss Weatherby."

Listening to his cool, measured tones, she felt like weeping. "Zenobie and Sir Rupert seem to have forgotten the time," she murmured.

"Lovers lose all track of time," he said, and wondered, now, why in the name of all the devils did I say *that*? "We could go down to them," he suggested.

Zenobie's chatter would help her recover her senses. Melinda hastily agreed and followed Lord Hartford down the long, narrow stairs until they came to the closed workshop door. "I don't hear voices," she commented.

"No." Hartford knocked on the door and called loudly, "Blyminster—Lady Darlington—are you there?"

Still no answer. Hartford gave the door a little push, and it creaked open. "It's empty," he exclaimed.

To her surprise, Melinda noted that the workroom had been tidied up. The *Subaqua* had been polished and readied for its trip to London, and the boxes and barrels of nuts and bolts had been pushed to one side. In the center of the room, the table was covered with platters of food and bottles of wine. Comfortable chairs had been pulled up around this table.

"Are we going to dine down here?" Melinda wondered. "It is like Zenobie to think of something unusual. But the table is set only for two."

Hartford raised his eyebrows. "We had better go back upstairs and see what all this is about." He paused and said, "Odd—I thought I left the door open."

He walked up to the heavy wooden door and turned the knob. "Even more strange," he exclaimed. "It's locked."

"You don't think that Dr. Gildfish—"

"He's on his way to London under guard." Hartford rattled the doorknob and shouted, "Open the door, Blyminster!"

Nobody replied. "Perhaps they are playing a joke on us," Melinda said uncertainly.

Hartford put his shoulder against the door and pushed. It didn't budge. He picked up one of the chairs and slammed it against the door, but it splintered against the heavy oak. "Nothing short of cannonfire is going to open that door," he said grimly. "I begin to smell a plot."

"But who would want to—" She broke off, eyes widening as a possibility occurred to her. *"Zenobie?"*

"Blyminster is putty in her hands."

"But why deceive us and lure us down here, and—" Melinda stopped talking and looked at his lordship in total horror. "They mean to leave us here together, to compromise us. Oh, that Zenobie could be so base—I will never forgive her!"

She stormed across to the door and kicked it. Hartford could not help laughing. "Oh, do stop laughing in that odious way," Melinda cried. "We must find a way out of this place."

"There's only one other exit, and that's by way of the lake." Hartford began to run his hands up and down the doorjamb. "The door is opened by a lever someplace—ah, here it is."

The door swung ajar with a creak, and Melinda saw that it opened onto a ramp that sloped directly into the by now dark water. There was no landfall for at least a hundred yards on each side.

"There's always a rowboat moored here—" Hartford broke off. "It's gone. They thought this out quite carefully, it seems. We're trapped."

"I never expected such shabby treatment from Zenobie," Melinda exclaimed wrathfully.

Hartford watched as she began to prowl about the workroom, and as he did so, the hard knot within him began to loosen. He walked over to the table, poured wine into two glasses, and tasted his. "Excellent champagne," he pronounced.

Melinda had never felt less like drinking champagne and said so. "Sit down," Hartford went on. "Please. There's no use flying to pieces over this. What we need to do is think this through."

Recognizing the logic in this, Melinda sank down into one of the chairs. It was soft and most insidiously comfortable. "Well?" she asked.

"Let's look at our situation. They've locked us down here and stolen the rowboat so that we will have to spend some time together. Since your reputation would be compromised, they feel that I'll offer marriage—"

"That will not happen," Melinda interrupted.

"But if we aren't married, you'll be ruined," Hartford pointed out. His face had softened, Melinda noted, and his eyes were as merry as they had been when first they met.

"No, I won't," she retorted. "Who will say anything against me? Not you, and not I. Certainly not Zenobie or Sir Rupert. They can't be entirely without scruples."

Hartford put down the glass of champagne, and walking over to Melinda, took her hands in his. "Don't look so distressed," he told her quietly.

"Think of this not as a trap but as a second chance. Melinda, you must have guessed that I'm in love with you."

Her heart thudded once with blinding joy—and then again in misery. "You needn't pretend, my lord," she whispered. "You needn't offer for me, either. This is a trick, an illusion, nothing to do with real life. I intend to be an independent woman. You are the son of a duke—"

As if she had not spoken, he went on. "Lady Darlington did us a great favor, my love. If it weren't for her, we would both have parted and gone our separate ways and been miserable for the rest of our lives. You would have been too proud and I too stupid to understand that the only place for us is with each other."

Melinda felt her foolish heart yearn toward those words. It cost a great deal to reply, "I beg you will not say such things."

Hartford frowned. "I'm trying to ask you to marry me."

"And I tell you that I will not accept." Melinda added, even more miserably, "I can't marry you when—when you are offering for me only because you are being forced to it."

"But, damn it," Hartford exploded, "I'm not being *forced* into doing anything."

Looking him straight in the eye, Melinda asked, "Do you stand there and tell me that you would have asked me to marry you if we were not trapped together?"

Hartford thought of Sir Orin's lecture on the folly of his tendre for Miss Weatherby. The memory of that irritating conversation still rankled, and he spoke more curtly than he intended. "You're twisting the facts."

No, of course he would not have proposed. Melinda watched him with mounting misery. She loved Anthony Hartford too much to force him to do anything, and she had too much respect for herself to accept a proposal that sprang from trickery. In days to come, perhaps he would begin to think that she, too, had been in on the plot.

"I have seen marriages of convenience," she said at last. "My parents' was so unfortunate that I promised myself I would never—oh, please, let us not argue. We must find a way out of this prison."

She was near tears. Useless to pursue the matter, Hartford thought gloomily, when she obviously did not want him to do so, but there really was no way out.

"Except by water," Melinda exclaimed, and he realized he had spoken this last thought aloud. When he looked at her in astonishment, she added, "I'm a very good swimmer."

Determinedly, she walked to the open door of the workshop. He followed. "It's an extreme way of escape," he pointed out.

Melinda could not help flinching as she saw the expanse of dark water. Hartford went on. "It's quite some distance to shore, and the lake's sure to be cold. Are you sure you want to do this?"

For answer, she jumped into the water. Hartford swore and plunged in after her. A moment later they surfaced and looked at each other, and he began to laugh.

"I knew from the first moment I met you that you were a highly unusual female," he said. "The Briddles would be proud of you."

Melinda's tension eased at the amusement and appreciation in his tones. As she began to swim toward shore, he fell in beside her, and their long, easy strokes matched perfectly. "Are you getting tired?" he asked.

"Not at all. Are you?"

Hartford flipped onto his back and began an easy backstroke, and she followed suit. They swam in companionable silence for some time, and in spite of the cold water, Melinda felt her heart grow warm and light. So light, in fact, that she confessed, "When I first met you, I thought that you were an unlikely kind of St. George."

"Vanquishing the Kendle dragon, you mean?" Hartford smiled into the darkness. "Speaking of which mythical beast, I hear that the locals are all abuzz over the *Subaqua*'s public debut. They believe that Blyminster's machine was the dragon emerging to warn them of impending war with the French."

"If the creature lives up to its promise, England will never be conquered," she said stoutly. "But I don't think we need a dragon as long as Sir Orin Calworth is on guard."

She paused for a moment and then added, "I have not truly thanked you for coming to my rescue the other night."

"You did write me that letter," he reminded her. When she did not reply to this, he added, "I'd have come after you even if I had to swim the lake. You do know that, don't you?"

His words were simple, sincere. "Yes," she said softly. "Yes, I know you would have come."

"Melinda," he went on, "we were both saying good-bye for absurd reasons. You were afraid of the difference between our stations. I was leaving Dorset full of stiff-necked pride and indignation that you refused even to see me." He paused and then added, "Neither of those arguments make much sense."

"No," she murmured. "No, I suppose not."

"I love you and I want you to be my wife," Lord Hartford said. He spoke with such conviction that Melinda felt a surge of exultant joy. Even so, she hesitated.

"Are you certain you are not offering for me because you think I have been compromised, and—why are you laughing?"

"No one would ever dare to compromise you," he told her, "so put that out of your mind. I love you, and that's the long and short of it. Will you marry me, Melinda?"

He reached out a hand to her and, catching her arm, suddenly stood up in the water. The water was shallow enough so that his head and shoulders were above water, but she was still beyond her depths. She remedied this by putting her arms around him and holding tight.

"Yes," she said joyfully. "Oh, yes, Anthony, I will marry you—now!"

Their kiss was like sunshine after storm, like joy and deliverance and homecoming. It drew them deep into a happiness so rare and profound that it effectively wiped out every other thought. When finally, reluctantly, they drew apart, they smiled long and mistily at each other.

"Well, my love?" Hartford asked at last. "Shall we go and tell your cousin that she's to wish us happy?"

"Indeed, I will have more than a few words to say to Zenobie when I see her," Melinda promised. Then she tightened her arms around her lover's neck and gave a sigh of great happiness. "But must we go immediately, Anthony? The water is really not cold at all and the night is beautiful."

"Very beautiful," he agreed, and bent his lips to hers.